Aleppo Tales

By the Author

Adjusting Sights

Haim Sabato

ALEPPO
TALES

TRANSLATED FROM THE HEBREW BY
Philip Simpson

The Toby Press

The Toby Press Edition 2004

The Toby Press LLC
POB 8531, New Milford, CT. 06676-8531, USA
& POB 2455, London W1A 5WY, England
www.tobypress.com

Originally published as *Emet MiEretz Titzmach*
Copyright © 1997, Books in the Attic
& Miskal Publishing House, Tel Aviv
Yediot Aharonot / Sifrei Hemed 2000

Translation Copyright © Philip Simpson 2004

ISBN 1 59264 051 6, *hardcover*

A CIP catalogue record for this title is
available from the British Library

Typeset in Garamond by Jerusalem Typesetting

Printed and bound in the United States
by Thomson-Shore Inc., Michigan

Contents

*Hebrew words have been transliterated according to the
Sepharadi pronunciation and italicized throughout.*

Truth Shall Spring From The Earth

Chapter one

The people of Aram Zova are proud of their city, and unstinting in its praise. They are as proud of its air and its fountains as of the acumen of its tradesmen; proud of the poets and the cantors of their city, proud of the lyrical supplications and the *Sefer HaPizmonim*, the Book of Hymns, which they wrote, with their melodic scales. They believe there is no cantor in the world to compare with their cantors, no hymn to compare with their hymns.

There is a saying that goes: He who has not seen the sons of Aram Zova in their joyful chanting does not know the meaning of true joy. It is characteristic of hymns that they seem pleasant to the ear only on Sabbaths and festival days, at betrothals, circumcisions and celebrations of mitzvot. The people of Aleppo extol the food of their city and its delicacies. They do not eat to excess, but they expend inordinate effort, and employ meticulous precision, in the preparation of dishes. The saying goes: *If you want to judge the quality of someone from Aleppo, uncover his pot and inspect his food.* They are even proud of the name of their city, calling it Aram Zova, as it is known in scriptural parlance, and in this historical allusion they add more than a veneer of grace to their locality.

But the essential pride of the sons of Aleppo is derived from their sages. Aleppo was a city of sages and scribes, and its sages are distinguished by the depth of their genius and the sharpness of their intellect. A sage of Aleppo hates meaningless ostentation or affectation and loves clear judgment. He is sparing in speech and makes a virtue of silence; his speech is brief. He is meticulous in his dress, and meticulous in his dignity; he strings pearls together in a sermon, and is bold in declarations of *Halacha*. Forthright and making no pretenses to anyone. It is not in the nature of a sage from Aleppo to follow the crowd; he stands by his opinions, and knows his own value. He disdains a saintly fool, and loves the intellectual. He enjoys a jest, and his talk, even on non-religious subjects, is worthy of study.

My grandfather of blessed memory was a sage in the classic mold of the sages of Aram Zoba, and all the qualities we have mentioned were present in him. He too was proud of his city. To him, "Aleppan" was a prestigious title. Whenever he mentioned one of the illustrious sages of Aleppo, he used to stand up as a mark of respect. And although he was nine when he went down to Egypt, and although he spent the final years of his life in Jerusalem, he associated himself with the sages of Aleppo and was counted among them. He was especially proud of his grandfather, considered one of the great scholars of Aleppo.

Even in us, his offspring, the same Aleppan pride was firmly fixed, even though neither our parents nor ourselves ever saw Aleppo or Tedef with our own eyes. We never saw them with our mortal eyes, but saw with the visions of the heart. In my imagination I stroll through the markets of the city, explore its alleyways, loiter in its courtyards and taste its delicacies. I read in its places of learning, hear its sages and their exposition of the Torah, and hear its cantors leading the worship. I sit down to write and my pen writes of Aram Zova, returning to Aleppo as if of its own accord. Who knows the way of the spirit?

This attachment of the heart led me to the discovery of a wondrous story from the annals of Aram Zova and its sages, some six or seven generations ago. It is a story diffused amid the lives of the entire community, its scholars and its leading townsfolk, its tradesmen and printers of books. For several months, I have been engrossed in this story. Chapter by chapter it has been made known to me, sometimes revealed, sometimes obscured. Some portions of it were supplied to me by scholars knowing our history, others became known to me by chance, in haphazard fashion. One episode was explained to me in a dream. With every hint deciphered, my eyes have been opened further. As it has been revealed to me, so I shall tell it to you, chapter by chapter.

Chapter two

I t was my grandfather of blessed memory who opened up the whole of this episode for me, without meaning to. This is how it happened. It was a source of great regret to me that grandfather never wrote a dissertation on a topic of Torah. I was studying at the *yeshiva*, and I knew that every scholar, even a *yeshiva* student, writes a dissertation. I used to think that a scholar is only recognized on the basis of his dissertations. I often asked him about this, and mostly, he used to brush me off. However, once he answered me: "If you had been fortunate enough to hear our teacher and our master, Hacham Ezra"—and on mentioning his name he stood as a mark of respect—"you would understand what clear judgment is. And if you had been fortunate enough to know my esteemed father, my guiding light, you would know the meaning of true innovation."

By which he meant, if they did not write, then why should he?

Another time he answered me: "This is my understanding, as inherited from my ancestors. The Rambam's *Mishneh Torah* is a dissertation. *Beit Yoseph*, by *Maran*, the illustrious Yoseph Caro, is a dissertation. Anything less than these, is not a dissertation."

It was only toward the end of his life that he admitted to me that he was sorry he hadn't written a dissertation. At that time he was in great pain, his eyesight heavy, his memory failing and his loneliness overwhelming. He, who used to walk at the head of his students like a king with his army, issuing new interpretations of the Torah like an inexhaustible spring, impressing all who heard his sermons, sat alone. It was then that he tried, tried and tried again, to study the whole of the Talmud afresh, thus upholding the saying, *Blessed is he who comes hither with his Talmud in his hand; Gemara, Rashi, Tosafot, Maharsha, Maharam Schiff, Rambam and Beit Yoseph.* And analytically too. Analysis in the style of Aleppo. Study of the Talmud without analysis was no study at all in his opinion.

Sometimes, it seemed he had succeeded. He would dive into the depths of a problem and come up with jewels, as in his former days. Then he would wait until I returned from the *yeshiva*, and the moment I arrived he would tackle me with an abstruse question regarding the interpretation of the *Tosafot*, or of *Maharam Schiff*, a question to which it seemed there was no answer. And he was exultant, seeing that his power was undiminished, and he was as capable as ever of going forth and fighting the wars of the Torah. It was then that he plucked up the courage to enter into a discussion of *Halacha*, corresponding with the greatest scholars of the generation, as he used to do in his youth. And when the dialecticians answered him and rejected his arguments, he would gird on his weapons, beginning peaceably and in courteous terms, and setting out the issue in all its elements, analyzing the words of the commentators in meticulous detail and with acute logic, and then attacking with all his might.

If for some reason they were slow in replying to him, this made him very bitter, and he would write another letter, protesting at the insult to the dignity of the Torah, and adducing further proofs in support of his argument. The great men of the generation were aware of his power, even though he had not written a dissertation. But there was always a shadow of a suspicion in his mind that they were in no hurry to reply to him because his failure to write a dissertation had harmed his reputation as a scholar of the Torah.

After studying a few chapters of the Tractate *Berakhot*, he submitted to his infirmity and returned to his loneliness. At first he felt resentful, but then he regretted his resentment, and finally accepted Heaven's judgment. He clung to his prayers. It was his habit when at prayer to speak out the words as if counting gold coins, and he retained this habit, for it restored his spirits in old age.

This was the time he admitted to me that yes, it would have been appropriate to write a dissertation. And he even said: "With the help of the Almighty and by His grace, *you* will write a dissertation, for you are the seventh generation. The vow is annulled." My grandfather went on to say: "My grandfather, after whom I am named, was one of the greatest sages of Aleppo."

On hearing him mention Aleppo, I listened even more intently than usual, as I was always eager to hear about Aram Zova and its sages. And thus he related:

"The sages of Aleppo, when they used to sign books, always signed according to the order of their official stature, so when you see the sages of Aleppo listed anywhere, pay close attention to the order of their signing. On the endorsement of the book *HaEretz HaTovah* ["The Good Land"], my grandfather was the seventh to sign. And in the book *Eretz Zavat Halav* ["A Land Flowing with Milk"], he signed fifth. And don't be misled by what you find in the famous ban, where in signing he is ranked seventeenth out of thirty-six, as there is a reason for this, one that I cannot explain. And my grandfather wrote a great book of legal decisions which would have enlightened the whole world, but was not published for the familiar reason."

I thought grandfather was referring to a shortage of funds. How many wonderful theses, in which the greatest scholars of Israel have invested all their spirit, have remained in manuscript for this reason and been lost forever? But there was the hint of something mysterious in the tone of his voice, something slurred, and I realized that here there was a secret, of the kind to be revealed only to the meek. I tried to induce him to say more about the unpublished book, and the familiar reason that he had spoken of, but he cloaked himself in his silence. His big black eyes deepened in the void before him, as was his wont when he was contemplating. I knew that grandfather's silence was conversation, and deserved to be studied, and I listened

9

to it. After a few moments he looked at me and said: "I'm sure you know that his hymn was included in the *Sefer HaBakashot*."

From the tenor of his words I deduced that the inclusion of a poem in the *Sefer HaBakashot* was almost as prestigious as the publication of a dissertation. For the *Sefer HaBakashot* of the good people of Aram Zova was composed by the greatest of their sages. It is full of longings and yearnings for our Father who is in Heaven, and sorrow at the exile of the *Shekhinah* and the exile of Israel, and in every plea and poem there are allusions to the *Mishnah* and the Talmud based on both literal and arcane meanings. It was then that I knew that it was for some obscure reason that my grandfather hadn't written a dissertation, and my great-grandfather hadn't written a dissertation. It was on account of the large book of legal decisions written by our ancestor and not published. There was a mystery about this book, and its whereabouts. I took it upon myself to seek out the hidden book and bring it out into the light of day. I wanted to reveal the things that were concealed, and I didn't know how far my quest would take me.

Chapter three

The arcane is not our concern. But from experts in the esoteric we have heard: a man's character is in his name, and it is in his name that his destiny is bound up, and in effect, a man's entire life is nothing but a living out of his name.

Sometimes it is the name of a book that determines its fate.

Sometimes, even the streets of a city resemble their names. Who it was who named the streets of Jerusalem I do not know, but it was a fine piece of work. There is a street in Jerusalem near the Mahaneh Yehuda market—and far from it. Just a few paces separate them, but the distance in atmosphere is immense. It is called Rashi Street, and it suits its name. The sound of the bustle of the city is not heard there, although it is situated in the very heart of it. It is a hospitable place, and imbued with purity, its residents industrious and happy in their work. Some of the elderly worthies of Jerusalem live there. The place enjoys their company, and they enjoy it too.

I went to Rashi Street, to visit my great uncle, Hacham Isaac Vidal. Hacham Vidal Haspanioli married my aunt, my grandfather's sister, Senora Victoria Vidal. Hacham Isaac Vidal was advanced in years, and had a fine head of white hair. He suffered no sickness and no pain, and the hint of a smile was always on his face. Life loved him, and he smiled at it in return.

My great aunt, Senora Victoria, had been a typical native of Aleppo: shrewd, acute, caustic and prickly. Her statements were brief and pithy, and sometimes irritating, but when she married Hacham Isaac Haspanioli, she adhered to his ways. The many years she spent in his company, and the many years she lived in Jerusalem, on Rashi Street, made her calm and placid, complacent and relaxed, in the manner of the worthies of Jerusalem.

Entering their house, you passed into another world, a pleasant and tranquil world. There was a festive taste to visits at the home of Hacham Isaac and Senora Victoria Vidal; the taste of red dates stuffed with almonds and smeared with honey, the taste of baked quince covered with cinnamon and dipped in fragrant rose-water, the taste of lemonade and exotic fruits.

We used to visit them twice every year: at *Pesah* and at *Succot*, toward the close of the festival. I had never seen their home on a normal day, or seen them wearing weekday clothing. In my eyes they were always dressed for a festival.

It never occurred to me that my great aunt knew anything about the hidden book and its mysteries. I assumed that such things were not shared with the female side of our family. But I thought she might let drop, in passing, some reference to our great-great-grand-father. I say 'in passing' because from my great aunt Senora Victoria you could expect to hear nothing in any other form. She was more accustomed to speech than my grandfather was, but she too knew the value of silence. Her conversation was as she chose it to be; you could ask her questions to your heart's content, and she would respond to you, but not to your questions. She would tell you what she wanted you to hear. However, I hoped to hear some hint about the life story of our ancestor. I heard a great deal more than I expected to hear.

I arrived in Rashi Street and entered their courtyard. As soon as my footsteps were heard outside, she called from the house, "Welcome, welcome!"

I pushed open the door and went inside. The whole house—courtyard, one room and kitchen—was whitewashed. The main room was spacious, with a high-ceiling, full of light. Not much furniture in it, but what there was was neatly arranged. There was a canapé—a big sofa running the length of the room, with round leather cushions covered with red and green home-woven fabric in its corners. Facing it, there was one deep armchair and a carved wooden chair. There were two small tables, each with six legs shaped like towers, and on them a white cloth embroidered with a pattern of stars. Hacham Isaac sat on the canapé, wearing a white caftan with yellow and gray stripes. A dark red sash was bound around his waist, and a gray turban sat on his head. His beard was white, his eyes big and humorous, and a book of *Midrash* lay open on the table before him. My great aunt, Senora Victoria, was sitting in a wooden chair, gazing out at the courtyard and the street beyond. Time stood still in the house on Rashi Street.

Hacham Isaac rose from his seat with dignity, put his hand to his forehead as a sign of welcome, and immediately commented on the numerology of my name. Such was his way. If my brother Nissim were to visit him, he would exclaim at once: "Ruby, sapphire and diamond—add up to Nissim." In my case it was: "Haim, whose fruit is sweet to my palate, to my palate—equals Haim." And so it was for every single name, without a moment's thought. My great aunt Senora Victoria made do with a nod of the head and went to the kitchen—partly out of modesty, partly to fetch a variety of delicacies.

The manners of Aleppo brook no deviation: one is obliged to begin with certain words, and to conclude with certain words. The conventions are rigid: who asks and who answers, and when. According to the etiquette of Aleppo, you are not asked why you have come, and you do not say why you have come. Everything must be explained by way of allusion.

After a few words of greeting I began by expressing admiration of their street, Rashi Street, broached the subject of the name and stature of Rashi, and so forth. I meant to draw my aunt into a discussion of her own name, Victoria, which always sounded strange to me.

Senora Victoria began by saying: "Young people today tend

to call their children by new names: Lior, Uri, Noga, Zivanit, and suchlike. Where they get these names from I have no idea. We always named our children after our relatives, and in order, of course. It is our custom that the firstborn son is named after the father's father, the second after the mother's father, the first daughter after the father's mother, and the second after the mother's mother, thus upholding the commandment to honor thy father and mother. Other sons and daughters are named after aunts, or eminent sages. As to my brothers and sisters, Aharon was named after our grandfather and Jacob after our other grandfather; Latifa after our father's mother and Zakkia after our mother's mother. I am the only one not named after one of our relatives. My name recalls no precedent in the past."

She paused for a moment, while I pretended this was a mundane story, and not what I had come here for; if she saw how interested I was, there was a danger she might stop. She went on to say: "We had a sister. There was none like her in all Aleppo for intelligence and for beauty. She was beloved of all. And most of all by our grandfather. Day after day he used to play with her. They say that at six months old she was already talking, at one year she knew *Come let us rejoice* by heart, and at three she was expounding on the *Parashah*. She was a prodigy. But then, tragically, at three years and three months old—she was taken from us. I'm sure you have never had the slightest inkling of this, for since the day she died she was never mentioned in our house. That day all Aleppo mourned for her, but our grandfather forbade mention of her name. They say that when he heard, he beat his head against the wall, accepted the judgment upon himself, and was silent. A heavy pall of grief descended on our family, and the decree of silence was the hardest to bear. But that was our grandfather's command. Many rumors were heard about this episode. Old people would whisper her name among themselves, saying she had been "bitten by a snake, a snake of the rabbis.[1]"

Senora Victoria went on to say: "Twenty years after this incident the rumor reached my ears too. I didn't know what a venomous

---

1 'snake of the rabbis', i.e., at rabbinic ban. Also, the letters that form the word 'snake' are the initials of the words "ban, curse, denunciation"—a strong hint at the denouement.

snake was, but I was terrified all the same. I once asked my esteemed father, but he silenced me with a rebuke. As for my mother, I couldn't ask her any questions at all. Several times I tried asking others about the episode, yet no one told me anything. More than ninety years have passed since then, and still I cannot speak of her without a shudder. Today I know more. I shall tell you what I do know.

"The day she was born, our grandfather had just finished writing his great book of rabbinic decisions. Everyone said: 'When the Book of Decisions is published it will shake the world.' There was great happiness in our house that day. Our grandfather laid out a sumptuous banquet and the family celebrated with these delicacies, singing hymns and even improvising poetry. Grandfather composed a special hymn for that meal, and it appears in the book of hymns. That day my sister was born. The entire house was full of light and we had double cause for celebration. Our grandfather asked his son, my father, to let him choose a name for the new baby. They say he named her after his great book. That same night a deputation of sages and elders on the town council arrived at our house. From the temporal council of the congregation of Aram Zova, and from the spiritual council. Everyone thought they were coming to congratulate him on his book, or to consult with him on some matter, as happened from time to time. But their faces were grim. After the customary salutations, they went with him into the little room. No one ever went into the little room. In this room my grandfather used to conduct the *Tikkun* of midnight every night, and afterward, he would sit at his desk and work on his great work of rabbinic decisions until daybreak. Even my mother never saw the inside of the little room. It was said to be full of old books and manuscripts. The community elders spent a long time in there with our grandfather; when they came out, his face was blazing like a torch, and his black eyes staring into the void. He was silent, and said not a word. No one dared to ask what had happened. They finished their meal, and blessed the food. Before the blessing, after the Psalm of David, *The Lord is my shepherd, I shall not want,* he referred to the verse: *Truth shall spring from the earth.* The next day my grandfather announced he was resigning from the spiritual council of Aram Zova.

"There was great commotion in the city. Deputation after deputation came to urge him to reconsider, but he was not to be swayed. Aleppans are aggressive and proud, and once they have given their word they never withdraw it. He gave the excuse that he was occupied with his book and with his trade, and he shunned them. After a while things returned to the way they had been before. Our sister grew and thrived, and our grandfather played with her every day. He used to set up her cradle in the little room and rock her. But when she was only three years and two months old, she fell ill. At first they thought it was a common childhood ailment, but the days passed and she did not improve. Women who dealt with these things came to our house and told my mother to hang on her an amulet made by Hacham David Orfali, whose amulets had proved efficacious in the past. Our grandfather was consulted and he refused to allow it. 'The healing of mankind is in the hands of the Creator of the world and the physicians who are His envoys,' he said. 'What business have amulets in a God-fearing household?' They asked him to whisper verses from the Psalms to her and he would not, because the Rambam forbids it. He wrote in a treatise that words of Torah are not healing for the body but healing for the spirit, and although there are some who disagree and allow it, here in Aram Zova we heed only the words of the Rambam. He even refused to neglect his studies to recite Psalms. The greatest and most skillful doctors treated her, but nothing helped. She died a month later.

"The world was murmuring: The book has been suppressed, the girl has died; ban, curse, denunciation—a venomous trinity. Our grandfather engrossed himself in study, scorning all the rumors. He said that they were fools: 'The Creator of the world gave us a gift, and now He has taken it back.'

"Two years later I was born, and the family was healed. Our grandfather gave me the name Victoria. An allusion to my sister's name, and an allusion to the triumph he anticipated. When I was a year old, our grandfather laid his hands on my head and blessed me with long life.

"He went on to say: 'In the lifetime of this girl, my justification will come to light, the mouths of the accusers will be silenced, and the book that has been hidden away will be printed.'

"More than ninety years have passed since then, and I'm still waiting. Before my older brother, your grandfather of blessed memory, died—he summoned me. I came to him. He told me the whole of this story. He went on to say that you would be coming to see me; he wanted me to tell you the story. To what purpose—he didn't say. I promised. So you have come, and I have told you. What you will do with the information, I do not know. And besides,"—she concluded her speech with a faint smile on her lips—"things like this were never meant for the women in our family."

Having heard what I heard, I knew that our ancestor's book of rabbinic decisions had been suppressed at the instigation of the community's elders. Why they wanted to suppress it, I didn't know. I knew our ancestor was a great scholar and a man of integrity. Why he resigned from the rabbinate, I didn't know. I felt I had to do something; but what exactly I would do—I had no idea.

Chapter four

Aman's books testify to his character: from his library there
is much you can learn of his nature. Grandfather had many books in
his library. Responsa, decisions and collections of customs, novellae,
poems and songs, works concerning the creation of the world and
the secrets of *Kabbalah*. Books old and new, large and small—after
his death they were dispersed. Every one of his relatives took some
books for themselves. Some said they needed them for research, some
said they were taking them as a token of remembrance. One way or
another, the bundle was split apart.

A man scrimps and saves all his life, collecting a treasury of
books from all over the place according to his taste. This affords him
peace of mind; yet as soon as he departs this world his books are
dispersed and their charm is forfeited.

After hearing the whole of that story from my great aunt Senora
Victoria, I went and visited all my relations, searching for the *Sefer
HaBakashot* of the sages of Aram Zova, the book my grandfather used
to have. I wanted to examine the poem written by our great-great-
grandfather the night he finished his book that he composed right
before his resignation from the rabbinate. I thought that it might

contain a clue to the mystery of the hiding of that book. Was this not what grandfather had said? That the sages of Aleppo used to invest all their spirit in their poems. I found the book in the possession of Hacham Moise Shayo.

Seven sons were born to my aunt Madame Jamila of the house of Shayo. Seven sons and one daughter. And they all married in *Eretz-Israel*. The sons brought seven brides into the family—each from somewhere else: one from Iraq and one from Morocco, one from Libya and one from Algeria, one from Iran and two from Aleppo. The daughter married an *Ashkenazi*. Every Sabbath, after the meal, Hacham Moise Shayo used to set out on the table ten books of hymns in the Aram Zova version, and a bottle of arak. Madame Jamila for her part would fetch a dish of pistachios and a brass basin full of ice, with peeled cucumbers floating in it. Hacham Moise would fill a glass with arak, set it down among the cubes of ice, distribute the books of hymns to his children and begin to versify in a hoarse voice: *My friend and my shepherd please save me/ From the kicking of people who mock/ Tell me why and for whom you have chosen/ To abandon what is left of the flock*—a poem originating from Rabbi Israel Najara, consisting in the main of supplications and sung to a captivating melody. After three verses, the sons and the son-in-law would skip to the last verse, and begin a fresh series of poems in the mixed 'Jerusalem' version. I don't know who named this mixed style 'Jerusalem,' for had Jerusalem been consulted, I seriously doubt she would have agreed to call it by her name; now, as she has not been consulted, and they have done the deed, all other tunes have been declared void in favor of the Jerusalem version, out of the respect due to the king's daughter, that is Jerusalem.

Sabbath after Sabbath Hacham Moise Shayo would begin, *My friend and my shepherd please save me...* and Sabbath after Sabbath his sons would prevail over him. The people of Aram Zova are proud, and lovers of music. His love of music prevailed over his pride. He forsook the tunes of Aleppo and he too became schooled in the Jerusalem style and sang with them. But my grandfather of revered memory did not forsake his ancestry. Neither the poem nor the melody. He used to say that the poems in the hymnal of Aram Zova were created by saints and men acting upon their religious beliefs, who invested all their energy in them; that there is grace in them, and there are pleas in them, and that they lead mankind to fear of Heaven. The saints who created them were close to the highest level of spirituality, and the *Shekhinah* used to tinkle before them like a bell, until they had written what they were writing. And each and every one of the sages composed a great many pleas, and only one or two of the very best of them were included in the *Sefer HaBakashot*.

A lover of poetry and song was my grandfather of blessed memory, and there were many supplications and hymns that we learned from him. The supplications, which called *bakashot*, are distinct from the hymns, and crafted from the Kabbalistic world of divine emanations. Their language is Hebrew and the Aramaic language, and their melody is fixed, and you find antiquity and dignity in them. And the congregation is in the habit of chanting them in the synagogues before daybreak, when they are huddled together and their hearts are pure, and the sage preaches before them, and after the *bakashot* they rise for the Sabbath prayers, and there is therefore an extra aspect of holiness in them. The hymns are distinct from them. There is lightness in them in that they are sung after a *mitzvah* celebration, when the participants are at their most mellow. There is gladness in them, their stanzas are short and some of them are written in the Arabic language.

My grandfather knew many poems by heart. But we never heard him recite a poem composed by his own grandfather that was included in the *Sefer HaBakashot*. Although he was always proud of his grandfather and showed us his name written at the top of the hymn, we never heard it in our house. I am surprised at myself, and wonder why it never occurred to me to ask him about this: What was the point of us chanting all those poems and hymns, when there was a poem that was written by our own ancestor which we did not perform? After I heard that story about our great-great-grandfather and the leaders of the congregation, and knew when the poem was composed, I realized there was a mystery there.

I promised Hacham Moise I would return the book to him, and he gave it me. I took in my hands the *Sefer HaBakashot* from Aram Zova. It was a small book, with red-brown binding and letters that had once been gold leaf embossed on it. The gold had long since disintegrated and only the impressions of the letters remained, a memorial to better days than these. Such is the way of the world; the gold melts and the impressions remain. The *bakashot* in this book are written not in the order of the alphabet, as is usual today, but according to the order of the *makamim*.

The supplication of our great-great-grandfather is written in the *makam* of Zaba. Introduced with the words: "A fine hymn created by the Hacham Bashi*, *makam* Zaba, to the tune of *Ya anta kalbi al-hanun*." And the hymn is as follows:

> *Delight of the nations, treasure of the world,*
> *You were blessed and you were fair;*
> *Hellas and Edom, Media and Babel*
> *What realm on the earth is your compare?*
>
> *Thorns hemmed you in and your blood was spilled,*
> *Your garments stained and dimmed your crown's fire—*
> *More charming the garb of your slavery grim*
> *Than your captors' festive attire.*
>
> *And the king will crave you for you are so fair*
> *And then your voice will be his delight.*
> *From exile's pit he will raise you aloft,*
> *Bring you as a bride to his palace bright.*
>
> *Then I, too, shall be built upon you;*
> *I shall go forth from the darkness to where the light lies,*
>
> *In me all your people shall rejoice*
> *Truth from the depths will yet arise.*

---

* a Bashi sage, Hacham Bashi, was the title of the chief rabbi of Syria

A sapling will flower in your garden,
Beauteous of eye and ruddy of gaze;
And for your sake he will go forth and crush
The head of the serpent of ancient days.

The redeemer will send and redeem you
As the king reclines on his bed;
In the courts of your holiness we shall walk,
As the king reclines on his bed.

The lines of our great-great-grandfather's poem and the terrible story told me by my great aunt Senora Victoria mingled in my imagination. Darkness and depths, a venomous snake and primordial serpent, the death of the little girl and the concealment of the book. I wanted to bring the truth out into the light, and didn't know then that truth would spring from the earth.

I looked at the poem again, and was amazed, seeing that in the closing verse our ancestor had written the same line twice: *As the king reclines on his bed.* And although this was an acceptable line and might have been pleasing to the one who wrote it, could he really not have found a suitable rhyme at this point? My heart told me this was an inaccurate version. At that time I didn't know it had been intentionally corrupted. I decided to seek out an old *Sefer HaBakashot*. I thought that perhaps I would find a version that had not been spoiled. And I found more than I meant to find.

Chapter five

The neighborhood of Rehavia is highly regarded in Jerusalem. It has a number of good qualities, which it well knows and is justly proud of. Its streets are broad, the houses spacious, the gardens pleasant and the air pure. Yellow leaves cover the courtyards there; the footsteps of those strolling about are swallowed up by them, releasing a fragrant aroma. The rays of the sun flicker in the branches of the trees, and the place is poised constantly between light and shade. Only Gaza Street separates the neighborhood of Rehavia from her sister neighborhood, Talbieh. They say the sister is prettier than she, but Rehavia is joined by a thread of grace to her neighbor, Sha'are Hesed, a devout place with devout inhabitants.

Rehavia's greatest asset is its proximity to everywhere. If you are a resident of Rehavia you can rise early on a Friday, the eve of Sabbath, to pray at dawn with the pious *vatikin* in the synagogue of the Gr'a in Shaarei Hesed, study in the *Beit Midrash* of the ascetics of Rabbi Harlap, buy your Sabbath groceries in the Mahaneh Yehuda market, sort out your business affairs in King George Street or in the Ben Yehuda pedestrian mall nearby, stroll in the evening through the enchanted olive groves of the Valley of the Cross, and greet the Sabbath in the *minyan* of devotees of Bratslav at the Western Wall.

The neighborhood of Rehavia is well known in Jerusalem, and yet there are secret places there that not many people know of. There is a broad street in Rehavia with a tomb in the center of it, an ornate and sculpted tomb, belonging to one of the priests of the Second Temple era. Alongside this tomb is a house with many rooms and cellars. The old folk of Jerusalem know what is not known to many: this was the house of the Turkish hangman, a man once dreaded by the Bey's prisoners. His name and his abode were not made known publicly, for fear of reprisals on behalf of his victims. In spite of this, the old folk of Jerusalem used to whisper to one another: "That's the hangman's house."

Two generations have passed since then, and I only heard this by way of a whisper. Inside this house is a big hall, with two smaller rooms beside it. The hall and the rooms are dark even by day, with a single electric bulb to light them all. And they are full of boxes of books. Old books, and ancient books. Passover *Haggadahs* from Amsterdam and hymnals from Aram Zova, books of responsa literature rescued from the valley of death in Europe, illustrated writings, monographs of eminent rabbis, books no longer in print, books printed on blue paper, forms for obtaining meat on credit, and transport coupons. The one unifying factor is that there is no order to the books. They are piled up in boxes, and in every box you will find books new and old, books of our teachers of blessed memory and books by intellectuals of previous generations, books published this year, and books printed centuries ago.

This is now the store of the Gordine brothers. There are many who claim to sell old books, but true bibliophiles know there are only three true antiquarian bookshops. The Gordine brothers in the hangman's house in Rehavia, Naftali Hirsch Schreiber in Meah Shearim, and Issachar Heder of Djerba in the Bukharian quarter. You will find in one what you fail to find in another, and book lovers frequent all three.

There are two more that could be added to the list: Steinitz on King George Street, a specialist in out-of-print academia, who paces about his shop with an irascible expression on his face, as if customers are an irritation to him and he has no interest in selling anything, and Akiva Steinberg, who buys up entire libraries from heirs whose fathers loved books but who themselves prefer cash, and sells books piecemeal. Sometimes a real bargain falls into his hands and he sells it for an exorbitant price to the book-buyer of the Hebrew University or the Ben-Zvi Institute for Research.

The ways of conventional bookshops are not the ways of antiquarian booksellers. In conventional shops the proprietors make an effort to keep the shelves clean and clear of dust, arranging books in the correct places, and in protective wrappers. When customers arrive, the salesman approaches them with a smiling face and offers to help, and when purchases are made, he wraps their books in neat parcels and bids them a cordial farewell. But in an antiquarian bookshop, that is not the way things are done. Wrapping and parceling up do not exist there—they have mildew and dust instead. And any book that is older than another is more highly esteemed, even if it's torn and has been chewed by insects. Chaos is a virtue in these establishments. You go into the shop, stick your head into a box, reading, rummaging and disarranging, and no one discourages you. On the contrary, the bookseller gives the impression of one who is there solely to provide a haven for eccentric scholars. He knows each and every one of his customers, knows his personality and his preferences, whether it be for scriptural commentaries or homilies of the saints, the writings of eminent rabbis or *Haggadahs* for Pesah. Sometimes customers sell him books. Perhaps you wonder how he makes a living, but you need not worry on his account: lovers of old books are maniacs, and they invest a lot of money in their mania. And if they see a book printed in Venice in a certain year or in Istanbul in a certain year, they won't let such a jewel slip out of their hands, but pay a princely ransom for it.

I was familiar with these places, and now, wanting to decipher for myself the poem of our great-great-grandfather I went to the store belonging to the Gordine brothers. I thought I might find an old version of the poem in an old hymnal. Gordine senior approached me; he exchanged words of wisdom with me, and brought me a bundle of books of poetry dating from medieval times. He knew what usually interested me. I said to him, "I'm looking for something else today. A book of hymns from Aram Zova."

Here I was doing something that lovers of books should never do. For as soon as a man says what he's looking for, it becomes known to Schreiber and to Steinitz and to Heder and to Akiva, and the price soars, as there is no such thing as overcharging where old books are concerned, and what buyers of books tend to do is pretend they have come upon a book by chance, and that it's of no great importance to them, but they might be prepared to buy it at a reasonable price. The sellers know them and know they are being less than sincere. They have seen for themselves how, once the book has come into their hands, they won't let go of it for a moment until they have ransomed it for all the money in the world. And anyway, the higher the price rises, the more they covet it.

Mister Gordine showed me a number of hymn books; the one I was looking for wasn't among them. I went on my way. A few days later he asked me to return to his shop, and when I arrived he showed me a book of hymns in manuscript from Aram Zova. I knew at once this was the book I was looking for. I hastened to open it at the poem "Delight of the Nations," and saw that my assessment was correct: the version we had was corrupt. In the corrupt version the closing verse was*:*

> *The redeemer will send and redeem you,*
> *As the king reclines on his bed,*
> *In the courts of your holiness we shall walk,*
> *As the king reclines on his bed.*

And the manuscript version read:

> *The redeemer will send and redeem you*
> *And let your teachers not be misled*
> *In the courts of your holiness we shall walk*
> *As the king reclines on his bed.*

I remembered that this hymn was composed by our great-great-grandfather at the ceremonial meal that he organized after finishing the large book of rabbinic decisions. The questions began revolving in my head: why did he write, *and let your teachers not be misled*? Who are the teachers who might be misled, and what was their mistake, and why was the book hidden away, and why did the elders of the community come to his house and talk to him at length that night, and why did he resign from the rabbinate that day? And what did his little girl die of? And what was the venomous snake?

It was then that the truth began to bubble in my heart, although I didn't yet know where things were leading. I paid the full price that Gordine asked for the book, and went home. All that day I pondered the matter, and continued into my dreams at night. In my dream our great-great-grandfather, with a radiant face, and clad in a white rabbinical gown girded with a broad red sash, was holding an inkwell and using it to crush the head of a snake. He turned to me and said:

"The vow is annulled.
The primeval snake is crushed,
And the hidden will come to light.
You are the seventh generation,
And it is for you to resolve this matter.
It is permitted for you,
It is permitted for you,
It is permitted for you,
And as you have been permitted by an earthly court below,
So will you be permitted by a court above.
And truth shall spring from the earth."

It seemed that the solution to this dream came to me by way of a miracle. When the antiquarian booksellers realized what I was looking for, they began showing me pamphlets and hymnals from Aram Zova, which I bought from them at quite exorbitant prices. Then, some three months after my dream, Issachar Heder of Djerba brought me a certain pamphlet, not knowing what he was bringing me. If he had known its value, I wouldn't have been able to afford it.

This pamphlet was a judgment. And one of the sages of Aram Zova had written it, and sealed it with his seal. The judgment was written in a very florid calligraphic hand, the script habitually used by the sages of Aram Zova, in which I am no expert. So I turned my attention to the seal. The seal was round and colored red. The writing on it was blurred, and I could just make out a letter *aleph* and a *tzaddi*, and what looked like a ring encircling the letters. I looked again and saw that this ring was a snake curled around itself. With a start, I remembered the dream I had had. I looked again, and saw the snake's head was crushed.

By this time I already knew this judgment had been written by my great-great-grandfather, and I considered it miraculous that this pamphlet should have come into my hands. Later it became clear to me how this came about. There are things we take to be miracles, and they are nothing but straightforward events, and there are things we take to be merely straightforward events, which in truth are the greatest of miracles.

I went to see Hacham Ezra Alfiya in Jerusalem's Bukharian quarter, to ask him to decipher the judgment written in the pamphlet for me.

Chapter six

King David, may peace be with him, loved Jerusalem dearly. In his love for her, he wrote verses in her praise. And every verse is interpreted in various ways, and the praise of Jerusalem is found to be doubled and redoubled. David wrote: *Jerusalem is built as a city that is at unity with itself.* And our teachers of blessed memory interpreted this to mean—a city that makes friends of all Israel. Therefore, when a neighborhood in Jerusalem is named after one of the communities of Israel, this is considered shameful. By *halachic* ordinance it has been decreed—Jerusalem is not divided between tribes. An exception to the rule is the Bukharian quarter, since this name stands to its credit. Jerusalem remembers her sons who came from Bukhara and she delights in them, so she called one of her quarters by their name.

Innocent and upright are our brothers from Bukhara. Wealthy too, and happy in their lot. Devout in observance, and generous in their charity. And the commandment to honor thy father and thy mother they uphold with all their might, and for this reason they are blessed with long lives.

Hacham Alfiya lives in the Bukharian quarter. He is of Dama-
scene origin, and yet he resides in the Bukharian quarter, and this
on account of his wife, Mistress Mazel of the house of Babayov.
Mistress Mazel is one of the charitable ladies of Jerusalem, and one
of the most industrious. She is at the fore of every charitable act; she
has bequeathed *tefillin* to many orphans, and many orphans has she
has brought to the wedding canopy, and many old folk have been
sustained by her. She has donated a Sefer Torah in her name to the
synagogue of Musayov, and in the synagogue of Ades she supports a
minyan of scholars of the Zohar and a *minyan* of scholars of the Psalms.
A young pupil in the *yeshiva* of Porat Yoseph owes his learning and his
livelihood to her. In the Midrash of the Mashhadim she serves coffee
to the old men, and she officiates at the memorial banquets for the
sages; the cloths that cover the holy arks at the Western Wall—they
are the work of her hands. And with all this we have mentioned not
even a small portion of her merits.

The house of Hacham Ezra Alfiya and Mistress Mazel is large,
and in every single room you are entertained by the variety of colors
present. There are carpets spread on the floor and carpets hanging on
the walls, colored wraps on the armchairs and on the tables. Silver
Sabbath lamps and a gold *Hanukkah* menorah, a dish for the *Seder*
night and the goblet to be offered to Elijah the Prophet all sparkle
in a small glass cabinet. And on the wall, a large picture of Zion,
David's Tower and the Western Wall in memory of Jerusalem, and a
picture of their parents to uphold the commandment to honor one's
father and mother. The father, adorned with a white beard, is sitting
on his chair, and the mother is standing beside him, a scarf on her
head, their faces pleasant and radiant.

I came to Hacham Ezra Alfiya hoping he would read for me the
judgment of my great-great-grandfather that I acquired by courtesy
of Issachar Heder, the bookseller from Djerba, the judgment written
in the ornate script known as 'half-pen.' There are many in Jerusalem
who can read the letters of this script, but most will not interpret for
you unless you tell them what it is about, and who wrote the pamphlet,
and why he wrote it, and to whom he wrote it, and how it came
to be in your possession. Whereas Hacham Alfiya, I knew, would

read and interpret and ask no questions, being a man of restrained temperament. He used to say: "Should we not be content with what we are obliged to know? Why should we embroil ourselves in things we are not obliged to know?"

Hacham Ezra greeted me warmly. I gave him the pamphlet. He read, and I strained my ears to hear. This is what he read:

> A question is asked of the honored and highly esteemed leader, the great teacher, majestic and mighty, illustrious judge, learned in all matters, master of Aram Zova, elder of laws, from whom no secret is hidden, may the Merciful One preserve and redeem him. May his days be long in the governance of his realm, he and his sons in the bosom of Israel. May he graciously enlighten our eyes regarding an issue of *Halacha* with which we have contended, we the humble congregation of Cochin, where disputation has been rife, and decrees have been renewed and troubles multiplied, and we have no ear to understand the words of Torah that are more precious than gold and rubies, and there is no longer a prophet and there is none among us who knows how long this situation will endure.
>
> Our first question concerns our practice over many years of chanting the psalm: *Lord, the king shall rejoice in your strength and in your salvation how greatly shall he rejoice, his heart's desire you have given him and the request of his lips you have not refused, Selah*—every day after the morning *amidah* prayer. And we are in doubt whether we should we say it before the psalm prescribed for the day or after it, and should we say *Kaddish* after that, or join it with the *Kaddish* that is said on completion of the psalm of the day. May our teacher be merciful to us, and instruct us by his grace. And may blessings alight on his head.
>
> The response: To the members of the glorious congregation, more precious than gold and rubies,

their hearts filled with the love of Torah, whether it be *Gemara* or whether it be *S'vara,* in utter reverence for Heaven, crown of the people of Israel, men of good tidings that you are, the house was filled with light when your sweet words arrived, and we are glad that Torah has not departed from Israel.

But as for what you have written to me—that every day you say the psalm, *Lord, the king shall joy in your strength and in your salvation how greatly shall he rejoice,* and that you are in doubt when you should say it—this alarms me very much. Know my lords, you are in grave error. Heaven forbid this chant be sung before the daily psalm or after it. The liturgy as determined by the sages brooks neither addition nor deduction. And when you write that this is your longstanding custom—the truth is, your sages may have been thus accustomed, but they fell into a trap. As a bird is snared, so they were snared by the hand of that wicked and foolish man who arose in Israel two generations ago, and tried to hasten the end of days and perplexed all minds, and turned fasting into feasting and made himself a king, until it became obvious his mind was deranged. And he and his foolish disciples used to sing this psalm because 'and in your salvation' is the numerology of his abominable name, and he thought to call himself a king. Alas for a wise and understanding people that has seen such folly. And you should know that even in Aram Zova a number of teachers fell into the trap—among them the Great Teacher of our congregation—the pre-eminent rabbi, followed them and likewise fell with him into error. And he greeted him in kingly style and sent letters in his praise to the congregations of Israel. And our grandfather opposed him with all his might. He wrote other letters, urging that the former letters be ignored.

In time, the truth became clear and the Great Teacher admitted his error. And our grandfather urged that he make his recantation public, and claim the credit that is due to those who admit error and profess the truth, but he refused. And there was a grievous rift between our grandfather and the Great Teacher, but for fear of profanation of the divine name we shall not dwell further on the subject, and may the Almighty save us from error in our teaching. And our grandfather designed the seal of our family as a result of this episode. Since that man's seal was a snake, and from Heaven it was intended he had dug his own grave, for he was a snake to Israel and his venom was bitter, and he was punished and his legs were cut off and dust was his food. And our grandfather made his seal a snake with its head crushed, to signify that he had gone forth against him and crushed his head. And this is the seal that you see on all my judgments.

So when you receive this letter, you must immediately cease to recite this psalm after the *Amidah* prayer! Those who say it are to be reprimanded and silenced with a rebuke, and anyone who continues to say it after the rebuke—then he should be suspected of adherence to that sect. Where we live, even a man who is called by the name of Shabetai is suspect until he chooses himself an additional name.

And may it be pleasant for he who obeys, and may these blessings reach you at a pleasant time, and may you receive many blessings, and may the Almighty prolong your peace forever and may He remove from you and from us the yoke of the Gentiles, and may we yet see the coming of the just Redeemer, the true Messiah, and may the house of our holiness and our glory be built speedily and in our times—may our eyes see it and our hearts be glad, amen.

To be added to the great book of rabbinic decisions, in responses to faraway congregations. Between,
section 390 and section 391.*—*Shin Tzaddi* and section
Shin Tzaddi Aleph.

The cup of tea set before me by Mistress Mazel was now cold. The
cube of sugar was untouched. I rose and went on my way.

* The Hebrew symbols for the number 390 are the letters *shin* and *tzaddi*, which
  are also the initial letters of the name of the false messiah, Shabetai Tzvi.

Chapter seven

Six months passed since the resolution in the previous chapter. I spoke of it to no one. On several occasions, I meant to go to my great aunt Senora Victoria and tell her what had happened, but somehow I didn't go. For her part, she too made no mention of the conversation, nor even hinted at it. As I have said before, she was fond of silence. The business remained stored in my heart. I knew from previous experience that this was one of those things that solve themselves, and I didn't want to force the issue. And so it was.

One day I was told that Mr. Issachar Heder wanted to see me in his shop, urgently. I thought he had found another pamphlet manuscript from Aram Zova. When I came, he told me, "You remember the manuscript of a judgment from Aram Zova that I sold you?"

"Yes."

"You should know that a certain man who works with me in the antiquarian books trade sold me that pamphlet, and he is looking for you."

"And who is this man?" I asked him.

"Oh, he's an extremely distinguished man. He comes from Brazil. He's the *Nasi*, the president and head of the Aleppan congregation in Sao Paolo, the worthy congregation of Aram Zova. There, they call him el Presidento. He's an extremely influential man. He's established a number of *yeshivas* and synagogues in *Eretz-Israel.*"

I asked Issachar Heder: "And what does this man want of me?"

"I don't know. Perhaps he wants a rabbi for his community or a cantor for *Rosh Hashanah* or a teacher for a Talmud Torah."

"And where is this gentleman to be found?" I asked.

Issachar Heder took out a white card, showing the man's name and qualifications and title and the name of his city and his congregation, in Hebrew and in European script, in gold letters. He gave the card to me. At the bottom was the name of a hotel in Jerusalem and a room number.

I went to that hotel, and said I wanted to speak to a certain gentleman in a certain room. He asked my name and I told him. The man came down and met me. By the cast of his features, it was clear he was Aleppan; his clothes were simple and betrayed nothing of his distinguished status. It is the way of the world that simple people like to dress up like gentlemen, and gentlemen prefer to appear as simple people.

We began with the customary polite questions, and then he began going through my family connections with me. He asked me my father's name, my mother's name, the names of my grandfather and grandmother and my grandmother's sister, and where was she born, and where my grandfather had died, and what his trade had been. The man wasn't satisfied until he'd asked me the name of my great-grandfather too. I told him as much as I knew, and where my information was lacking, I told him so. Then he said: "I hear that you are interested in manuscripts from Aram Zova."

I realized he was in possession of a precious manuscript. I supposed he was one of those émigrés from Aleppo who had kept a fragment of a page from the famous "Keter" of Aram Zova, expecting to make a fortune from it.

I said to him: "What is it that you have?"

He said, "I have a lot of material, but wait here a moment."

He went up to his room and returned with a chest. He opened

it and took out a box. He opened the box and took out a scroll wrapped in several layers of silk and bound with silk tassels, which he untied, removing the wrappings to reveal a scrolled parchment that resembled the Scroll of Esther. He took another box from the chest, opened it and took out three large volumes. I was aware of the shrewdness of dealers schooled in the Aleppo tradition, and assumed he wanted to sell to me directly and avoid paying commission to Issachar Heder. I said to him: "I'm a simple man, and I don't have a lot of money."

He was silent for a moment and then said: "I don't want anything from you. You are the seventh generation. You are taking what is yours. I came here only to do as I was commanded by my esteemed father of blessed memory before he died, in fulfillment of his oath to my grandfather, and I have been blessed with the opportunity to accomplish this in my lifetime. I have one small favor to ask of you; that you write me a note, confirming that you have received a booklet from me and three other volumes."

I wrote as he asked, signing with my name and my father's name and the place of signing, Jerusalem the Holy City. He asked me to add the name of our great-great-grandfather, and I did so. He laid his hand on my shoulder and said: "I must ask you to excuse me now, I have much business to attend to."

Then he got up and went on his way.

I took the text and the volumes and hurried to the Bukharian quarter and the home of Hacham Ezra Alfiya, hoping he could read it for me. Hacham Ezra made no mention of our conversation of six months before, being a man of reserved temperament. He started to read the booklet. It read as follows:

> By divine grace and assistance I have recorded these words, I the junior scribe of laws, Raphael Chabot, in our mighty city of Aram Zova in the house of the illustrious judge and elder of laws, our master and our teacher, when a meeting of the spiritual council was convened at his home, at its head our *Nasi* and teacher, son of the great teacher to his flock, master of

the land, may the memory of a *tzaddik*, a saintly man, be blessed. And they invited me to join them. And I have copied the text for preservation in the community room in the synagogue of Ezra the Scribe.

We have heard the saying, and we are greatly perturbed, that the illustrious judge and elder of laws, our master and our teacher, wrote a judgment to a great city of Israel, the congregation of Cochin—may it be built speedily and established in our day, amen. And our teacher included it in the great Book of Rabbinic Laws that he composed, in section 390, and there he mentioned things that we had agreed were never to be divulged or discussed, neither in speech nor in writing, and not by way of allusion, not under any conditions or circumstances in the world, for the sake of Heaven. And we sent a reliable messenger to relay this to him, the junior scribe of laws, Raphael Chabot, the Merciful One preserve and reward him, to examine the truth of these matters. And the elder of laws and illustrious judge replied that in the name of Heaven it was his duty to publish the truth, so that all might hear and be afraid, and be saved from the pitfalls of error, and turn aside from those who hasten the end of days and exalt themselves above their peers.

And we went after him to his house, all the members of the spiritual council of our great city of Aram Zova, and our president, the son of our Great Teacher and Master, may the memory of a *tzaddik* be blessed, stood and said to him: It is utterly prohibited to leave behind any memory of that messianic episode, lest others come and repeat his errors. And he adduced proofs from the Babylonian and the Jerusalem Talmuds and from Sifra and from Sifre and from Midrash, from the medieval authorities and the latter ones.

However, the illustrious judge and elder of laws stood and refuted our president's arguments, and adduced further proofs against him, and said that he was the one offering deliverance from those who deal in error. And the son of our Great Teacher stood and swore a powerful oath that it was not on account of his own honor or the honor of his father's house that he sought to serve—but that his purpose was only in the name of Heaven, and therefore not to be defiled. And the illustrious judge answered him that he too meant only to uphold the name of Heaven.

At length, Hacham Raphael agreed not to divulge the name of the great teacher, but he refused to delete the judgment that contained his advice to that community. And fiery sparks flashed from speaker to speaker, and all the sages of the spiritual council rose and said that if he would not excise Section 390, that section with the problematic initials, *Shin Tzaddi,* they would invoke a threefold denunciation—ban, curse and denunciation—demanding that the entire book be hidden away. And our Master and our Teacher the illustrious judge said: I have labored night after night over this Book of Rabbinic Laws these twenty-four years, and it is my fruit and it is my life and dear to me as life itself, for it is all new interpretations of the axioms of the Torah. And in spite of this, the book will be hidden away, for I will not sin against the truth and will not delete the judgment from its place here. And truth shall spring from the earth.

And he announced he was resigning from the rabbinate. And that day was bitter as wormwood for Israel. They imposed a fast upon themselves and debated the matter back and forth until they found a compromise: the book should be hidden away for seven generations from the time of that episode. This record too shall be hidden away seven generations. And they declared an oath that no man was to disclose anything of this business until the seventh generation, and I too, the junior scribe of laws Raphael Chabot, was included in the dreadful oath that they invoked. May the One who understands errors, cleanse me from secret faults, and hold back your servant also from presumptuous sins, and let them not have dominion over me, then I shall be innocent and cleansed of great transgression, let the words of my mouth and the meditation of my heart be acceptable to you Lord, my rock and my redeemer.

And the Lord will do as He sees fit.

This document is signed by the members of the spiritual council of the congregation of Aram Zova our city of strength.

The text concludes at this point. And the large volumes bear the inscription: *Truth Shall Spring From the Earth.*

The Wheel
Turns Full Circle

Chapter one

My grandfather, of blessed memory, was so strict that people feared him—his time was precisely ordered, his study was dignified, and he had no time for casual conversation. And yet there were times when he was agreeable, his heart wide open and his mind joyful, and those who knew how to seize the moment and were not afraid of a rebuke, came to understand from him the true nature of the casual conversation of learned men.

I attended him in his old age. If I had known then what I know today, I would have asked him to dispel some of my doubts about the philosophy of the Rambam, and to throw light upon certain troublesome questions regarding his perception of the world, or I would have asked to hear about his reading of the *Tosafot* as interpreted by Maharam Schiff. But such is the way of the world, that when we have someone we can ask, we don't, yet when we are minded to ask, it is our misfortune that we have no one to ask. I was a child, and I only exploited his cordial moments for the purpose of hearing his secular talk. A man seeks to hear stories of past events, and he does not know that as these events unfold before him, he need only open his eyes to see them.

One of the times when he was often in an agreeable frame of mind was on the Sabbath, after the noon meal, and the chanting of the *bakashot*. He would repeat the old saying that sleeping on the Sabbath is a joy. Then, on rising from his afternoon rest, and while the other members of the household were still asleep, he would sit at the table wearing a *jallabia*—a combination of cloak and dressing-gown, white with embroidery at the fringes—and he would bless and eat the fruits that were the pride of *Eretz-Israel*. Thus did he uphold the ordinance of the rabbinical authorities to complete the one hundred benedictions one is obliged to recite every day. He ate the fruit very slowly to show his appreciation of the Sabbath, and for his Sabbath reading, he would take up the Ramban's commentary on the Torah and read a passage. So it was every Sabbath. It was a time of goodwill, when it was quiet in the house, and the sweetness of the holy Sabbath hovered over everything. His face was radiant with joy, and the study of the Ramban filled him with delight.

At that time I used to sit before him. He might glance up for a moment from the book, see me and cried: *"Haim!"** And then he would quote the line from the Bible, which pivots around my name: *"Life he asked of you and you gave it him, length of days forever and ever!"*

Then, smiling, he would return to his studying.

Sometimes he would start suddenly from his quiet pose, rise hurriedly, the Ramban in his hands, pointing and crying out to me in great agitation: "See! See what the Ramban says about the Rambam, would you believe it? Saying those things about the Rambam!"

Then he would draw me into the debate between the Ramban and the Rambam on the meaning of the sacrifices. At times like these, I felt he saw them standing before him, engaged in virulent disputation: these two giants were the teachers and masters he most admired. Sometimes he would test me with the riddles of Ibn Ezra. If I was on target with my answers, he would say: "Blessings on you!" But if I tried to challenge his logic, he would raise his hand in a dismissive

---

* Haim means life

gesture and return to his studying. At these times I also used to hear from him something of the sages of Aram Zova.

Once, when I mentioned the name of the Hacham Hiyyah Sapporta, he looked up from the Ramban and said: "The Hacham Hiyyah Hacohen Sapporta was a great man, the son of holy people, a noted sage and a scholar in Kabbalah. His blessings bore fruit, yet even his friends had no idea what he was thinking. And what became of his sons after him?"

With that he returned to his texts. I knew that he meant every word he said, and I knew that this cryptic description of one of the sages of Aram Zova had something hidden behind it. What he left hidden was revealed to me by others, unfolded before me in a story which began in the village of Tedef near Aleppo, continued amid the rioting students of Paris, and ended at the Western Wall, the sole remaining relic of our house of joy.

Some time later, I visited my great aunt Senora Victoria, during *Hol Hamoed,* the intermediate days of the festival of *Succot.* I wanted to wish her a happy festival. At that time she was immersed in sorrow, since that year she had been twice bereaved, with the deaths of her husband and her brother, leaving her all alone. I knew there was no joy in her house, other than in the words of Torah or in the practice of repentance.

I said to her: "I have a piece of news for you."

She said: "Tell me."

I told her the story that had so enthralled me. She listened patiently and without emotion. When I finished she said to me: "Have you finished?"

I replied: "Yes."

She waved her hand lightly as if to say: Some piece of news! What kind of story is that? Then she said: "Did you think that the blessing of Hacham Hiyyah would prove fruitless? Furthermore, he is our relative," and what she meant to say was: "Did you think that the outcast would be banished by him?"

I had no idea what she was talking about. Yet such is the way of the world that things that we regard as astonishing, the aged matriarchs of the previous generation regard as quite straightforward.

Chapter two

The sages of Aram Zova are devoted to the Rambam. They study his teachings, revere his name, and direct the course of their lives by his wisdom. He was not at ease with the notion that the livelihood of sages should be dependent on the public, and their income derived from charity. He was deeply respected, and so his ideas were taken into account in Aleppo. And although Maran enunciated a contrary opinion regarding this matter, drawing a distinction between generations past and our generations, and although the sayings of Maran in Aleppo were like the words of the prophets that brook no dissent—in spite of this many respected the opinion of the Rambam. Thus many of the sages of Aram Zova, masters and saints included, could be found engaged in trade, making their work the subsidiary and their study the essence of their lives. Study was the real focus and business work was managed around it.

And when was their studying done? Such had been the custom of the congregation of Aram Zova, or Aleppo, for more than two hundred years: at midnight the *shamash* of the congregation used to wander among the houses, knocking on the windows with his staff and calling upon the sages according to their prestige and upon householders according to their rank. He called every one by name and would add rhymes that were drawn from the *bakashot* or the liturgy, or were of his own invention. In a highly musical voice he would intone the melody of the psalms of supplication:

"Hacham Rafael Pinto, it is midnight! The *Shekhinah* is tinkling like a bell. Hacham Yedidiya Dayan, midnight! The angels are weeping bitterly. Senor De Piciotto, at dawn I shall seek you, my rock and my fortress, I shall stand before you morning and evening. Senor Nechmad! May they find you rejuvenated in tassels and bandana, like a bride adorned in the morning."

And more in this style. And they, not only did they not berate him for disturbing their sleep in the middle of the night, but they blessed and thanked him: "May you earn the reward due to a *shamash*, and may your sons rejoice."

He was even allotted a stipend for this work of his. As soon as they heard his call, they would rise, wrap themselves up and gather in the great synagogue, and in the study hall of the Beit Nasi, and in the academy of Senor Moshe, and in other synagogues and academies. On Sabbath nights they sang *bakashot*, and on week-nights they studied the Torah. After midnight prayers they sat in groups to study sacred subjects. A group devoting its attention to sections of the *Hoshen Mishpat* and *Beit Yoseph*'s commentary on it included an elder of the law who was an outstanding judge and a president of the *Beit Din* of Aram Zova; another group was occupied with the *Mishnah*, one group studied ethics in the *Reshit Hokhma*, while yet another was reading the *Zohar*, and so they gladly engaged in Torah until daybreak. With the rising of the sun, they prepared themselves for *vatikin*, the *minyan* which met for the earliest, dawn prayer of the *Shaharit* morning prayer, and their devotion was very deliberate, like the counting of jewels; each syllable emerging from their mouths was radiant with meaning and precision.

Those passing before the *tebah* were great sages, men of eloquence, and their voices were sweet and melodious before the Holy One, blessed be He. And they purified themselves of sin before Him, as a son purifies himself before his father, that He would endow them with understanding, and return them to His law and forgive their evildoing, and redeem them from their captivity, and heal the sick, and bless the crops, and gather them unto Zion, and reign over them as one, and punish the wicked, and give a just reward to those who trust in His name, and make His presence dwell in Jerusalem, and there establish the throne of David and make him prosper. And they prayed that their prayers would come before the One who listens to prayer and that He be kind to His people, and they will praise His name and He will grant them blessing and peace. And they would confess their evildoing and reconcile themselves with Him, and turn toward the strength of His presence that is in exile. And after the prayer, still wrapped in their shawls and wearing *tefillin*, they would read the *Hok le-Yisrael*, in which there are excerpts from the Bible and *Targum* and *Mishnah* and *Halacha* and even ethics, and they would conclude with some precepts of the Rambam, studying and reviewing every day, and depart to their homes in peace. There they would take a light meal, rest awhile, then go out to ply their trade for a few hours of the day before returning to their Torah. Such was the practice of the devout and renowned congregation of Aram Zova.

Despite this there were some sages who derived their livelihood from the community. They were recorded in the list compiled by the councils, the temporal and the spiritual, which were entrusted with the leadership of the community, and every sage was allocated a stipend according to his degree. A sage recorded in this list was called a 'listed' or 'classified' sage. Some called them 'Noted sages'. Over time the reason was forgotten, and every sage of distinction was called a Noted Sage. And whence did the noted sages derive their livelihood? There was a community endowment, set up by the illustrious Senor Franco and Senor De Piciotto. It was they who established a charitable society and a sick-bay for the ailing, they who inaugurated a fund for the aid and support of bridegrooms, in addition to many other charitable deeds. They ransomed Jews who had been imprisoned by the authorities by sending donations that paved the way for the annulment of decrees.

The endowment for the sages by Senors Franco and De Piciotto comprised courtyards and houses, whose rents were distributed to the noted sages. Once the administrators sought to use this endowment for the needs of the community, but this provoked such an outcry that the scheme was thwarted. The endowment was revered as a legacy from the past. It was said that the grandfathers of Senor Franco and Senor De Piciotto had been partners, traders in scrap metal and had once made their rounds of the streets in a cart, buying up scrap and all kinds of utensils that nobody wanted. The bulk of their work was done in the Spring, in the month of *Nissan*, when it is the custom of the daughters of Israel to purge their homes not only of any suspicion of leaven but also of any lingering speck of dust, and therefore they polish and scrub the rooms and the stairs and the beams, and the authorities have declared that they are not to be scorned. For this reason they bring all their utensils into the courtyard. All the days of the year man spares his favorite utensils, and even if they are old and damaged he makes excuses: I might need them one day, and there is nothing that does not have its place. However, in the month of *Nissan*, when these things are removed from the house, they are examined. Everything necessary for the upkeep of the house they take back, and the rest is sold at a knockdown price to those traders, who take the discarded items, clean them, repair them and set out for the nearby villages to sell them door to door.

Senor Franco and Senor De Piciotto were extremely close and fiercely loyal partners, negotiating in good faith and setting aside time for their Torah studies, awaiting salvation, and trusting in the Lord. And their hearts were joyful and their hands open to offer any kind of charity. And their pockets were one pocket, from which they took cash for their needs, and into which they put their proceeds. Scrap metal businesses, like most small businesses, sometimes prosper but more often are in decline, spending much and earning little, a wheel turning full circle and turning especially toward poverty. Their commerce, too, diminished almost to the point of collapse.

It is the way of troubles that they love to travel in packs. Trouble chases trouble. A certain Ishmaelite bought a pan from them; it broke in his hand and he demanded his money back. While this was going on, the axle of their cart broke. At the same time, rolls of expensive fabric that they had bought were damaged by rainwater. And then the authorities arrived, demanding they pay the same tax that was levied on wealthy merchants. Protests and pleas were of no avail, not pleasant speech nor the offer of a bribe. By the day's end, they were losing money so fast that they did not know which way to turn. Borrowing money at acceptable rates of interest was not to their liking. Taking out a charitable, interest-free loan was not to their liking either, since all their days they had enjoyed the labor of their hands. They consulted on the matter, and decided to enlist another partner. He would invest money, and they would contribute their labor and their good name, and perhaps his luck would bring blessing and prosperity to their business, and the Almighty would look favorably upon them.

Said Senor Franco to Senor De Piciotto, "Tomorrow, you do the rounds by yourself and I shall go and look for a partner, and in the Lord's name we shall succeed."

They felt encouraged, trusted in the grace of the Lord, and went to their homes.

It is the custom of the people of Aleppo that whenever troubles arise, a pilgrimage is made to the village of Tedef, a pleasant village with olive groves and orchards of almonds and apples, a sweet smell in the air, and only a few hours walk from Aleppo. In Tedef there is one fountain called the Ein El Azir, and it is a tradition among Jew and Gentile alike that it is named after our master, Ezra the Scribe, who used to bathe there. There is also a synagogue, and a sealed cave. It is said that a Torah scroll written by Ezra the Scribe is kept there. And it is there that they light candles, and make vows and pray and there prayers are answered.

Don Franco rose early and went to the village of Tedef. He went directly to the cave, lit candles and recited the opening section of the words of Elijah from the *Zohar*. He held out his hands in prayer to God and prayed with his broken heart that he and his partner might succeed in their business, enabling them to do the Lord's work without tribulation, enabling them to earn a livelihood in which there is neither shame nor dishonor, and that they might need no charity from flesh and blood. And he claimed no merit on their part, lest angelic prosecutors should come to investigate their dealings, but rather prayed that he might freely be granted this as a gift from God. Then he recited the Psalms melodically, and suddenly he rose and the words flew from his mouth: "O Lord eternal! What need have I of a partner of flesh and blood? You shall be our trusted partner!"

Being a God-fearing man he was alarmed at his own words and feared he might somehow have blasphemed against Heaven. Upon reflection he felt more at ease and vowed that of all the profit they made, one-third—the partner's share—would be given as charity to the sages of their city. And at once he arose joyfully and returned to Aleppo.

He did not go to his home but went directly to the great and ancient synagogue, which according to a tradition upheld by the sages of Aram Zova was built during the time of Jerusalem's Second Temple.

In the synagogue there is one cave where according to tradition, a revelation of Elijah the Prophet took place, and thus candles are lit there in times of tribulation.

Don Franco made his way to this synagogue to pray *minha*, the afternoon prayer, and the prayer was fluent on his lips and his heart was joyful. He gave praise and thanks to the Holy One, Blessed be He, and then he went on his way in peace. Within the great synagogue there was a wide corridor that was called the Midrash, where humble sages sat studying the Torah. As Don Franco was about to leave for his home, he saw a sage sitting there studying. As he gazed at him, he saw the sage's face light up with radiance such as he had never seen before. He was almost alarmed, and drew back from him. Fumbling in his pocket, he found one valuable coin, laid it before the sage and left.

The sage Don Franco saw was a humble man. He never held out his hand, he never asked for anything. If he was given something, so be it, and if not, he continued to sit and study. Earlier that day his wife had pressed him: the needs of the house were many and where was their livelihood? Go to the market, she said, and maybe the Lord will be merciful. He listened to her words, which rang with truth, and set out for the market, yet somehow his feet led him to the great synagogue. The sage told himself: I sought to serve the needs of my household; but what am I to do if my feet lead me hither, despite my resolution?

So he sat down in his customary place and immersed himself in a problematic tractate of the Talmud. Laboring over the holy texts dispelled his worries. In his current studies, he was striving to find a basis for the words of Rabbenu Tam on the issue of the widow from the family of dubious probity. He looked in the *Maharsha* and did not find it; he looked in *Maharam Schiff* and did not find it. He exerted all his energy, sitting with both his hands at his temples and poring over every single word. He probed and probed again, and some hours later his eyes brightened as the words of Rabbenu Tam became clear to him, as incandescent and glorious as he was hearing them being given on Mount Sinai. The joy of the Torah illumined his face. This was the light that had so amazed Don Franco. He thought he was seeing the light of the world above, the light reserved for saints, and did not know that the wisdom of the Torah could shine so brightly in a man's face. Such is the way of the world: sometimes we look for the hidden light, not knowing that the light of the Torah is the brightest light of all.

For his part, the sage was glad to have arrived at the basis he had sought for the words of Rabbenu Tam. He looked up, and saw a hand laying a coin before him and disappearing. He rose to seek his benefactor but could not find him. He was concerned that he was being rewarded in this world with his portion from the next, as in the story of Rabbi Hanina Ben Dosa. The learned rabbi had seen a hand come down from Heaven and offer him a golden leg, but then he was shown in a dream all the saints dining at a table with three legs and he was sitting at a table with two legs, and so he begged for mercy and the golden leg was taken from him again. However, soon the sage felt more at ease, saying: "Why should I ponder the acts of the Holy One, Blessed be He, Blessed be He? I did not ask to be given a coin. Rabbenu Tam, whose words I was studying, must have seen me in my poverty and brought me the coin to ease my mind and relieve my wife's concerns."

The sage did not know that it was not Rabbenu Tam who laid the coin before him but Senor Franco, transfixed by the light that he saw on the sage's face. Such is the way of the world: we think a miracle has been performed for us, and we do not know that the Lord of deeds unfolds those deeds through the hands of men of action. The name of the sage whose face had been so illumined was Hacham Raphael Sapporta, father of the noted sage, Hiyyah Hacohen Sapporta.

Raphael Sapporta was one of the sages who sat and learned in the Great Synagogue. Many of the sages of Aram Zova maintain that Joab, the son of Zeruya, built Aram Soba's ancient synagogue. There are several holy arks to be found there, and many ancient manuscripts of the Scriptures, including the famous manuscript by Ben Asher that is cited by the Rambam. Anyone needing to swear on the Torah, swears on these; and it is the prerogative of the family of the Beit Dayan, and no other, to administer this oath. The family of the Beit Dayan is in possession of a scroll of ancient pedigree, passed down through the generations all the way back to the time of King David, may peace be with him.

From the outset, this family was also known by the name Beit Nasi, and there were many privileges that fell to this family alone in Aram Zova. They were responsible for writing all the documents of betrothal, and *ketubbot,* and texts for loan contracts, and they wrap the Torah scroll on Sabbaths and holy days and the eve of *Yom Kippur,* and they say the *Kal Nidre* on the eve of Yom Kippur and the *Havdalah* in the synagogue at the Sabbath's end and prepare the *eruv tavshilin* of food for the holy days for those who have forgotten to prepare them, and it is they who go up to read the portion of 'the Song of the Sea' from the Torah on *Shabbat Shira,* the Sabbath of the Song of the Sea, and they are called upon to read the Ten Commandments on *Shabbat Yitro,* and they who are also *Hatan Torah,* reading the last portion of the Torah on *Simhat Torah,* and they are the ones who are given the honor of the last circuit around the Torah on *Simhat Torah,* the circuit which corresponds to King David, and they who are entitled to send citrons on the Feast of Tabernacles to all the townships neighboring Aram Zova. Besides all this, as we have already mentioned, they are entitled to swear in anyone required to make an oath in the rabbinical court in the ancient synagogue of Aram Zova.

Chapter three

The evil instinct is jealous of all men. But it is most jealous of partners. And if the partners are trustworthy, it is irked all the more. It stalks them around and around, devising ploys to trouble them or cause them to err.

All day Don De Piciotto waited for Don Franco to come and tell him what he had done, his heart preoccupied with all kinds of thoughts; jealousy held him in its grip like a besieging enemy scouring a wall in search of a weak point. But De Piciotto and Franco had been fond and trusting partners all their days. And every single day, from midnight to sunrise, they had studied ethical texts. The sacred books *Reshit Hokhmah* and *Shevet Musar* and *Pele Yoetz* were their guides, and they knew all the secrets and wiles of the Old King and the Jester, as the evil instinct was known, and it could not get the better of them.

And although the evil instinct has never been deterred by ethical texts, and will find its prey even if he hides himself in ethical texts, yet whoever truly struggles with it, will be helped by the Almighty. So Don De Piciotto was able to banish all unworthy thoughts and his Creator helped him.

At last Franco came and saw De Piciotto standing before the cart and he saw it was empty of merchandise, and he was ill at ease. But De Piciotto, catching sight of Franco, brightened.

"Welcome my friend. Do you have any good news for us? Has the Lord made your way successful and found you a partner?"

Franco answered him, "Yes."

"A partner to be trusted?" asked De Piciotto.

"There is none more trustworthy than he," he replied.

"And he has money?" he asked.

"Money is His," Franco answered him. And thus it was, that one of the partners was referring to flesh and blood while the other directed his thoughts toward the Heavens.

"And may I know his name?" asked De Piciotto.

"I'm deeply sorry," Franco answered him, "but that I cannot tell you. He made it a condition that his name not be revealed."

De Piciotto found this hard to understand, as indeed Franco found it hard to say. They had been trusting partners for seven full years and had hidden nothing from one another, but because they were friends and men of good faith, the evil instinct was dispelled from them. De Piciotto said to himself: Why should his name matter to me, so long as he has funds that we can trade with, and the Lord makes our way prosperous, and we can share the proceeds in three parts?

They agreed that on the eve of the first of every month they would examine the accounts and divide the profit into three. Up to that point they had shared one purse and needed no accounts, but with a third partner joining them, everything had to be done properly.

As they sat there a certain middleman came to them with a purse full of coins in his hand. He said: "I have been looking for you."

Knowing that their cart was empty of merchandise they were embarrassed and did not know how to answer him. And such being the way of traders, they took care not to utter a syllable that might betray their sorry state of affairs. They were silent. He said to them: "May I tell you what happened to me today?"

They said to him: "Tell us."

So he told them the following: "After the dawn prayer I made my way to the market, thinking that perhaps the Almighty would find some trade for me, and I could earn profit for my household. I saw a man who was clearly not from these parts, standing with a bag of money in his hand. He looked like someone seeking a bargain. Straightaway I went to him and greeted him and he greeted me back. I looked at him and it seemed to me he came from another country. Judging by his accent he sounded Lebanese, but he was dressed in the fashion of Stamboul, while his temperament and innocence made me think that he was Egyptian.

"I asked him: 'Are you seeking trade?'

"He answered me: 'Yes.'

"I said to him: 'I can offer his honor textiles from London and velvet from Paris and silk from India and wool from Kashmir,' and he said to me: 'No.'

"I said to him: 'Perhaps it is ornaments that his honor is seeking? I know skilled craftsmen, working with precious stones and jewelry and making necklaces of pearls and rings of gold and silver.'

"He shook his head at me, a sign of negation. I said to him: 'Perhaps it is pistachios from Damascus that you seek, or the halva for which Aleppo is famed, or dried fruits, or tobacco?'

"He said to me: 'No.'

"I was perplexed. A man comes from a far country, a purse full of money hanging around his neck, and all the merchandise by which our city prospers and which I offer to him, he rejects. I said to him in jest: 'Perhaps your honor is looking to marry off his daughter?'

"He smiled and said: 'I have no daughter.'

"I was afraid lest he was in search of one of those things that are forbidden by the government—or perhaps he had been sent by the government to investigate us. Finally I said to him: 'Why don't you tell me what you want?'

"Then he laughed and said: 'Had you let me speak, I'd have told you. I'm looking for an old *Hanukkah* lamp. I collect *Hanukkah* lamps from the various congregations of Israel. Go and find some for me; the older they are, the more precious they'll be to me.'

"I told him: 'I know two partners trading in scrap metal. I'll go to them.'

"He put the purse into my hand and told me: 'Go at once and buy them, and don't waste time haggling, and I'll wait for you here.'

"I was alarmed. I said to him: 'How can you give me money when you don't know my name or my surname nor where I live?!'

"But he replied, 'That is not important to me. Go and do your job, and the Lord will be with you and I shall pay you a generous commission.'"

The partners looked at one another and said nothing. Their hearts told them this was a good omen, since the *Hanukkah* lamp commemorates a miracle, and the luck of the new partner had surely brought this new miracle about, but for fear of the evil eye they kept silent. Especially excited was Don Franco, whose prayer had been answered. He knew this was to the credit of the sage whose face he had seen illuminated so. At once he vowed in his heart that if the Lord should bring him prosperity, he would set aside a regular allowance for that man.

They rummaged among their utensils and found one old *Hanukkah* lamp, made of brass. The middleman told them to fix a price, and they said to him: "How can we put a price on it? For an old piece like this we used to charge very little, but for this customer age is an asset rather than a defect, and he only wants to have it because it's old." And although they were wary of fraud, there is no fraud in the pricing of antiques, since everything depends on the taste of the collector and things that are dear to the heart are priceless. They set a price and the middleman paid them. He went to the buyer and immediately returned to them. He told them: "Go to your suppliers and bring me more lamps like these and I'll pay you four times the price you set."

Franco said to himself: I shall go to that sage whose face I saw lighting up, and I'll do him a favor. He went to find him, and met him on his way from the *Beit Midrash* to his home. He said to him: "Peace be with you, Rabbi."

"Peace, blessings and good things," came the answer. "What are you seeking?"

Franco told him: "I'm looking for a *Hanukkah* lamp." The sage was astonished: "It's not yet *Pesah*, and you want to practice the *Hanukkah* ritual?"

Franco explained: "I am a trader and I have met a man from a far country who wants to buy old lamps and is offering high prices. I mean to uphold the injunction of our masters—to support scholars of the Torah and do business on their behalf. Perhaps you have an old *Hanukkah* lamp?"

"Come with me," the sage replied, thinking in his heart: Rabbenu Tam is still helping me. They came to his house. He conferred with his wife and she brought out an ancient lamp, many years old, inherited from his fathers and his fathers' fathers, men of the Spanish exile. It was old and damaged and could not hold oil, or be used for any ritual purpose. He saw that engraved on it was the name *Sapporta* and the picture of a ship. They went and showed it to the foreign trader, and when he saw it he was overjoyed and offered a generous price for it, enough to keep the sage solvent for months.

Rabbi Raphael Sapporta made a handsome profit from the lamp, as did the partners Franco and De Piciotto and the middleman, and the man from the far country was delighted with it. And what was special about it? It was made to accord with a custom maintained by many of the people of Aleppo, that rather than light one candle, they lit two, thus on the first day of *Hanukkah* three candles were lit instead of the more usual two, up to the eighth and last day, when ten candles were lit.

This custom has been vouched for by my father, who saw his late father following the practice, and to this very day, in the Aram Zova community of New York, I have seen many doing this and not knowing why. I have heard it said that this tradition was instituted by exiles from Spain, who arrived in Aleppo at *Hanukkah* time and were saved from shipwreck by a miracle, and added an extra candle in memory of the miracle. So this ancient *menorah* belonging to Hacham Sapporta was designed to hold ten candles, and few of its type remained in the world. It was for this reason that the man was so delighted to have it and was prepared to pay so much for it. And he too did not lose on the deal, as it was eventually bought from him by the Louvre, for a substantial sum.

This was the *Hanukkah* lamp that was destined to be displayed in the Paris museum, where it would be seen by the grandson of Hacham Hiyyah Sapporta, son of the Hacham Raphael whose face had so lit up when he understood the opinion of Rabbenu Tam. And recognizing the family name on it, he would be reminded of his grandfather, and his thoughts thrown into confusion. But we shall let events unfold by themselves.

⅊

Following this episode, fortunes changed for the partners Franco and De Piciotto. Every deal they touched turned to gold. An old carpet that they bought at a knockdown price was coveted by a certain sheikh, who paid a handsome price for it. A table with broken legs cost them only a few coppers, but once they had repaired and restored it, it was seen by one of the villagers and reminded him of a table that used to stand in his father's house. He had been searching for something like it for years. This deal, too, yielded a respectable profit.

As their resources swelled, they began dealing in more expensive goods, and here too they were trading profitably. All in all, within a very short time they were riding high, but they showed no pride, nor any inclination to boast, and they treated everyone with integrity and humility and proved to be generous contributors to many charities. It is told that barely a year had passed since that first episode when they bought themselves a shop in the market and stocked it with all kinds of goods. Within a few more years they were appointed local agents for several overseas companies. Eventually they were awarded government warrants and titles of honor, becoming Senor Franco and Senor De Piciotto, and the kingdom of Spain even appointed their sons honorary consuls of that state in Aleppo.

And on the eve of the first of every month they worked out their accounts meticulously, setting aside a third of the profits for their anonymous partner. After some years, Senor De Piciotto could restrain himself no longer, and he pressed his partner Senor Franco day after day—where was the third partner and when did he take his share?

At first Franco put him off with reasoned argument: "Why should you care? Don't you see with your own eyes how his luck has worked for us, and how the wheel has turned to our advantage, and that all this wealth of ours is due to him?" But when he saw that his partner was not satisfied, and nothing that he said would convince him—for whoever heard of a partner who for years had neither taken his money nor checked the accounts—Senor Franco became afraid lest the evil instinct overcome his partner and incite him to blaspheme against Heaven. So as to *maintain innocence in the eyes of the Lord and of Israel,* Franco told De Piciotto the whole story of what had happened in the village of Tedef and in the great synagogue. De Piciotto was a God-fearing man, and not only was he not angry, but he loved Franco all the more and was exceedingly glad to be in such a partnership.

So together they gave praise and thanks to the Creator Blessed be He, and decided to finally use the saved third of the income for charity, as Franco had promised. First they went to the village of Tedef and hired many laborers and brought in masonry and timber, and they enlarged and embellished the synagogue by the cave. Then they went to the sage whose face had been so illuminated by the light of his Torah studies, and allotted him a regular monthly stipend. Then they founded charitable and benevolent societies, and still their hands remained outstretched to give. Not only did they give away the full third, for fear lest the devout be defrauded, they added further sums to the third, until their consciences were eased. Such was the conduct of the partners Senor Franco and Senor Piciotto, and at every *Purim* feast they would tell their sons and sons-in-law the story. And when they departed this world they left substantial wealth to their heirs, who carried on the ways of their fathers. And their commerce grew and spread worldwide, and their charity and generosity were legendary. And their grandsons, those celebrated grandees Senor De Piciotto and Senor Franco, whose praises are sung by all of Aleppo, did not content themselves with the deeds of their ancestors and sought to add to them. They dedicated a number of courtyards and houses with all of their produce, to go to the noted sages, and this was an endowment that no power on earth could foil. One of the noted sages who enjoyed the fruits of this endowment and immersed himself in Torah and divine worship was Hacham Hiyyah Sapporta, son of Hacham Raphael Sapporta whose face had been so illuminated when he understood the thinking of Rabbenu Tam. This was Hacham Hiyyah, of whom my late grandfather had said he had been versed in silence and that his friends could never fathom what he was thinking. It was with Hiyyah's grandson that the whole of the episode in Paris and at the Western Wall was to unfold, as shall be presently explained.

Chapter four

Hacham Raphael Sapporta was a humble man. He was meticulous in respect to the Torah and devout in his observance. He dearly loved the Torah, and it was his greatest fear that he might inadvertently neglect it. Whenever members of his family would urge him to rest a while, he would remember the sayings of our teachers regarding a sage who separates himself from the study of the Torah, and he would shudder and return to his studies. He used to say: "He who neglects the Torah is as one who sheds blood." Another favorite saying of his was: "What is the life of a man, other than his strength and his time. To dissipate one's strength or fritter away one's time is akin to destroying one's soul. Neither is subject to restitution or can be restored." Since the day that Senor Franco and Senor De Piciotto allotted Hacham Raphael a regular stipend for his sustenance, he had become all the more anxious, for now he was not only afraid of neglecting the Torah, but also nervous of the possibility of theft—lest he neglect the Torah for a moment and thus be accepting payment under false pretences. He even withdrew his hand from communal affairs. To every request that was made of him he would reply: "There are others who can do this." Then he would return to his studies.

He was often asked to ordain candidates for the rabbinate, and he would decline, or to inspect the credentials of scholarly emissaries from *Eretz-Israel* and he would again refuse. He would not solemnize a wedding or preach to the bereaved, give advice to merchants or pray for women in childbirth. He paid no heed to individuals or to leaders of the community. Even our Teacher and Master, the Chief Sage of Aram Zova, came up against his reticence. Our Teacher—who knew the status of Hacham Raphael and was aware of his strengths, and had installed him in the place that was most fitting to him—eventually invited him to serve as a judge in the financial court, but Hacham Raphael refused. An invitation to serve on the spiritual council was likewise spurned.

It was known in Aleppo that our Teacher and Master, the Crown of our Community, was acquainted with every single one of the sages of Aram Zova, was aware of their strengths and set them in the place most fitting for them. There were sages who tried to conceal their activities and keep them secret from all men—yet our teacher would uncover their hidden treasures, as happened in the case of Hacham Nissim Muhadeb.

Hacham Nissim Muhadeb, whose father died after begetting him and whose mother died giving birth, had been left a lonely and destitute orphan. His mother was the daughter of a sage from Tiberias who had come to Aleppo as a fundraiser for the community in *Eretz-Israel* and stayed there, unable to raise enough money to make his return worthwhile. His father had been a simple artisan. Since there was no one to take care of the orphan, the trustees of the *Somekh Noflim*, the 'Charitable Fund for Those in Distress' looked after him, until he reached the age when he could be sent as an assistant and an apprentice to a goldsmith's workshop. This workshop belonged to Ezra Farhi, who was from a family of highly reputable goldsmiths.

Do you suppose that a goldsmith's workshop is sparkling with precious stones and lit by shining jewelry? Well, it was not the case, for it was small and dingy and crammed with all kinds of instruments—wicks and hammers and pincers and files and pliers, and screws and nails of all different sizes. It was a busy place too, with customers coming and going and conferring with Ezra, clutching jewels that they wanted to be mounted on gold chains.

Nissim's employers were kind to him, and trained him in all the tasks of the goldsmith's trade: gripping with the pincers and straightening with the pliers, beating with the hammer and heating ingots in the furnace until they glowed white. There was only one task not entrusted to him, and that was inlaying, which is an art and not a craft, and a secret that is handed down confidentially from father to son. For inlaying requires true expertise and a good eye to gauge the quality of every jewel, to know which facet will catch the light, how to display its full beauty and where to set it, since if it is set in a place that does not suit it, a precious stone will never shine. Such is the way of artists, that they always hold back one of their secrets and do not teach it to their apprentices, lest those who learn from them eventually outstrip their masters. If their apprentices learn these secrets by themselves, so be it.

Nissim Muhadeb felt no pressure to learn the things that were not taught him, because his heart was not in the trade. The lad worked hard, but with tears in his eyes. His heart longed for the Torah, and this was more precious to him than rubies. While his hands crafted precious stones his lips uttered verses from the *Seder Taharot* which he had learned by heart. His day was for work and his night for the Torah. Every night he would hide himself away in a different synagogue and study the code of the *Hoshen Mishpat*, from the medieval authorities to the post-medieval rabbinic legal authorities, the responsa literature, delighting in the Torah, and no mortal in the world knew his secret, since he hid himself away and was wary of any prestige he might be given on account of the Torah.

On attaining his thirtieth year, he went as usual to study by night in the Beit Midrash of the Nasi Synagogue, intending to commemorate his mother, who had died the very same day that he was born. That night he did not study with his accustomed pleasure. A thread of grief was woven into his learning, as he reminded himself that he had no friend in the world other than the Rashba and the Shach and the Taz, and dearly as he loved them, he longed for a friend of flesh and blood in the here and now. Before sunrise he felt his head tilting and his forehead touching the Talmud. With an effort he raised his head and it fell forward again. He saw the letters of the *Gemara* dancing before him and the *Tosafot* going round and round the page. He feared this was the fulfillment of the saying regarding one who dozes off in the Beit Midrash—that his learning is torn to shreds—and he was close to panic when he saw our Teacher and Master was standing before him, laying his hand on his head and blessing him. But then he was glad, seeing in this dream a good omen, a sign that he would not be punished, Heaven forbid, nor all his learning forgotten. Nissim said, "A good dream, a good dream I have dreamed." But then he opened his eyes and saw that our Teacher and Master was still standing there. Such is the way of the world, sometimes what we think is a dream becomes real before our eyes, and sometimes what we think are great events prove to be nothing but dreams. Startled, Nissim stood up, took the hand of our Teacher and Leader and Crowning Glory, and kissed it.

He mumbled: "I thought I was dreaming…"

Our teacher smiled and said to him: "I came to hear your learning and to bless you, because it is time for you to take your rightful place, so that others may benefit from your wisdom. We are setting up a new court for financial matters, because there are many traders in Aleppo and the disputes between them are complex, and in all Aram Zova I have found no one as well versed as you in the *Hoshen Mishpat*."

Hacham Nissim accepted the appointment and achieved renown as a conscientious judge with a deep understanding of the law, held in awe by all litigants as one who had the perspicacity to expose all their deceits and machinations. It was he who brokered a settlement in the long-standing lawsuit between the heirs of the minister Farhi in the matter of his wife's jewelry, a case in which all the sages of Aleppo had become embroiled over two generations. It was he who reached a decision in the case of the widow of the house of Chabot, who had bequeathed land to the synagogue, leading to a dispute between her heirs and the congregation. If our Teacher had not discovered him he would have remained Nissim Muhadeb the jeweler's assistant, and we would not have reaped the benefit of his erudition.

Once I asked my grandfather of blessed memory about this incident, and he nodded to me as if saying, I know. I summoned up the courage to ask him:

"Was this an instance of the spirit of Divine intuition?"

Grandfather fixed his black eyes on me and said reproachfully: "You're asking for a miracle? The incident cannot be detached from its literal meaning. Have you not learned that a sage is superior to a prophet? Just as the expert knows the quality of jewels, so the sage knows the quality of sages.

"Such was the genius of our Teacher and Master and Crowning Glory," he continued, "that from the moment he heard any of the sages of Aram Zova speak, our Master could cite that sage's degree and could tell if he was a judge or a preacher, a teacher or a scholar, and set him in his place."

And after some further reflection he added: "You seem to think Our Teacher was like the leaders of the community today, where someone who is not a sage is appointed to a sage's office, and a preacher is made president of the court and a sharp-witted sage is made a preacher, and an arbiter in matters of *Kashrut* is appointed head of a *yeshiva*, and an expert educator is set to issuing divorce papers—may the Merciful One spare us."

He fell silent. His eyes were dark and sad.

※

As in the case of Nissim Muhadeb, the strengths of Hacham Raphael Sapporta too were not concealed from Our Teacher and Master, the head of Aram Zova. There was one occasion in particular when the Hacham Raphael asked him to clarify a saying of Rabbenu Tam, and from Raphael's question, our teacher immediately understood his stature and character and his way of thinking. He urged him several times to take on an appointment, but Raphael always refused. And although they were friends, there was once a certain coolness between them. It was when a great assembly for the sake of Heaven was convened in Our Teacher's house to protest the outbreak of unruly behavior in the new school founded by the Alliance Israelite Universelle, the philanthropic society headquartered in Paris. All the sages gathered to debate the issue, and it was agreed that they would protest on behalf of the Holy One, Blessed be He, whose glory had been desecrated, and the respect to be accorded His teaching which had been besmirched, and they wrote a petition beginning *Lift up thy voice like a shofar* that was signed by thirty-two sages. And the Crown of our Community asked Hacham Raphael to join with them and sign the petition, but he refused, saying: "I'm not a sage of the community. The verse *'Surely oppression maketh a wise man mad and a gift destroyeth the heart'*—is it not interpreted by the wise to mean that the work that a sage does for the sake of the public corrupts his wisdom and destroys it?"

Hacham Raphael Sapporta, who loved our Teacher and Master, sought only to use the words of our masters to excuse himself, and no other thought had occurred to him, but to Our Teacher it seemed to be a statement of grievance. He thought that the words of Hacham Raphael were directed at him. He, Our Crowning Glory, who in his youth had been renowned for his diligence and had been an expert in the secrets of the Torah, had been forced to give up his study time for public works once he became the head of Aram Zova, to sit with the spiritual council and the temporal council, visit religious schools and examine the students, ordain candidates for the rabbinate, confirm important legal decisions, appoint judges, supervise the charitable societies and those charged with the visitation of the sick, placate the governor, intervene with the consuls on behalf of a member of the community who had offended, reprove the community—all this and much more—until, as a result of all this, his time for studying was severely curtailed. All his days he was pained and distressed over this; how he envied the sages sitting over the Torah and writing their commentaries!

So when our Teacher and Master heard the words of Hacham Raphael concerning the oppression that makes a wise man foolish, he was angered. He declared: "Does Hacham Raphael know whether his son's son will not need this thing, is it not a wheel turning full circle?"

Then he concluded: "Hacham Raphael is a sage—all unto himself."

The word Our Teacher and Master actually used was the Arabic word *Lahalo*, and by calling Rafael, 'Hacham Lahalo'—he implied he was someone who was not involved in the community.

Hacham Raphael understood him at once, and used all the appeasements in the world in an effort to placate him. And although this was not the intention of Our Teacher and Our Master, the son of Hacham Raphael, Hacham Hiyyah Sapporta, used to say: "My sons, see how great are the words of the wise men who said, *Beware of the embers lest you be scorched, for their bite is as the bite of the fox, and their sting as the sting of the scorpion*, since it was on account of the punctilious nature of our Teacher and Master that my son, Master Jacob Sapporta, or as he calls himself—Monsieur Jacques Sapport, left the *Beit Midrash* and went to study with the Alliance Israelite Universelle society, and his Torah learning is no longer his major preoccupation—his trade—and in the end his eldest son became a clerk in the warehouse of Franco and Piciotto."

At that time Hacham Hiyyah Sapporta had no idea that another son of Jacob would go to Paris, lay aside his learning, and desert his family, and become involved with that famous group that reckoned it could set the world to rights and overturn the old order, and nearly destroyed his own world, until the Lord reminded him of his ancestors who had laid down their lives for the Torah, and lit up a way for him with a *Hanukkah* lamp, in the episode which we will soon relate.

Chapter five

Hacham Raphael Sapporta was as diligent as he was pious. It was said that in those days he upheld all the precepts of piety in the *Reshit Hokhmah*. In spite of this, he was not immune from the gossip of the populace. Because he did not involve himself in the community and did not officiate at their daughters' weddings, nor bless their sick, nor eulogize their dead nor give merchants advice on the increase of their profits, householders used to point their fingers at him, as if saying: "What use is he to us? All his reading, is just for himself, all his learning—for himself." And they would add in a whisper: "Why should he receive a monthly allowance?"

Only Senor Franco objected to this attitude, for he saw how the face of Hacham Raphael was illumined with sublime light and knew that in him the saying was fulfilled, the injunction to extend help and give blessing to erudite scholars, and Franco silenced Hacham Raphael's detractors with a reproach. He said, "What do you know of the qualities of sages? Does he take anything from the public purse?" And so on and so forth. But it is the way of those who slander that they will not be silenced with words of reason, such as: "What pleasure is it to the snake when he bites, and what profit is there for the slanderer?" They nod and wink as if saying, "It isn't for nothing that Senor Franco is supporting him. There must be something behind it."

Such is the habit of the gossipmongers, that after praying the dawn prayer of *Shaharit*, they go to drink coffee. The proprietor of the coffee house sets out low chairs made of wicker and they sit on them, and he circulates among them, with an oval brass tray in his hand and five small cups on it made of thin-lipped white porcelain, decorated with painted roses. In the middle of the tray, there's a bronze coffee pot with a long handle and a jug of cold water. And he wishes them good morning, addressing each by name and by status, and they drink, and bless him and engage in trivial conversation about the rains and the winds, one speaking and another replying, and they discuss the ways of kings and their wars, the King of Germany who prevailed and the King of France who was vanquished for want of troops, and after that they talk of livelihood and economics and rising prices. Such is the way of the evil instinct, that it begins with idle talk and passes on to forbidden things, and so their mention of prices leads on to a Senor So-and-So, and "Have you seen the diamonds and the sapphires that his wife was wearing?" To which another replies, as if speaking in all innocence but plotting treachery in his heart, "Are his dealings wholly proper, whether in things relevant to authority or in other areas?" He implies that these matters are known but he is careful of his honor and so does not want to clarify. And a third continues, "What is there left to say if the heads of the community act in this way…. I actually have quite a lot to say about members of the temporal council and in particular a certain merchant," and he says the name and then adds, "I'm afraid lest I stumble into calumny, silence is best."

So after they have reviewed, parading before their eyes the members of the council and the heads of the community like so many sheep, they survey them one more time, and one of them says, "What have we to do with such people? They have their affairs as we have ours, and why should we care what they do?" And all nod their heads at this, drink up what remains of their coffee, wipe their mouths and go their way.

At first, the evil instinct relents, but eventually it rules, for their minds are not at ease until one day they began slandering the sages.

One of them said: "I shall tell you about that saint, Hacham Raphael, whom many call the Hacham *Lahalo*, and you shall know whether he is sincere. Why does he differ from the other sages— because he receives an allowance from Senor Franco. This allowance has corrupted his integrity."

There was much dissension among the sages of Aram Zova on the matter of the Francos, because the Francos who came to Aram Zova were distinguished and sophisticated people, lovers of wisdom and possessed of fine qualities, but they were unwilling to mingle with the congregation. They made themselves a congregation of their own and appointed a sage of their own. So the remuneration that should have gone to someone who was of the Beit Dayan family, being of the lineage of the House of David, was not given to him but to their own sage. And they conducted themselves according to their own norms and refused to adopt the customs of Aram Zova. And even the contributions and rates imposed upon the congregation of the faithful they did not want to pay, giving only a fixed sum to the council of the congregation. In the end, they detached themselves from the community and formed a community of their own. The sages of Aram Zova were furious at this rift, complaining of the Francos and advancing arguments against them. Only Hacham Raphael Sapporta stood by them, and delivered a lengthy judgment declaring that justice was on their side, since they were a congregation in their own right.

Yet the slanderer in the coffee house alleged that this saintly man had been corrupted by wealth, adding that it was for this reason his eyesight was dulled. When the purveyors of gossip brought these things before Hacham Raphael Sapporta, the man was mortified. He, who throughout his life knew nothing whatsoever about money, and hated wealth and asked for nothing—neither from the community nor from benefactors, neither for himself nor for his household—if they gave to him they gave, and if they didn't give he sat and studied, until Senor Franco saw his eyes light up with the joy of the Torah and was moved to give him a coin, and when his business prospered, allotted him an allowance—was he now to be suspected of taking bribes? Perish the thought! He, who feared for his sight on account of the dimness of the prayer house where he studied all day, straining his eyes over the tiny letters of the commentaries—would it be said of him that he had perverted justice? He laid his sanctity aside and said, "I do not forgive this man, absolutely not, not in this world nor in the next."

When the matter became known, there was uproar in the community. People recoiled from the man who had slandered Hacham Raphael; many thought that this slanderer would be ostracized by the community, if not worse. Even the man himself and the members of his household were alarmed by the rebuke, for the power of Hacham Raphael Sapporta was well known, as was the story of how he came to have his regular place in the *Beit Midrash*.

The sage's place was in the corridor of the great synagogue, and opposite his place was a window, overlooking the cave of the saints. The cave of the saints was a patch of ground in the courtyard of the synagogue where the greatest of the sages and the dignitaries of Aram Zova had been buried for many generations. And not only were the sages buried there, but manuscripts of fresh interpretations of the Torah as well, for this was also the *genizah*, the place where vessels containing the archive were deposited. This archive was like any other archive; it contained sheets of Torah scrolls that had decayed and *mezuzot* in which a flaw had been found, and had therefore been consigned to burial in the tomb of the saints. But in one respect the cave of the saints was superior to other archives. Here jars full of entire manuscripts were also buried, for many of the sages of Aram Zova wrote new interpretations of the Torah, and responsa and verdicts and matters of *Kabbalah*, but few had succeeded in having their works printed. Consider the difference between our days and those. In modern times, money is available and printing is cheap, and anyone who gathers together a few anecdotes regarding the sages of Israel will see them printed as a book and will receive payment, whereas in those days the sages themselves were eager to write their interpretations of the Torah but were unable to have them printed. And although some succeeded in gathering funds from public benefactors and sent them off to Livorno or Constantinople where the printing took place, many manuscripts were lost between Aleppo and Livorno and between Aleppo and Constantinople. And even when Ribi* Isaiah Dayan established a printing press in Aleppo—which was a day of celebration for the sages—they still lacked the means to have their own works published.

In Aleppo, when a sage saw his end drawing near, and still there was no one to publish his texts, he would moan piteously and hide the manuscripts over which he had labored all of his life, burying them in the ground in the cave of the saints near the great synagogue, by the tombs of the sages of Aleppo, praying that the One who redeems the saints of Israel might redeem his manuscripts also. The whole of the world is nourished by the wisdom given us by the great in their books, but who knows how many thousands of manuscripts that would have illumined the world have perished over the generations because the money to publish them could not be found? Some were lost, some destroyed in house fires, some eaten by mice, to the extent that the joke circulating among the wags of Aleppo had the mouse reciting daily the verse: *To do thy will is my desire... and thy law is in my belly.*

So, it was opposite this cave that Hacham Raphael Sapporta was accustomed to study. Just as there is no incense without resin, so there can be no quorum without dissension. Some malcontents were jealous of Hacham Raphael, and complained to the trustees, saying that by sitting opposite the window he was obstructing their light. The trustees thought that their grievance was justified, and they came to Hacham Raphael and asked him to change his location. He raised no objection, and moved to another place in the corridor, a place known as 'the *Midrash*.' A few days later, one of the trustees arrived in a state of great alarm and told his colleagues how some of the saints buried there had appeared to him in a dream and had rebuked him: "We used to enjoy listening to the learning of that diligent scholar so much, day after day. Why have you deprived us of this?"

---

* Ribi—reverential form of address used by Syrian Jewry for their rabbis, "Rabbi" is not used, since in Arabic it denotes "God"

So Hacham Raphael was restored to his place. The episode was reported at large and the community saw how great was the power of the mighty sage that even the saints, crowned in glory and delighting in the glow of the *Shekhinah*, were leaving their places and coming to hear his discourse.

Members of the family of the slanderer also saw the power of the Hacham Raphael and were afraid, and sent deputations of friends to make peace with him. They wept before him. He said to them, "Have I ever protested over my honor? I protested only over the honor of the Torah. Go and ask the Torah's forgiveness."

Finding himself utterly spurned by Hacham Raphael Sapporta, and abandoned by his friends, the slanderer was at a loss. He began thinking thoughts of what is above and what is below and what is before and what is behind. He began reading worthless books, *internal* books as they are known, books of esoteric lore, where improper things were revealed to him, and he began painting pictures and imagining images, and gradually took leave of his senses. Day by day his mind became more confused. His son, an aggressive man of incisive intellect, was protective of his father's dignity, and from that time onward the son was like one who has separated himself from society. While his father read esoteric books, while he read books that are frowned upon in religious circles. He came across a number of pamphlets, printed overseas. No one knew how they had reached Aleppo. Some said that the founders of the Société Alliance Israelite Universelle had brought them with them from France, and some said they were found in the archives of the French consul. One way or another they fell into the hands of the son and he became engrossed in them, fired with enthusiasm. Pardon the profane comparison, but he began poring over them as a learned student pores over the Torah ... indeed, it was not long before he was the leader of the group of world-reformers of Aleppo that tore a number of families apart. At first their activities were conducted covertly and no one knew their identity. By the end all was revealed. And this was the group that was joined by the son of Monsieur Jacques Sapport, son of Hacham Hiyyah Sapporta, the illustrious son of the saintly Hacham Raphael whose deeds we are now relating.

Chapter six

The face of winter is forbidding. The days are short and the darkness abundant. Rains keep the marketplace empty, and people are confined to their homes. The joy of *Succot* has long been forgotten, and the Torah has ordained no festival to sweeten the days. That is why the lights of *Hanukkah* are so beloved of Israel.

It is said that a special love accrues to these lights, for bringing the hearts of a household's members closer together. The language of the sages heals, and since the day the sages said: The obligation of *Hanukkah* is for every man and his home to have a lamp, this quality has been instilled in them. And though their light is small, it warms the heart; and though the sages have not given us dispensation to use them for their light, warmth of the heart is not forbidden. Moreover, they remind us of times of deliverance and times of mercy, and testify that the wicked are destined to be delivered into the hands of the righteous, the many into the hands of the few, and the evildoers into the hands of those who observe the Torah.

On the eve of the start of the month of *Tevet*, after we had lit the lamps and sung a psalm of David, a song at the dedication of the Temple, in the style of Aleppo, my mother was in a cheerful mood, and she said to me: "Son, the month of *Shevat* is close at hand, and then you will start wearing your *tefillin*. Go to grandfather and ask him to help you prepare a sermon." I relished the prospect, and was thrilled with anticipation.

I went to grandfather's house. My grandmother, Nona Sarina, opened the door to me with a beaming face. She thought I had come with the sole purpose of being treated to *zalabya*, the little sweet buns that we eat at *Hanukkah*, and she turned straightaway to the kitchen, to warm a pan. But I was thinking about the sermon. I went to grandfather's room. Cotton wool wicks floated in glasses full of olive oil and by their pure light, he was sitting and perusing a book. I took his hand and kissed it, he laid it on my head and blessed me, and returned to studying his book.

I said to him: "Grandfather, *Ima* sent me to ask you to help me with a sermon." He turned his dark eyes to me and said: "Your mother asked me to help you with a sermon; but I was thinking you could preach on your own account, for isn't it high time that you learned the art of preaching? Why, at ten years old, I was already preaching in the synagogue of Aleppo," and he returned to his book.

I was afraid I would leave empty-handed and rebuked, but suddenly he smiled and said: "You are putting on *tefillin*—this is a festive day for our sages—of course I shall help you with a sermon." He was silent for a moment, then put his hand to his temple and said: "Not only that, you shall preach the words told to me by my father of revered memory the day that I put on *tefillin*, and he told me they were spoken by Hacham Hiyyah Sapporta, quoting his father the saintly Hacham Raphael, at the *tefillin* ceremony of the firstborn son of Jacob Sapporta," and he concluded his address with the verse: *"They shall not depart from your mouth, nor the mouth of your offspring, nor the mouth of the seed of your seed, from henceforward and for ever.* From this time onward the Torah is seeking her lodging, *and the outcast will not be expelled by him.* And people did not realize at that time which way things were leading."

I knew my mother had chosen the time in the days of *Hanukkah* when grandfather's heart would be open wide, and I strained my ears to hear more. He sensed this and said: Again you are asking for a story, but have I not told you that stories unfold by themselves, and mortals need only the eyes to see them? And grandfather began to relate:

"This was the story. Hacham Raphael Sapporta was not content with the method of teaching at the Talmud Torah in Aleppo (which they called the *Kuttab*) because once a youth had gained understanding of the Talmud, he would cease studying and begin analyzing, and for love of analyzing he would become engrossed in it and would not revise his study of the *Mishnah*, and would neglect his reading of the Bible too.

For this reason, when his son Hiyyah came of school age, he upheld the commandment of education himself, and was unwilling to send him to the *Kuttab*. Furthermore, this son of his was dearly beloved of him, since his conception was a miracle and his birth a miracle of miracles. And there was another consideration, in that he saw him as shrewd and strong in memory and perception, and feared lest the evil eye take control of him. When others said to him they feared the evil eye, he used to mock them and dismiss their words, but to himself he said: Here there is reason to fear. And although his wife said to him: "Leave the child alone and let him learn with his friends and let him discover something of humanity," he paid no attention to her words. If truth be told, many years later he admitted to her that she had been in the right, and that if he had heeded her voice the things that had befallen him would not have happened. Hacham Raphael treated his son in the manner laid down by the sages in the *Mishnah*, introducing him to the Bible at five years old, and over the next five years he read the whole of the Bible from beginning to end. Alongside the holy texts he learned the science of grammar and cantillation and the hints of the *Massora* and the *Targum* of Onkelos and the commentaries of our master, Rashi, with Rabbi Eliahu Mizrahi, and the Prophets with Rabbi David Kimhi, and the commentaries of the disciple Rabbi Shmuel Laniado, of whom tradition has it that when the elders of Aleppo asked our Master, the Beit Yoseph, to send them a sage, he wrote to them: "I am sending you a man who is my equal." And on Sabbaths he taught him chapters from the wisdom of Ibn Ezra and from the Ramban. By the age of ten he had been through the whole of the *Mishnah* with him, with the Rambam's commentary, and over the next five years he read and reread it.

And when Hiyyah came of age, the night before he put on *tefillin*, his father called him to his room. His mother laid her hands on his head and blessed him. She kissed him and wept. She wept for emotion and she wept for destitution, as their house was empty and she had nothing with which to entertain the worshippers on the day that he would ascend the podium. And she also wept because she had nothing to give him as dowry other than one handkerchief on which she had embroidered a series of letters, an acrostic to remind him of the verse: *Hear my son the teaching of your father, and do not forsake the law of your mother.*

She gave him the handkerchief and said weeping: "My darling son, there is only thing for which I have pleaded all my days, that my son will be a lover of the Torah and a God-fearing person. I know your hidden depths, and I know you are a thoughtful person. Pure thoughts you have. But it is the way of thoughts to stray by themselves and encounter fancies and blend with them. Please, if you should come to such a time, think of your mother's love and her tears. And do not say, what has love to do with thought, and an aged mother to do with the free exercise of intelligence, and what are tears compared with scholarly enquiry, for great is the power of a sigh arising from a broken heart, and great is the power of a tear welling from a pure spring, for what comes from the heart enters the heart, and he who bathes in a pure spring will be purified."

And so saying, she kissed him and left.

His father, the saintly Hacham Raphael, called to his son to approach. He took his hand and held it tight. He said to him: "I heard the *Gaon* Pne'ai Yehoshua had a favorite pupil who studied with him for many years. One day he came to take leave of him. The *Gaon* took his hand and said to him with a smiling face: *Rejoice in your youth young man, and may your heart cheer you in the days of your boyhood, and walk in the ways of your heart and in the sight of your eyes,* and suddenly, he gripped his hand tightly and said: *And know... that for all these things the Lord will call you to judgment.* And the pupil said that throughout his life, whenever he was about to commit a sin, his hand would feel the grip of the *Gaon* as he said to him: *And know...* and he would see the image of his master before him and desist."

And as the saintly Hacham Raphael told his son this story he held his hand, and when he repeated the words, *"And know..."* he shook it vigorously, like one accepting a handshake to conclude a deal. At that moment Hacham Hiyyah resolved to conduct himself virtuously.

And as my grandfather of revered memory told me how the saintly Hacham Raphael dealt with his son Hiyyah he held my hand and shook it and when he said, *And know...* I felt it in my heart, and knowing that saintliness was beyond my ability, I resolved to be a lover of the Torah. Grandfather went on to say: "At that time the saintly Hacham Raphael began preaching to his son, and he was stringing verses together, from the *Halacha* to the *Aggadah*, and his face was aflame. He said to him: My son, stand and I shall give you hints for the outlines of a sermon. They both stood. He preached to him things to do with the mysteries of the world, and the *tefillin* of the Lord of the World and what is written there, and the binding of the *tefillin* that the Holy One Blessed be He enjoined upon Moses, and about the *yod* of the *tefillin* and the tip of the *yod*."

Grandfather said: "We do not concern ourselves with mysteries, but a little of what Hacham Raphael said overtly I shall pass on to you and you shall preach it. And thus he preached: It is the custom of Israel to bind the tape of the *tefillin* three times round the finger and to repeat the verses from the Book of Hosea: *I shall betroth you to me for ever, and I shall betroth you to me in righteousness and in justice and in grace and in mercy, and I shall betroth you to me in faithfulness and you shall know the Lord.* And why the three bindings? For the three betrothals whereby the Holy One Blessed Be He betrothed Israel. And in three ways He betrothed them, as we have read: there are three ways whereby a wife is bought—with money, with a document and with cohabitation. With money—as he ransomed them from servitude in Egypt and gave to them the spoils of Egypt and the spoils of the sea; with a document—for this is the Torah; and then there is the Absolute Unity—as it was said in the writings: The Almighty and Israel and the Torah are all one. And though a wife may be acquired by any one of these ways, Israel was acquired by all of them. For there are some for whom acquisition means the acquisition of wealth, they are its slaves and obey its commandments; and there are some for whom the document is wealth, and those are the wise scholars who devote themselves to the Torah; and there are some whose wealth is in the Absolute Unity, and those are the saints who wrap their souls in the *Shekhinah*." And grandfather went on to explain to me what Hacham Raphael said of this, and what Hacham Hiyyah added to this, and what new interpretations were made by Hacham Menahem, my grandfather's father.

I stared at grandfather, astonished. I had never heard him tell a story at such length. He went on, and told me the following story:

After the saintly Hacham Raphael finished his sermon he said to his son: Hiyyah my son, sit and I shall tell you of the mercies and the miracles shown to me by the Lord and why I devoted my life to the Torah. The Sabbath that I came of age was the Sabbath when the month of *Elul* is proclaimed. There was a scent of supplication in the air, and the gloom of the month of *Av* had not yet dissipated. The day that I went up to read from the Torah was the fifth of the week. Father took me to the *Midrash Dabbah* where I would put on *tefillin* and read from the Torah. Father didn't want me to miss one moment of the *tefillin* ceremony, so we prayed with the veterans who time their prayer to coincide with the sunrise thus upholding the saying, *Let them see you with the sun.* The *hazan* chanted the *Shaharit* prayer to a tune on the Makam Zaba scale, to hint that here was a bridegroom for *Bar Mitzvah.* When they brought out a Torah scroll from the ark the *shamash* said: Give honor to the *Bar Mitzvah* groom. They set up a stool for me to stand on, as the *tebah* in *Midrash Dabbah* was very high. Father stood to my right. I made the blessing on the Torah, and read, *See that I set before you this day a blessing and a curse* and I concluded, *May you sit at ease.* The *hazan* appointed someone to make the blessings over the Torah on my behalf, according to custom, and the congregation sang an anthem, and the women in the gallery showered us with sugar sweets and almonds. The congregation had not finished singing the anthem when a thunderous sound was heard, and I saw the *tebah* swaying to the right and the left, and my head was spinning. A moment later, the big *Menorah* that hung above the *tebah* fell and was smashed. I put my hand on the *tefillin*, sought refuge beneath my father's prayer shawl and we fell together. More than this I do not remember, only what father told me, and I am not in the habit of telling other than what my eyes have seen, so I shall not dwell on everything that happened, except that we were graced by a miracle the day I went up to read from the Torah and we fell beneath the big ark, and stones and planks fell on it and did not touch us. At that time father swore that if it was decreed we should live, he would dedicate me to the Torah. On account of my father's virtue, and on account of the *tefillin* of which it is said, *By these you shall live*, we were spared and were allotted life instead of death. That day was the last remnant of the month of *Av*, and there was a mighty tremor in all the cities in our lands. The earthquake caused even walled houses to collapse. One third of the city of Aleppo was ravaged, and in that moment close to six hundred souls of Israel perished. And everywhere there was mourning and grief and lamentation and wailing and sighs, for there was barely a household without its dead. And the living were broken and shattered, and there were many widows and orphans. But the hand of the Lord touched us and we were spared the horror. That winter they built houses of paper and planks, and heavy rains fell and flooded them, and we were assailed by all manner of torments and troubles such that the tongue cannot relate. For those who had sat at their ease the wheel turned—merchants became mendicants and the wealthy begged for bread.

Despite this, my father upheld his vow and put me into the hands of my teacher and my master, the great and illustrious Hacham Nissim Muhadeb, who instilled in me the flavor of the Torah for its own sake. So I learned with fearful urgency, and the Torah that I learned with great difficulty and in poverty stayed with me, and set me on the way. And Hacham Raphael said to his son in a whisper: "Your conception was a miracle. For how many years had I prayed for a son, until I did what I did and was blessed by whosoever I was blessed, and I saw Elijah in a dream, and knew that I was brought good tidings. I have a great deal more than this to tell, but I am neither worthy nor willing to do so. And the day you were born was a day of many miracles for us." The eyes of Hacham Raphael seemed to be dreaming, and he went on to tell his son Hiyyah:

"That was a day of tidings for me and for the community of Aleppo and for all our brothers, the children of Israel. This is what happened. One night before midnight, as the members of the household were asleep and I intent on my study, I heard a knocking at the door and could tell this was the knocking of the *shamash* of the *Beit Din*. I opened the door to him in alarm and he said to me: "Our Teacher and Master and Crowning Glory, the chief sage of the land, has summoned you at once and without delay, and for the Lord's sake let this not be known to anyone, for there is mortal danger in the affair."

I rose and followed him and already gathered there was a quorum of noted sages and associates of the *Beit Din*—saints and men of commerce. One lamp was burning and there was a great silence in the place. Our Teacher and Master addressed us in a broken voice, saying: "My lords, sages of Aram Zova, direct your hearts toward Heaven, for the accusation against us is severe and this is a time of danger and the decree has been decreed."

We directed our hearts accordingly, though we had no idea what was being discussed.

Our Teacher opened the door of the room, and a man entered, his beard and side-burns shaved and dressed in the garb of a Gentile. We were stunned. Never had we seen a Jew in Aleppo dressed as a Gentile, with side-burns shorn. He moaned tearfully, quaking at the knees and said: "My teachers and masters, do not be shocked by my appearance, for there was great need and many lives are in danger. I am a Jew from the community of Damascus. I arrived just now. I have been riding on my donkey for twelve days, and at night I have had neither rest nor repose. How much danger have I risked to inform your worships of the dreadful decree! On the eve of the holy Sabbath in the glorious month of *Adar* when there is much rejoicing, our rejoicing was blended with affliction, when a certain priest and his acolyte perished, and the malicious and accursed uncircumcised laid against us the familiar libel that our brother Jews spilled their blood to bake their *matzas*. And there were some among the uncircumcised who testified on oath. All our leaders were arrested, including our Teacher and Master, the revered judge Ribi Jacob, and they inflicted severe torture on them, and they confined our teacher inside a dark pit, just one cubit by one cubit with no light, with lice swarming there day and night and flies great and small, and afflicted him with torments that cannot be described. And among other harsh decrees, no child of Israel is permitted to come or go or write letters that will make our sorrow known abroad. I was consumed by the zeal of the Lord and I shaved off my beard and the locks of my head and put on Gentile garments, and came to you to report the plight that we are in. And you, sages of Israel, the eyes of all the communities are turned to you."

The Crown of our Community spoke, saying: "*Look down from Heaven and see, from the abode of your holiness and your beauty, where is your zeal and your valor, and the noise of your bowels and your mercies toward me, are they restrained? Will you restrain yourself Lord over these things and afflict us sorely?*"

He asked us to stand and we stood. We recited the passage concerning the blending of incense and the loosing of vows and then we invoked the great ban that is written in the miscellany, the *Book of Colbo* against the accursed and wicked accusers, and imposed on ourselves a private fast. And we appointed one of our number to bless our brothers, for every household of Israel in the community of Damascus was given over to oppression and captivity. Said Hacham Nissim Muhadeb: "Brothers in adversity, this is no time to be praying at length, we have debated the matter and decided that I shall dip my pen in tears and write letters, to make our suffering known in the cities of Europe, to the lords of the house of Senor Rothschild, and to His Excellency the minister and diplomat and benefactor of his people, Moses Montefiore. And I shall entrust the letters to Senor De Piciotto and he will take the risk of delivering them to one of the consuls for conveyance."

From that day forward we broke our silence and moved heaven and earth with *shofars* and with fasting and with prayers and with letters.

One night I dreamed of Jacob our father going up to Jerusalem.

I went to see our Illustrious Leader. He was happy to explain to me that Hacham Jacob had passed from the realm of conjecture into the light and would go up to Jerusalem. The next day we were informed that the Lord had been merciful to His people and the decree had been annulled, and we rejoiced with great gladness, and sang the full *Hallel.* It is in the nature of joy that it cancels out violence, and joy engenders joy, and I had not yet said: *I love the Lord for he has heard the voice of my supplication, for he has inclined his ear to me,* before the messenger came with the news of your birth.

And still His mercies were manifold. Your breathing was heavy and almost stopped and the women despaired of you, until the Lord showed us His wondrous mercies and gave you life, and we called you by the name Hiyyah, that the Lord may make your days long in goodness and your years rich in pleasantness. Your life was given us as a gift, and the Almighty does not perform miracles for no return. Know what is before you and the Lord be with you. *And the outcast will not be expelled by him.* He put his hand on his head and gave him the priestly blessing and went.

Grandfather gripped my hand and said: "I was told all these things by my parents, they were passed down in the family, so it was as if I heard them myself when Hacham Raphael told them to Hiyyah his son the day he came of age. And I heard more, that from that day forward Hiyyah was a changed man. He rose and excelled until he became a noted sage and the community allotted him a portion of the fruits of the endowment founded by Senor De Piciotto and Senor Franco when the wheel turned for them.

Grandfather concluded his speech and resumed his perusal of the book. Many years later these things were supplemented by what I heard from others regarding Hacham Hiyyah and what became of his sons after him.

From all of them I heard that the special art of Hacham Hiyyah had been his silence. All his days he held on to the crutch of silence. It is said that sages and community elders once came to his house to consult him. Each one of them had his say, and he was silent. One of the sages rebuked Hacham Hiyyah for this, for is silence an end in its own right? Hiyyah took up the Rambam

88

and opened it at the place where it is stated: *"Man should always be abundant in silence."*

One hand Hacham Hiyyah raised to signify a question and the other he raised to signify an answer. "After all, the Rambam could have written: *'Man should always be sparing of speech,'* but this was not what he wrote, but rather *'Man should be always abundant in silence.'* Hence it follows that silence is an art in its own right."

I heard a number of entertaining stories from the old folk of Aleppo, regarding the silence of Sage Hiyyah. I will relate two of them. I was told by my great aunt, Senora Victoria: When I was a child I was silent for much of the time. On my own account I never said a word, and when I was asked a question I answered as briefly as necessity allowed. And although it is typical of the people of Aleppo that they are parsimonious with their speech, and even the women of Aleppo are not the garrulous kind, it seems that I was reticent even by their standards, and I used to be scolded for my behavior. Once we were visited by Senora Nazli, the wife of our uncle, Hacham Eliahu, who composed a commentary on the hymn *Lord, the Healer of Pain*, written by Ribi David Pardo, which is full of allusions to the Talmud. She engaged me in conversation and to everything she said I answered briefly: Yes or no. When she saw this was my habit she laughed and said: "Victoria, you're a quiet one! Let me tell you a story that I heard from a neighbor of Hacham Hiyyah's wife. Day in and day out, Hacham Hiyyah used to go to the *Beit Midrash* after the dawn prayer, and return after the evening prayer. At midday his wife used to send him bread and soup by the hand of a certain boy who was studying grammar with him. One day the boy didn't come and she had no one else to send with the food, so she wrapped herself up and went herself. As she approached the *Midrash*, she heard from the window a clear and limpid voice, debating with the sages and asking and answering and expounding, rising and falling and accentuating, and she recognized the voice of her husband, Hacham Hiyyah. She stood still to listen to his voice a while longer. Although wedded to him for more than forty years, she had never heard him converse at any length, either in his home or in the homes of others, and this was her first visit to the *Midrash*. She waited for him to finish and asked that he be called, gave him the soup, and went. She turned back and said: Hiyyah, you have the voice of a nightingale. He laughed, and said nothing.

And she told me another story. When a daughter was born to one of her relatives, Hacham Hiyyah's wife said to him: Let us go and bless them on the birth of their daughter. He put her off with the words: *Ziyarat al-bint tawila*—visiting a newborn daughter can be done at any time; it is not limited to eight days.

She pressed him again and again: We are relatives, and this is the custom of the land. In the end he gave in to her. They went to the house. The master of the house offered them all kinds of delicacies and a cup of almond juice. They blessed the food and tasted. Hacham Hiyyah's wife was silent out of modesty, not wishing to speak before the sage her husband; Hacham Hiyyah was silent out of habit, and the host was silent because they were silent.

After a few minutes Hacham Hiyyah rose to leave, his wife whispered to him: Hiyyah! Say something! He replied: Why did I come here?—and continued on his way.

The husband of my great aunt Senora Victoria added to this, telling me: You know, because silence was his art, and because his mind was not in tune with humanity, and his studying was for his own benefit, his colleagues could not fathom him. They knew him as a great sage but a sage of a different kind, unlike the other sages that they were accustomed to. While they were wrestling with the *Halacha* and putting forward testimonies from the former and the latter rabbinic authorities, from the author of the *Beit Yoseph* and from the author of the *Sifte Cohen*, he was putting forward testimony not only from the Talmud and the commentaries but also from the Talmud Yerushalmi and the *Tosefta* and even from the *Targum* of Onkelos or from the exposition of the Ralbag—and returning to his silence. And his colleagues were shy of him because they were not accustomed to testimonies such as these and didn't know how to answer him, and they used to show him that this was not in accordance with the latter authorities. And it was not his way to argue with the sages, but he would say, I am not one to answer their sayings, but you see the testimony set out clearly in the Bible, that is my humble opinion, and the truth shall show the way. And in their hearts they knew he was in the right, but they wanted to harmonize their opinions with the opinions of the *Poskim*, the rabbinic authorities. For this reason, they used to say, discomfited, that this is the way of the world, that they were trying to find the golden mean, by which everything was reconciled; and with him it was otherwise, as he sought only to pursue the truth.

Even when he preached, his colleagues could not fathom him, since it was the custom of the sages of Aleppo to preach on the Bible in mellifluous style, and to sweeten their sermons with fables, and draw ethical lessons from them, and crown them with numerology. And this was not his way of preaching; rather he would expound on the simplicity of the Bible, and support this with meditations derived from the *Moreh Nevukhim* and from the *Kuzari*, and go deeper than the intellect of any other man could reach, and not only this but he would even quote the sayings of learned Gentiles. And the sages were bemused. And there was no one ready to argue or dispute with him, as they knew he was a great sage and a great *tzaddik* and the son of devout parents, with a hand in the mysteries, and laboring over the Torah for its own sake and pursuing the truth. What sages know, their pupils do not; for when they saw their teachers perplexed at heart, they would speak out, telling one another that here is a sage unlike all the other sages.

Chapter seven

For those who are truly devout and God-fearing, their reverence arises from their joy, and their joy from their reverence. A thread of sorrow is stretched across their faces, grief for the exile of the *Shekhinah* and the exile of Israel. When their faces light up, this thread of sorrow also glows. And when do their faces light up? When they succeed in finding a genuine and new interpretation of the Torah—at such times, their soul clings to the Torah, and their spirit is blended with its spirit. It is a blessing and a privilege to catch a glimpse of them at times like these.

The holy Sabbath is like the world to come; the *Tikkun* of Midnight is not said then, nor the *Tikkun* of Rachel nor the *Tikkun* of Leah. For this reason there is no grief to be discerned among the devout, and the joy infused in their midst is revealed on their faces.

Even my grandfather of revered memory, who was a God-fearing man and went about with an air of dignity, was affected by the Sabbath. His face, too, was illuminated on the Sabbath, and in his somber eyes the hint of a smile appeared. And this hint of a smile was most often revealed when he was humming a refrain from the hymnal of Aram Zova.

The hymns written there were created by sages and saints, distilling them from their reverence and their joy. And when worthy sons of Israel chant them with dutiful gladness, the reverence with which those saints were imbued returns, and takes hold of them. At this time their table is adorned with a garland of holiness, and they are inspired with love brimming over for their Creator.

Every Sabbath without fail, grandfather would give some hint about the hymn, whether it had to do with the composer, whose name was sometimes revealed and sometimes concealed by an acronym, or the story upon which, according to our tradition, the hymn was based, or the origin of the tune, and who recommended it, and so forth. And all this by means of allusion, since it is the way of Aleppo that its citizens converse only in hints, as if saying, if you have taken the hint you have taken it, and if you haven't taken it, you have no right to know.

One time he stopped abruptly in the middle of a hymn, and said: "Hacham Taboush…Turkish…soldiers of the House of David…." He raised his hand aloft, in a gesture of yearning and expectation, and returned at once to the hymn. Anyone listening who understood would realize that he meant to say the tune of this hymn was composed by the poet and Hacham Raphael Taboush, when he heard soldiers on the move singing a Turkish marching song, and his head was filled with longings for redemption, and he resolved to correct the tune, and refine it and set it to accompany the poem of redemption by Rabbi Israel Najarah.

One Sabbath we sang the hymn: *Be well prepared for what lies ahead, with charity and healing, blessed are the enlightened and the vigilant, who holds their hand…* Grandfather showed us the line: *Hasten, Comforter, to save them,* and he said: "My late father, Hacham Menahem that is, wrote this hymn, and hinted at his own name in this verse.* And when did he write it? It was at the inauguration of the company founded by those grandees Senor Piciotto and Senor Franco, an organization which they named 'Charity and Healing,' and Senor Silvera became part of that enterprise, joining them. Silvera was

---

* Menahem, in Hebrew, means "the one who gives comfort"

that heroic and godly man Senor Silvera, who built the great house of study, Midrash Silvera, where I too had the privilege of studying Torah, which he filled with books and manuscripts from Italy.

"That day the benefactors held a ceremonial banquet, and they invited the sages and the heads of the community and even the Italian consul, Marcopoli, was there. That's the consul who took out an injunction against our Crowning Glory, the chief of the sages, complaining that he and his followers were disrupting his sleep with their early morning songs of supplication, and asking them to cancel this practice that had been established by the great men of Aram Zova. But he was stung by the scorpion-whisper of our teacher, who whispered to himself: 'Marcopol, Marcopol, Marcopol—why don't you fall?' The story goes that at that time the consul would often go out horse-riding, and one day he fell off and died."

Grandfather continued for longer than was his wont, his eyes dreamy. He said: "When the affluent people of Aleppo held a banquet they used to invite sages to grace their table. True sages would decline the invitation for fear of neglecting the Torah, and to avoid eating to excess in too many places, and in particular having regard to the saying of the Talmud, that before uneducated people a sage resembles a goblet of gold; if he accepts a favor from them, he resembles a pitcher of clay."

All sages are like this, and Hacham Hiyyah all the more so. In spite of this, when Senor De Piciotto invited him, he accepted, on account of what Piciotto's father had done for Hacham Raphael, his father, and what he had done for himself. A degree of gratitude was very precious in his eyes, and he held on to it with all his strength, for he who acknowledges the goodness of his friend, in the end will acknowledge the goodness of the Lord, and he who denies the favors of his friend, in the end will deny the favors of the Lord.

All the leading sages of Aleppo preached at that banquet, to honor the peerless precept of rewarding the just, and to honor the illustrious benefactors, in whom reverence and greatness were combined.

Hacham Hiyyah Sapporta likewise preached, on the Bible and the *Halacha* and the *Aggadah* and scholarly enquiry, and he

said things that no ear had heard before, and he concluded his oration with a poem of twenty-two stanzas, following the order of the
alphabet, every stanza beginning with a verse from the hallowed
texts and closing with a rhyme on the theme of healing, and the
sages and the congregation were amazed. The poem's title, *Before the
Plague the Flower of Healing has Bloomed*, was 'altogether lovely' in the
words of the Song of Songs, and in spite of this, my father, Hacham
Menahem Choueka, rebuked him for it, saying to him: "Hacham
Hiyyah, have you not taught us that the mouth should not be opened
to speak of evil things, and that in this even the utterances of saints
are unavailing. Yet he forbore to mention the word 'plague.' And at
once my father, Hacham Menahem, composed that poem of his, *Be
Well Prepared…* to mitigate the omen, and although he was unable
to cancel the decree he may have assuaged it."

It came to pass not many months after Hacham Hiyyah's poem
about the flower of healing blooming before a plague, that a fearful
plague really came upon Aleppo. Many of our brothers of the House
of Israel perished. The epidemic, may the Lord preserve us from cruel
decrees, must have been granted dispensation to wreak slaughter in
Aleppo, and it made no distinction between the virtuous and the
wicked. Good people from the 'Charity and Healing' society put
themselves in danger by going from house to house to tend the sick.
This was the great plague on account of which many left the city and
fled to the countryside and lived in tents. When calm returned to
the land, the government praised the company for helping Gentiles
who were sick as much as it helped the sick of Israel, and awarded
it a gold medal.

The banquet in honor of the 'Charity and Healing' organization was attended by a very distinguished gentleman, his shoulders
broad, his face clean-shaven, round and gleaming, oval spectacles
with silver frame perched on his nose, a silver thread hanging from
them. He wore an English suit, and his manners were French. His
name was Monsieur Nuri Pinseau, and he was the headmaster of the
Ecole Alliance Israelite Universelle.

While all the other sages preached, dissecting the *Halacha* and
offering clues shrouded in numerology, he dozed, but when he heard

the preaching of Hacham Hiyyah, suddenly he was wide awake, and caught every single word, and knew at once that here was a great sage and a scholar and a pursuer of the truth for its own sake, and a man of eloquence and precision, and one who both understood the writings of the philosophers and was familiar with poetry too. From then on he sought his company, and every Sabbath Eve he came to him and said: "Rabbi, I have a question to ask." So Pinseau asked questions drawn from scholarly research and from poetry and Hebrew, and in every matter Hacham Hiyyah would say to him: "Ask my son, ask," and he would answer him and resolve all his doubts. When he saw their opinions converging, he began talking with him on matters that were the concern of the hour, the education of children and the administration of congregations and methods of teaching, and so forth.

One Sabbath Eve he came to his house and said to him: "Hacham , I have a question to ask." And Hacham Hiyyah told him: "Ask my son, and as Heaven directs me, shall I answer."

Said Monsieur Nuri Pinseau, "I am one who mingles with consuls and with ministers, and in their eyes it is shameful to be other than clean-shaven. For this reason, should I shave on *Hol Hamoed*, the intermediate day of a festival? The sages forbade it only so that a man should not enter the festival defiled, telling himself 'I shall shave on the day of the festival,' but for a man who is accustomed to shave on a daily basis, the degree of his beard growth will make him defiled throughout the festival. For such a man, how should he uphold the rule laid down by the holy convocation? Perhaps what I am asking is: What is the point of this decree today—and why is it that the sages did not debate it and abrogate it?"

Hacham Hiyyah looked at him with penetrating eyes, as if seeking to probe him deeply, and determine if it was justice that Pinseau sought and if there was reason behind his question and he deserved a considered answer, or if he wanted only an excuse and should be fobbed off lightly. Monsieur Pinseau was disconcerted by this look from Hacham Hiyyah, to which he wasn't accustomed, and he lowered his eyes, lest this sage, a man who had pursued truth all the days of his life, might detect some deceit in him, and rebuke him severely.

After some consideration, Hacham Hiyyah said: "For my own part I would not address this point, for many and diverse reasons, and my heart tells me I should not answer you, but since the day I came of age I have not refused to dispense judgment to anyone who asks for it, and all that is above me is the fear of Heaven, for the Torah commands us: *Be not afraid of man*—meaning any man. Listen my son, today is Sabbath Eve and the answer to your question—although it is simple in your eyes and concerns neither a capital offence nor a solemn prohibition but only a ruling of the sages—is in fact of such import that much depends on it. At any rate, its significance is such that I need to settle this matter, so that no disaster befall on account of me, Heaven forbid."

Hacham Hiyyah began to study this rule of conduct, putting together all that the former and the latter authorities had said of it, and the masters of *Tosafot* and the *poskim*, and what the sages of previous generations had said in their responsa, what had been printed and what had not been printed, since Hacham Hiyyah had a collection of many manuscripts which he kept stored in his house, and knew precisely what was in all of them, and whenever he needed a citation, it would appear of its own accord as if saying, Here I am.

After weighing all the answers on the scales of the intellect, and arranging the questions that fitted them and adducing proofs such that no sage had adduced before, he felt more at ease. He decided to write the answer so he could pass it to the questioner before the festival. He set out before him the books and the scrolls, took the pen and dipped it in the ink bottle, but before he had written a single letter his son Jacob entered the room and sat down before him.

Usually, when he was writing responsa in procedural matters, his wife allowed no one to disturb him, and even his sons stayed away from him at this time, but Jacob was the son of his old age and especially dear to him, and he never sent him away empty-handed. He entered and his father said to him: "My son, what do you seek?"

Jacob told him: "Father, I have a question to ask."

Then he began asking him about the commandment to heed the words of the wise and the commandment not to deviate from the rules laid down by the *Beit Din*, as interpreted by the Rambam, and what the Ramban had to say on the subject.

Hacham Hiyyah took his time explaining the issue to him, smiling brightly and using the reasoned arguments that he knew would satisfy him, since Jacob his youngest son was of sharper intelligence than all his brothers, and broad of understanding, and he would accept no answer in the world if it did not accord with his mind. It is said he had many of his father's qualities, being a thoughtful person and a lover of inquiry, apt to philosophize about each and every topic, to such an extent that his mother called him by the pet name, *Philasuf*, little philosopher. For this reason Hacham Hiyyah used to settle all matters for him, and encouraged him to develop his intellect, explaining to him the meaning of every commandment according to the writings of the Teacher and Master, the Rambam, and according to the Ralbag, and inducing him to love the Torah and the words of the wise.

One way or another the conversation with his son was prolonged, and Hacham Hiyyah set aside the answer that he was working on, and did not write it.

Whenever he heard the answer tinkling before him to remind him of its existence, other matters arose and he deferred it. And once deferred, it was deferred again. Although he wanted to return to it, the idea of going back over his earlier work was wearisome to him, since when he addressed the subject other sides to the argument were revealed, and he had to weigh them all in the scales of logic. As time passed, still having written nothing, the problem became hazy in his eyes.

When the days of the festival were approaching, he remembered the answer, excused himself from all his other business and went back to studying the issue from the beginning, making some pleasant new discoveries along the way. He meant to arrange it, to write it and to refine it, and apparently he did succeed in producing a finished piece of work. He signed his name at the end, and went to pick up the container of sand to scatter over the ink to dry it. His hand mistook the bottle of ink for the container of sand, ink was spilled all over his answer and it was ruined. He was mortified by the waste of all the effort expended on the answer, and the laborious study invested in it. He said: From Heaven they are hindering me. Although I taught the truth, the sages that dispute are hindering me. There is no true judgment that does not have its time, and I thought the time for this judgment had arrived. In Heaven they thought otherwise.

That festival was the Feast of *Succot*. On the day of *Simhat Torah*, it was the practice to invite all members of the congregation to come up and read from the Torah. When they sought to bring Monsieur Nuri Pinseau to the podium, the *tebah*, to read from the Torah, the warden, called him: "If you please, sir!" Monsieur Pinseau prepared to make his way to the Torah. Seeing that someone clean-shaven was about to go up to the podium to read from the Torah, one of the more meticulous members of the congregation shouted at the wardens: "How can you let a sinner approach the Torah?"

At this, others began shouting back at him: "How can you call him a sinner, after all this is only one of the sages' rulings!"

But the man stood his ground and said: "Anyone who transgresses the words of the sages is a sinner." Others rose to their feet and railed against him: "What is your reason for maligning him in this public fashion? For has not the Torah declared, *Do not bear sin against him*, and the sages have interpreted this as meaning, 'you should not embarrass him.'"

But the man was adamant and stood his ground, saying: "No honor is allotted to those who transgress the sayings of the sages, for there is no counsel nor wisdom nor understanding in opposition to the Lord," and one of them rose and answered what he answered, and every member of the congregation had something to say. One person answered from the Bible that he had read in his childhood, and another from things he had studied in his youth, and another spoke from his inner instincts, since even those community elders of Aleppo who are not rabbis know their books, and even he who does not know, is convinced that he does know.

From out of the din and chaos, one voice rang out: "Did Hacham Hiyyah Sapporta not allow this?" When this voice was heard, all were silent and sought to hear who had spoken. Such was the confusion of voices, with everyone interrupting somebody else, that there was no knowing who had spoken these words. The wardens silenced the congregation, and Monsieur Pinseau went up to read the Torah.

After the festival the sages summoned Monsieur Pinseau and rebuked him severely, warning him not to defy convention, nor exceed the bounds.

Since the day the Alliance Israelite Universelle school had been founded, the sages had had misgivings about it, but for numerous and diverse reasons they had not taken up arms against it, and for his part Monsieur Pinseau had been careful not to provide them with any grievance which could be used as a pretext for opposition to the school. He had warned the teachers a number of times that they must treat the sages with respect and must say nothing against the law or against the customs of Israel, and when they were studying varieties of wisdom, and some statement was heard from one of them that might be at odds with the sayings of the sages, it would be suppressed. He even employed a noted sage to teach the Talmud.

There was an instance when a student was about to be examined, and this student was a veritable prodigy. He saw that the test had been scheduled for the *Hol Hamoed*, the intermediate day of a festival, since the timing was established in Paris, and all the schools of this society held their examinations on the same day, and once decided, the timetable could not be changed for any reason in the world.

This student came to Monsieur Pinseau and told him he would not under any circumstances take an examination on that day. He was warned that all his studying would go to waste, but he was adamant. Monsieur Pinseau did everything in his power to help the student, and urged and cajoled, and went as far as Professor Maurice Halphi in Paris, and he succeeded in reaching an agreement that had never been reached before, that this student need not *write* his examination answers—two professors were sent from Istanbul to examine him orally, and this student obtained the highest marks awarded in any of the society's schools, anywhere in the world. He was sent a medal from Paris and was given a scholarship to study for five years at the Sorbonne.

This student was the son of Hacham Hiyyah Sapporta, grandson of the saintly Hacham Raphael, whose face lit up when he deciphered the system of Rabbenu Tam, Jacob that is, son of Hacham Hiyyah's old age and his favorite, a master of research, who in later times would call himself Monsieur Jacques Sapport.

How the sage's son came to be enrolled in Monsieur Pinseau's school, and what befell him in Paris, we shall presently relate. We have departed here from strict chronology, merely to demonstrate the care taken by Monsieur Pinseau not to affront the dignity of the sages.

After the senior judge had warned him, he said to him: "Monsieur Pinseau, it has been alleged that Hacham Hiyyah gave you permission to shave on the intermediate day," and he replied: "I never said any such thing, and I am not a purveyor of gossip." He told him: "That is well said, Monsieur, and we too have no interest in hearing the faintest trace of slander, and we do not believe that Hacham Hiyyah permitted what is forbidden, but the voice was heard, and we have to determine the truth of the matter."

It is the way of a voice that if it is not silenced, it is not silenced, but if people attempt to silence it, not only is it not silenced, but on the contrary it gains in volume and in currency. There were students whispering that they had seen Monsieur Pinseau coming and going to the home of the sage. Some came forward and said they saw him visiting the sage before the festival and asking him questions. Another came forward and said: I testify that some days before the festival Hacham Hiyyah went to the Midrash Silvera, searching for manuscripts of the Hachams of Italy. They were not content until they had impugned the honor of the saintly Hacham Raphael. One said: I remember hearing from my esteemed father that our teacher urged his father Raphael to be counted with the sages in the matter of the Alliance Israelite Universelle, and he answered him: I am not a sage of the community. Another came forward and averred that Hacham Hiyyah had been known to read 'external' books and works of philosophy. Other tales were told, some of them utter fabrication, some with an element of truth and some of them entirely true, but the curled lips of slanderers distort even the truth.

The sages tried to silence them, warning them lest they be

scorched by his burning coals, saintly man that he was, yet in spite of this the voices grew ever louder. All this time Hacham Hiyyah heard nothing of all these things, being engrossed in his study.

When the sages saw that the voices had not been silenced, they feared for his honor, and said, we have no other choice but to go to him and ask what the crux of the matter was. They conferred among themselves as to whom to send. At that time one distinguished sage was present there, Menashe Muhadeb, son of old Nissim Muhadeb. Hacham Nissim had been the teacher of Hacham Raphael, and his son Hacham Menashe had been the teacher of Hacham Hiyyah. Hacham Menashe Muhadeb told them: "Better that I go, than another go and fail."

They all agreed to this, as Menashe was a humble man, beloved of all, and the first teacher of Hacham Hiyyah.

Hacham Menashe Muhadeb went to the *Beit Midrash*, and into the presence of Hacham Hiyyah. Hacham Hiyyah rose to his full height to greet him. Hacham Menashe began with pleasantries and Hacham Hiyyah was silent. We have already noted that he was not by nature verbose. Hacham Menashe said to him: I shall tell you of one thing that I have struggled with. He began unraveling problems with him, he asking and Hacham Hiyyah replying, he raising difficulties and Hacham Hiyyah resolving them. He discussed with him the problem of an edict that no longer has a valid purpose, and whether the edict is thereby annulled, and the question of a sage who forbids something that another sage permits.

Hacham Hiyyah connected one thing to another, and it became clear to him that Hacham Menashe had not come to discuss the Torah for its own sake. Hacham Hiyyah said to Hacham Menashe: "What is it that is before us?" Hacham Menashe told him: "It seems that your colleagues are concerned about you. A voice has been heard in the town, declaring that your honor has granted permission to shave on festival days." Hacham Hiyyah said to him: "You know sir, that I do not deny what I have said. I have never told any man that it is permissible to shave on the intermediate day of a festival. The truth is that I wanted to write a judgment but I was not helped by Heaven." He added: "I could leave it at that, but I obey the injunction to speak the truth in my heart, and I shall say what is in my heart. If I had been able to write the response, I would have permitted someone who shaves every day, to shave on the intermediate days."

Hacham Menashe rose to his feet and said: "The proof has come from Heaven." Hacham Hiyyah said to him: "The Torah is not in Heaven—it has been given to us!" Hacham Menashe replied: "Since finally Heaven has helped to prevent an offense occurring here through our agency, and nothing has been done, allow me to debate with you." Hacham Hiyyah said to him: "If it is your wish that we debate by reasoned argument, as we did in our boyhood, when we rejected every proposition that was not upright and spurned any insubstantial sophistry, then let us debate."

Hacham Hiyyah began and put forward testimony for his words, Hacham Menashe replied with numerous rebuttals; Hacham Hiyyah once again put forward his testimony, the other repeated his refutation. One raised difficulties and the other explained, one proved and the other denied. They had no need of books; Hacham Hiyyah quoting from the works of the Rambam by heart, and Hacham Menashe citing columns of *Halacha*, and all the sages of the *Beit Midrash* stood and watched them from afar.

It is said that some were privileged to see a ring of fire enfolding the two of them.

When Hacham Menashe saw that the round of testimonies and rebuttals would produce no decision, he broached another matter and said: "Even if the truth is on your side, we still need to erect a wall and a fence about it, so that they will not say, 'the Pharisees have permitted this thing'—otherwise others will come and permit other things, and the masses will say, to this day the sages have not allowed us to shave, times have changed and now it's allowed, and just as this edict has been relaxed, so they are bound to rescind other edicts. Moreover, there are those who do not distinguish between rulings of the rabbis and outright prohibitions, and thus in this way forbidden things will be allowed, and the whole of the Torah will be in peril. Our generation is not like the generations of the past, when insurgents came to make breaches in the wall, and it was enough for a sage to understand an allusion, (and who knows if in essence the enquirer only asked the question for the sake of it), and my master is wise in the wisdom of the Lord, but he spends his days among those who sit in the *Beit Midrash*, buried under layers of *Halacha*, and not being involved with the community, and therefore the goodness of one and the innocence of another can, Heaven forbid, be the occasion whereby some irreparable damage be done."

Hacham Hiyyah closed his eyes and said: "I know, I know, I too have a path that I must steer, and all the suppositions you suppose I too have wrestled with, arriving, however, at the opposite conclusion. For if we do not allow what is allowed, and edicts become things of no value, unacceptable to the intellect, what will the enlightened say about the Torah and about the ordinances of the sages? On the contrary, it is indeed because this is a lawless generation that it is impossible for us to issue edicts that do not accord with the intellect, and if we do not permit them what is permitted out of fear and fear of fear, in the end they will allow it by themselves, and will say, just as we have relaxed this prohibition, so we shall relax the other prohibitions, and we will not have the strength to put the Torah back in its place. This is a libertarian generation, and it is impossible to force upon it anything that is unacceptable to its mind, but if we allow them what is allowed, we can forbid them what is forbidden."

Hacham Menashe Muhadeb said to him: "A majority of the sages have already voted to forbid it."

He told him: "You cannot speak of a majority except in a place where people debate face to face, and every sage has his say." Hacham Menashe told him: "*Truth and peace they love*, for there is an element in truth alone which is capable of destroying the world, if it is not sweetened by an element of peace." Hacham Hiyyah told him: "Peace that does not have the capacity to establish the truth of the law is no peace. How can I forbid something which my mind is inclined to permit?"

Hacham Menashe Muhadeb said to him: "You know the affection I have for you, and what is in my heart I have revealed to you. Remember the covenant sealed between your grandfather and my esteemed father, Hacham Nissim, at the time of the great disturbance, when the people of Aleppo were beaten and bruised and broken, and no one was found who could teach the son of his friend, and your grandfather asked my revered father to teach your father the Torah, and remember the covenant that we sealed between us when your revered mother broke down in tears before me, saying that if you did not learn the Torah, her life would be no life, and at once I complied with her, and we devoted ourselves to the Torah out of humility, and I revealed to you all its secrets, and exposed all its charms to you, and bound your soul to its soul. And I never said to you, I am your teacher, for I knew your strength, and I knew your scruples, and I knew that all your intentions were directed toward Heaven. Listen to me in this matter and do not deliver this judgment, for no sage can rely on himself in this question even if his stature is as that of the cedars."

And Hacham Hiyyah was silent.

Hacham Menashe left.

Hacham Menashe whispered to himself, Farewell to you my teacher and my pupil. My teacher in wisdom, and my pupil in that you have taken in my words.

Chapter eight

My grandfather of blessed memory admired the Rambam. There was not one sermon in which he did not mention him. He used to recite the sayings of the Rambam by heart, and in his style. He used to say: "The Rambam had a tongue of gold. It is impossible to exchange one word of his for another."

If quoting from the book of the *Mishneh Torah*, he recited in Hebrew, and if from the letters or from the commentary on the *Mishnah*, he recited in the Arabic tongue. Often he told us: Many mistakes were made by the copiers, who were not fluent in the Arabic language in which the rabbi wrote. Anyone who is fluent in a language knows how many problems there may be, over which so many pens have been broken, which are merely due to errors on the part of translators.

And by far his favorite book was the *Moreh Nevukhim*. One time I asked him a question about something he had quoted from it. He looked at me with his solemn eyes, as if saying: "What do you know about the *Moreh*?" and made no answer.

When we rose after the sermon and returned home, he took out an old text of the *Moreh* for me and showed me that there was a different version of the matter. He saw me looking at the book in his hand and said: "This text of the *Moreh* I received from my wise father, who received it as a gift from Hacham Hiyyah Sapporta, at the ceremonial meal which they held when they finished the *Tur*, Rabbi Jacob Ben-Asher's Book of Laws, which they had been studying together a whole year."

Grandfather went on to say: "The Rambam was admired by the sages of Aleppo, and his words were seen by them as the words of the prophets, but the devotees of *Halacha* were engrossed in the *Book of the Fourteen*, and the *Book of Precepts*, and no one was concerned with study of the *Moreh*. This was because most of the sages of Aleppo were engaged in *Kabbalah*, and *Kabbalah* and philosophy were regarded as incompatible. The exceptions were Hacham Hiyyah and my esteemed father, who had an interest in *Kabbalah* and also studied the *Moreh Nevukhim*.

He had a chest, Hacham Hiyyah, and many books of *Kabbalah* and philosophy were kept in it. Every time he finished looking at them, he locked the chest with a key, and put the key away.

The sage's sons were accustomed to entering his study and perusing all the books there, with the exception of the books stored in that chest.

Jacob, son of Hacham Hiyyah's old age, was a lad of inquisitive mind, and always eager to look at these books. And he was forever trying to open the chest.

One time Hacham Hiyyah hurried to the Beit Midrash, and forgot to lock the chest. On arriving at the Beit Midrash he remembered, broke off from his studies and ran home. Upon entering his room, he found his son Jacob perusing a book. He looked, and saw that he was reading the *Moreh*. Jacob was unaware that his father was in the room. When he saw him suddenly he was startled, and dropped the book. Hacham Hiyyah said not a word, but picked up the book, returned it to the chest, locked the chest with the key, and returned to the Beit Midrash.

There was another instance, when the sage was summoned to the *Beit Din* to deal with a certain case, a marriage that the sages wanted to annul urgently, and in his haste, the sage forgot to lock the chest, and when he returned he found his son reading the *Moreh*.

He said to him: "To study the *Moreh* is your heart's desire? Wait for me, and I shall fix you a time, and I shall teach you the book."

Hacham Hiyyah kept his promise, and at the close of every Sabbath, after the *Havdalah*, he studied the *Moreh* with his son Jacob. And every single detail in the book he interpreted, and showed him the source, that which was explicit, as well as that to which our teacher alluded only by way of parable. And he explained to him that many things the teacher wrote were nothing other than, as the saying goes, *silver images concealing golden apples*, and that not one word had been written by chance, but everything had been set down with intention and prior thought. Those deep matters, which not every man's mind is capable of conceiving, were matters that our teacher had had the wisdom to conceal.

Often they used to consult the works of Greek and Arab philosophers, to understand what our teacher wrote. And every study session ended with devotional instruction.

A lover of wisdom was Jacob, and these hours that his father spent with him were precious to him. He was drawn more and more toward esoteric sciences. Every Sabbath Eve when Monsieur Pinseau came to visit his father, and sat before him, Jacob was waiting for him. Monsieur Pinseau used to produce books and pamphlets from his case, and give them to him, and Jacob devoured them.

His mother was sensitive to her son, and although she did not know what was happening to him, her heart told her. She saw he was eating little, and spending little time studying with his friends, and even when she spoke with him, his eyes were dreamy, as if he were in a different world. Many times she wanted to speak of him with her husband, but refrained. When he was occupied with the Torah, she was reluctant to interrupt his study, and she had no wish to speak out in front of her sons. In any case, she knew Jacob was very dear to him, and she didn't want to distress him. She said to herself, perhaps I'm mistaken.

One night, during that time of which the rabbis have said, *it is then that a wife may speak to her husband*, she made up her mind to tell him. She sighed, as if to herself: "Hiyyah, Jacob our son," and fell silent. Before she could say more, Hacham Hiyyah replied to her with anger: "You don't think I know how to educate my son? He's quick-witted, and a thinker, and a God-fearer, and not everyone can fathom what's in his mind. He loves secular studies more than his brothers do, and what of it, have I too not dabbled in esoteric studies?" And at once he rose to wash his hands.

His wife was silent. In her heart she had something to say by way of reply: The times we live in are not as former times, and it is a dangerous path that he is treading, and the devil lurks in times of danger, up to all kinds of foolish tricks, augmenting the problem, producing pamphlets that were not written in purity.

But it is the way of the sages' wives of Aleppo, that they do not answer their husbands face to face. All the wives are thus, and the wife of Hacham Hiyyah, who was never accustomed to speaking with him at any length, all the more so. She kept her grief in her heart. She said: Would that I be proved wrong.

A few days later Jacob came to his father, and said to him: "Father, I have a question to ask. Is it appropriate for me to engage in the study of secular subjects?" His father answered him calmly: "There is the opinion of the Rambam and there is the opinion of the Rashba, and there are different kinds of secular study... There are some which equip mankind for the ways of the intellect, and there are some which are in themselves the gateway to the understanding of Creation, and there are some from which man emerges to practise mystical speculations, and there are those of which the sages said that man should find a time which is neither of the day nor of the night to engage in them, as it has been said in the Torah: *And you shall meditate thereon day and night*. And there are some the study of which is permitted on account of the saying: *Know what you will reply*, and there are those of which it was said: *Remove your way from them*. In the end, it all depends on who the man is, and on the areas of study that he is engaged with, just so long as he directs his heart toward the Heavens. As it says in the Bible: *In all your ways know him and he will make your ways straight*."

Jacob was silent a moment and then he said: "Father, I want to study with Monsieur Pinseau at the Alliance Israelite Universelle school." Hacham Hiyyah bowed his head and laid his temple on his right hand, sorrow rising to his eyes, and said nothing.

He knew what the sages said, that he should not push his son away with both hands, but the matter seemed very hard to him. His son Jacob, his precious son, whom he dearly loved, of keen intelligence, who he had thought would continue in the way of his own father, the saintly Hacham Raphael, and be one of the greatest in the land—was he to leave his Talmud behind and go to study with Monsieur Pinseau? Hacham Hiyyah did not know what he should do, whether to expel him, in which case the matter would be decided definitively, and he would go of his own accord, and who knows what the end of it would be, or whether to consent—but how could he consent to the notion that his son would not be working on the Six Orders and the precepts? His son sensed his feelings and said: "Father, is this not what you have taught us? Shall a man always study in the place of his heart's delight? I'm not abandoning my studies into the small hours, but holding on to the one, and not letting the other go. You know my love of the Torah, and my joy in it. I promise you she will always be my steadfast wife, beautiful doe and graceful gazelle, and all the philosophies are nothing more than spices and condiments compared to her."

Hacham Hiyyah was silent. He wanted to say: And yet her season is short. I made my study of the Torah the essence, and esoteric wisdom the seasoning, and he is making his Torah casual. And what is more, there is a distinction between the one whose foundation and the beginning of his learning are in study of the Torah and in its purity, and the one whose root is planted outside it. He said to himself: Better I say nothing, and hold him close, and in the end his love for me and his love for the Torah will bring him back to his study. The virtue of my father will prevail for us, and fulfill in us what was said by the sages, of one who is an erudite scholar and the son of an erudite scholar and the son of a son of an erudite scholar, that from here and henceforward the Torah is seeking out her lodging, as it was said: *They shall not pass from your mouth and from the mouth of your seed and the mouth of the seed of your seed for ever. And the outcast will not be expelled by him.*

After this episode a cloud of sadness dominated the face of Hacham Hiyyah, and every single day he waited for his son Jacob's return. And although he used to tell himself that he was an absolute God-fearer, working on the Torah at every possible moment, his mind was not wholly at ease. To others he would say: "He is studying the sciences that are also a duty to study, and they will help him when he is a sage, and when he associates with the enlightened, and he can lead them toward love of God. He will still be using them when he is a great judge, for if a question regarding matters that time has brought about is brought before him, or things dependent on the sciences are brought before him, he can determine them." And even to himself he used to say: "Haven't there been many illustrious sons of Israel who have engaged in the sciences and excelled at them? These were the kinds of things he would say to himself, at hint at when talking to others, yet his mind was still not at ease. The joy of the Torah, which had always shone in his face, shone no more. And although he did not neglect the Torah and his devotions, the Torah is not the same when a man studies it joyfully or in sorrow.

Monsieur Pinseau greeted his pupil with both hands out-stretched to him, having known him for many years, knowing his strengths and his love for all things to do with wisdom. Pinseau was cautious, warning all the teachers to beware, lest, Heaven forbid, they diminish his awe of Heaven. He himself arranged special times to sit with him and plumb the depths of wisdom.

From the moment Jacob arrived to study at the school, he was not like the other students. It is the way of students to do their work as if under compulsion, and they drop out from classes if they can, and every canceled lesson is a cause for celebration, as the sages said of the infant fleeing from school, but there was a different quality about Jacob Sapporta. He ran to every single class, like a *tzaddik* hurrying to fulfill an obligation, and he regretted every cancelled lesson. He pursued his studies diligently until he made a name for himself, and all the teachers singled him out for praise, saying: "We never had a pupil like the son of Hacham Hiyyah."

On arriving home, he finished his homework quickly, and straightaway ran to the *Beit Midrash* to study Torah. His mother, who had been grieved at first when he enrolled at Monsieur Pinseau's school, was proud of the exercise books that he brought home, all of them containing marks of distinction awarded by the teachers, and to everyone who visited their home she showed what the teachers had written about him. And already people were used to the idea that the sage's son was studying at the Alliance Israelite Universelle School, and the world carried on in its usual fashion. Hacham Hiyyah alone was bereft of his happiness. There was a short prayer that he used to pray every day: that the Lord would enlighten the eyes of his son Jacob through the Torah, and he would be an erudite scholar, and a God-fearing man, and his learning would not surpass his faith.

Jacob found that all kinds of spiritual challenges were placed before him, and he passed them all. The story has already been told of the examination paper that he even refused to write on a day of *Hol Hamo'ed,* despite all the multifarious threats and inducements and promises brought to bear on him. Jacob used to say to himself: when I finish the study of philosophies, I shall return to the *Beit Midrash* day and night, and devote all my strength to the Torah. The philosophies that I have learned will serve me, and perhaps I shall be privileged to compose a work worthy of inclusion in the literature of the Torah and of wisdom, approved by sages of the Torah and intellectuals alike, and I shall display the wonder and the beauty of the Torah before the eyes of the nations.

Not everything that man seeks to do is aided by Heaven.

When Jacob Sapporta concluded his studies, scoring outstanding success, he was sent a medal from Paris, and awarded a scholarship for five years, to complete his education at the Sorbonne. The directors of the society made this offer conditional upon his agreement to teach for three years in Aleppo, instructing boys in the French language, and in the writings of French thinkers and philosophers and poets, and other related subjects designed to broaden the mind. Jacob didn't want to distress his father, and tell him he had made up his mind to travel to Paris. He said to himself: One way or the other

I've taken it upon myself to teach here for three years, and after that I shall find some means of reassuring my father.

In those times some of the affluent wanted their sons taught the French language. Among the sages there were some whose daughters already studied French. The education of sons, which was an obligation, was taken seriously by their parents, whereas daughters, excluded from scholastic pursuits, had little interest taken in their education, their parents' only concern being to get them to the bridal canopy. According to the old saying, women had but one thought on their minds—marriage. And these girls used to speak French, and read French poetry and fiction, so much so that the time came when decent women of Aleppo regarded the speaking of Arabic as something shameful, and they conversed only in French, and even formed a kind of club for themselves, where they used to gather together, hear lectures, debate, and read pamphlets distributed by the teachers of the Alliance Israelite Universelle school, or obtained from the consuls.

Jacob used to go from house to house, and teach the language, and if he found a talented pupil he would introduce him to poetry as well, reciting before him verses of the great poets, and cultivating in him a love of learning. At times he was also invited to address that club, and would accept. Behind his back, some of his pupils took to calling him Monsieur Jacques Sapport, which they thought of as a mark of respect, not knowing that he considered it a greater honor to be named after his saintly ancestors. After some time they began calling him this openly, and he did not object; eventually this name of his came to be accepted by the whole community. Affluent patrons treated him with great respect, since in all Aleppo there was no teacher to equal him. In this way, two years passed. His father the sage was engrossed in the Torah, he busy with his teaching, and his mother anxious to find him a wife.

The affluent of Aleppo used to honor the sages, and strove to be close to them. *Cleave unto him*, as the Torah commands, and how is a man to cleave to the *Shekhinah*? Our teachers have explained, he who cleaves to wise scholars will thereby cleave to the *Shekhinah*.

Senor Franco had a daughter, a child who loved wisdom and

feared God. Her father called her Rachel, while the women of the club called her Rachelle. She was well schooled in the Bible, and was an intellectual and an avid reader. Senor Franco tried to think of was looking for ways to cultivate the friendship of Hacham Hiyyah, for he had thought of marrying his daughter to Jacob, the sage's son.

Senor Franco found an excuse to invite Jacob to his house, saying that he wanted Jacob to help him with a text that he had received regarding business dealings; it was written in Italian, a language in which he was not fluent. When Jacob came to Senor Franco's house, he greeted him cordially and spoke to him about various things, so as to get his measure. The merchant dropped a hint to his wife, and she dropped a hint to Rachel her daughter, suggesting she fetch coffee and delicacies as refreshments in honor of the guest. The daughter was familiar with her mother's wiles and, understanding the purpose of this visit, blushed and brought him the coffee. Senor Franco seized the opportunity, and asked Jacob a philosophical question concerning matters of secular wisdom in the French language, and Jacob answered him. The Senor said: "Do you hear, Rachel, how Jacob has interpreted it? Your opinion was otherwise."

She gave her reply, mustering evidence to support her argument. Jacob refuted her argument, and she bowed her head modestly, replied once more—though sparingly, with a couple of words—and left the room. The Senor perceived that they were of like mind, and was satisfied. He talked further with Jacob over matters of Torah and matters of wisdom, and Jacob saw this was a pleasant time for him, and did not know why. He blessed him and went his way.

A few days later Hacham Hiyyah called Jacob his son and said to him: "My son, I ask one thing of you, and I ask you do not disappoint me. I want you to take a wife. According to the tradition I learned from my father, in our family they used to uphold the ordinance of the *Mishnah*, that eighteen is the age to go beneath the wedding canopy. And they respected the saying of the Talmud in the tractate *Kiddushin*, that by twenty years old the Holy One Blessed be He expects a man to marry. After this age, there is a kind of obstruction, almost a heavenly ban, that comes into force."

Hacham Hiyyah went on to tell his son: "For a long time we

have known Senor Franco, who is one of the leaders of the community, a lover of the Torah and a God-fearing man. My saintly father told us how the father of Senor Franco came by his wealth, which the Lord shared with him, and how he supported the sages all his life. He has a fair and dutiful daughter, a worthy match for you."

His mother added further words of her own, some of them to the point and others not to the point, to appeal to his heart, and in the end the business was amicably settled.

There was great joy in their house in those days. First betrothal and marriage preparations, and then night after night the Wedding Week celebrations. And every sermon that Hacham Hiyyah preached was new and full of delight, and *hazanim* composed special anthems for the betrothal, and others for the wedding, and others still for the Sabbath when the groom went up to read from the Torah, and there were allusions there to the name of Hacham Hiyyah, and the name of Senor Franco. And the poets produced rhymes in praise of God, who brings couples together, and in praise of the bride and in praise of the guests, and the women baked and stewed and blended, concocting all the delicacies of Aleppo. And the heads of the community and the sages congratulated Hacham Hiyyah and wished him gladness of heart, and our Teacher and Master blessed the bride and the groom with a priestly blessing. But in spite of this there were those who sensed that Hacham Hiyyah's heart was not at ease. In his sermons he was trying to give his son the hint to return to his studies, but without success, and his joy was not complete. His revered wife was always aware of what was in his heart, for between them silence was open and affection concealed. Now too she was aware. So many times she wanted to tell him not to mar the celebrations, and hadn't dared speak with him. The days of the wedding passed, and all returned to their business.

Israel in Exile is never at ease. The sages said: If they found ease they would never return. Hard times came upon Aleppo, this town that was once the mother of commerce, situated on the crossroads, its merchants trading with East and West. Now it was in steep decline. The new Suez Canal had long since been opened, and already traders were used to it. New routes were opening and new traders emerging. Many of the formerly wealthy descended into penury. All their lives they had been involved in commerce, and they knew no other employment, and livelihoods were shrinking. In those days many members of the community left their homes and wandered faraway. The boldest of them traveled across the seas, the average ones went down to Egypt, and the devout made their way to *Eretz-Israel* to enjoy the grace of its soil. They said: Why should we cling to the bosom of an alien land? If it is decreed that we must leave our domicile, then let us make our habitation the Land of Israel, of which it is said, *Whosoever dwells therein is absolved of sin.*

And to whatever place they came, emigrants from Aleppo would join together in one community, praying in a *minyan* of their own, appointing sages of their own, and cantors of their own. For a native of Aleppo only prays to the tune he knows from his father's home.

Those who traveled overseas engaged in whatever business was practiced in that place, and those who went up to *Eretz-Israel* likewise engaged in the local business. And what business was practiced in *Eretz-Israel*? Torah, and worship of the Lord. And they occupied themselves with Torah and their reverence was elevated to new heights, since being in the anteroom of a king is not the same as dwelling in his palace. For the one who dwells in the palace is subjected to the most exacting standards; he must have no blemish on his garment.

The sages in Aleppo worked hard to help the poor who had been left behind, and many questions relating to the issue of *agunot* were submitted to them for judgment. When reports were heard, that those who had traveled abroad were prospering, everyone wanted to go there. And anyone who lacked the means to take his family, went by himself. And he would say: If the Lord increases my property, I shall send for them and bring them to me. And there were some who feared their wives might prevent them from going, so they deserted them and went on their way. And the deserted wives would come to the sages and weep before them.

I was told of those days by my great aunt, Senora Victoria, that when a wife saw her husband taking with him the *tallit* and the *tefillin*, she feared he might be planning to leave, and watched his every move. Such was the case of the nephew of Hacham Hiyyah's wife, who had four grown-up daughters, and was in financial straits. When his wife bore him his fifth daughter, he took his *tefillin* and went on his way, abandoning his wife and leaving his daughters destitute. Some time later they were told he had been seen in America. Hacham Hiyyah tried hard to locate him, but without success. He asked his son Jacob to write letters to those he was acquainted with in Europe, asking for news of him, but still no trace was found. His wife was left an *agunah*—neither married nor divorced—and hired out her services as a seamstress, sewing curtains in wealthy households from dawn till dusk to support her daughters.

Barely had the sons of Aleppo learned to cope with the scourge of poverty, when they were hit by another blow. Kingdoms were in dispute with one another, and the smell of the tumult of war was in the air, and the entire world was in ferment. It was not until many years later that they learned just how terrible that war had been, the war that came to be called the Great, or the First World War.

Every affliction that the Gentiles suffer, Israel suffers twofold. Because of the affliction, and because Israel is Israel. As the prophet lamented: *For she has taken from the hand of the Lord twice over for all her sins.* In times of tranquility people smile at one another, and in times of trouble they frown and quarrel, and to make matters worse, the state too begins to curb their freedoms. Troubled times are also the season of the rumor-mongers, who told people what they heard from someone who knows, who heard it from a certain Gentile associated with the Ottoman government. It was said that the authorities suspected that some members of the community were spies, and in particular they suspected the teachers of the Alliance Israelite Universelle school, where the language of instruction was French, and France was seen as a hostile nation. And although the sages preached in the synagogues, warning the congregation not to defy the government, lest the actions of one endanger the peace of all, not everyone heeded their appeal.

At the same time the government called upon the spiritual council and the temporal council, and warned them. It was also said that the government had posted agents of the secret police force to keep watch over them, and no one knew who could be trusted and who was an informer. Though this was not all that the purveyors of rumors said, but they had heard from those who knew, that the army was going to take youths from the community into its service. There could be no more frightful rumor than this. Never had we seen or heard of a Jew, one of the sons of Israel in Aleppo, conscripted into army service.

In short, rumor chased rumor, and worry chased worry, and joy drained from the world. *Hazanim* cut their anthems short, women restrained their chanting, sages engaged in lengthy discourse over ethics so as to rouse the populace to repentance, and amid all this, the sermons were full of woe, the devout added their pleas and *bakashot*, and synagogue administrators formed yet more committees charged with setting the world to rights.

There was one man in the community who capitalized on the fears of others. People said he could foretell destinies, and crowds used to come to him. Women used to come to him to help them find husbands, young men asked him if they were to be conscripted into the army, girls asked about their loves, old people asked how things would be after they had gone—and everyone wanted to know if war was imminent and what would be the outcome.

And although our Teacher and Master commanded Hacham Menashe Muhadeb to speak out publicly in all the synagogues on this matter, and warn them that they were transgressing the Torah's injunction: *Be pure of heart with the Lord your God*, and not only were they breaking a prohibition, they were also acting foolishly, and were unworthy of the Torah's description: *Surely this great nation is a wise and understanding people*, this made no impression on the populace. And there were even members of the Gentile community who came to this soothsayer, calling him by the honorific title Sheikh el-Yahud. And when Gentiles were in consultation with El-Yahud, he would hear from them about affairs of state, and he would then go and convey the report secretly to the sages, and no one in the world knew how these things were known to the sages.

One night he came to Hacham Hiyyah in a panic and said to him: I have a secret to tell you, and whispered in his ear. When

Hacham Hiyyah heard what he heard, his face turned pale with worry. He turned to face the wall and prayed a short prayer of supplication. Straightaway he asked that one of his sons be called, and he told him what he told him. All that night the sage had neither rest nor repose, until he had done what he did. And people were coming to his room, and conferring with him in whispers, and leaving. And no one knew what was happening. Before midnight Senor De Piciotto arrived, and the sage told him what he told him, and he left, with his mind more at ease

What was the rumor he heard? That a certain policeman had secretly told the fortune-teller that Jacques Sapport, Jacob that is, Hiyyah's son, was suspected of spying on behalf of the French. That night Jacques and Rachel fled to France.

Before dawn five secret policemen came to ask his mother about him. She said she didn't know where he was, and they left. She sent word to the sage at the *Beit Midrash*, where he had been studying since midnight. He stood and said: "Blessed is he who bestows good on the guilty," and returned to his text.

Chapter nine

The tribulations of travel are hard for everyone, and for the sons of scholarly households and the daughters of wealthy parents, even more so. When a man is in his place, everyone knows him, and respects him according to his worth and according to the rank of his forebears. He, too, is familiar with his surroundings, knowing what he should say and what he should not say, what he should do and what he should not do. Once uprooted from his landscape, a man is at a loss, bewildered and perplexed.

This was not the way Jacques and Rachel had imagined their arrival in Paris.

Jacques and Rachel had spent much of their time studying the language of France and the philosophy of France, and they knew the names of its rivers, and the names of its mountains, and the kings who had reigned there and the dates of their reigns, and who had rebelled against whom, and when the masses seized power, and where the universities were situated, and they even knew by heart the names of Parisian streets. This being so, they expected to feel at home in France, reckoning themselves versed in its customs and its manners.

Yet on their arrival, they saw that the mountains of France in

Aleppo were not the same as the mountains of France in France, and the things that imagination shows to man are not the same things that his eyes show him. The France they had drawn for themselves was the France of the teachers of the Alliance school, and of those girls who used to affect French conversation and French mannerisms at the club that they formed for themselves. The France that they came to was a different country.

They did not know which way to turn or where to go. They had arrived in 1914, a time of national crisis for France, and people were wary of anyone who was not of local origin. Although Senor Franco had given Rachel his daughter the names of merchants who traded with him, and Monsieur Pinseau had provided Jacques with a letter of introduction to Professor Farreur, who was an important figure in the Alliance Israelite Universelle, and furthermore he had in his possession a certificate confirming the scholarship that he had been awarded—despite all this, the time was not opportune.

Because they had left Aleppo in haste, there had been no time for Senor Franco and Monsieur Pinseau to give their contacts notice of their arrival. The merchants that Senor Franco sent them to were busy with their own concerns, and treated them rather evasively, for although the merchants showed friendly faces, and offered them a place where they could lodge for a few days, Jacob and Rachel were clearly not made to feel welcome.

Even finding the office of the Alliance Israelite Universelle cost Jacques considerable time and effort. When he arrived, he was told that Professor Farreur was visiting a university in Germany, and because of the state of emergency he could not return. The staff in his office, receiving Jacques with blank faces, told him they had no idea what he was talking about, and until the professor's return they could do nothing. When Jacques mentioned the name of Monsieur Nuri Pinseau they said: "We've never heard of him, there are many teachers employed by the society, and we can't possibly know them all." Finally Jacques showed them the certificate of his scholarship. They passed it from hand to hand, turned it over and upside-down, winking at one another as if saying: What is this meant to be?—until one of them said to him: "Pardon, Monsieur, we have never seen a document like this, and we don't know what a scholarship is."

They asked him to leave his papers with them until they could find a solution to the problem, and they would let him know. He went away in low spirits.

When a Jew is in low spirits and has nowhere to go, he goes to the synagogue. Jacques made his way to a place where his brethren of the House of Israel could be found, in the Troisième Arrondisment, near the Seine, and went into the small synagogue there. It was the time of *minha*, and the synagogue was still closed. With the setting of the sun a meager *minyan* assembled, and prayed in haste, without Psalm 84, and without the prayer 'Blending of Incense.' They didn't even say the prayers of supplication. Jacques was amazed. He was accustomed to afternoon prayer as conducted in Aleppo, with the *hazan* enunciating every word, pronouncing every letter and stress and accent, and starting from the section of the Zohar "Elijah began…" and arriving at the *Shmoneh Esreh* prayer, the Eighteen Benedictions, not only in a dignified fashion, but also with the joy of a duty well carried out. Yet here the man who was leading the prayers rushed through into the *Ashre* prayer and *Kaddish*, and they stood for the *Shmoneh Esreh* prayer. He hadn't reached the phrase 'Bestower of Knowledge' and the cantor was already finishing the silent prayer. It was clear that this cantor was waiting for no one, and he started the Repetition of the *Shmoneh Esreh*. Jacques had not yet finished when the entire service was over, and they all sat down at a long table to study passages from the *Mishnah*. One of them was reading the *Mishnah* and the commentary of Bartenura, and expounding upon them. When Jacques heard how he was interpreting the *Mishnah*, he was mortified, for the whole of the interpretation was utterly wrong, and even the reading was flawed. He did not know if he should speak out or maintain his silence. He chose silence. It was then that he saw before him the image of his father, Hacham Hiyyah, studying the *Mishnah* with him, and he felt suddenly homesick. His already crushed spirit became yet more dejected.

After the session one of the worshippers approached him, shook his hand vigorously and bade him welcome. He would not leave Jacob alone until he had told him who he was, where he had come from and when, and where he was lodging, and what he intended to do, and whether he had a trade, or was looking for accommodation, or for a generous and charitable patron (he was acquainted with some such) or did he need papers, a permit to reside in Paris, or did he have money to change. Jacques sensed that this man could be dangerous, as is one with a finger in every pie and with whom everyone is involved in some way, so he cut the conversation short and spurned him thereafter.

Jacques returned to the house of the merchant who had provided he and his wife with temporary lodging, and told Rachel the story. They saw that the upshot was that matters would depend on their efforts alone, and they resolved to rent an apartment on their own.

They found no one who would lease them property, because the French only let their apartments to their fellow citizens. They had to go to a great deal of trouble before they managed to rent a tiny garret on the fifth floor of a tenement in the Rue De Rousseau. It was typical of the buildings there, all built with five stories and garrets to let on the top floor.

Rachel, born into a wealthy family and spoiled by her parents, suffered dreadfully in this garret. Everything about it was wrong. But it did have one thing in its favor; it was close to the Louvre, that great and world-famous Paris museum. This was the museum that had been the final destination of the ten-branched *Hanukkah* lamp with the engraving of the ship, which Hacham Raphael Sapporta had given to the father of Senor Franco, who traded in scrap-metals, to sell to the man who came from a far country to buy old *Hanukkah* lamps. This was the *menorah* that was destined to bemuse the son of Jacques, but we will let the story unfold by itself, and let Jacques find his place.

In this way, a few weeks passed. More than he pitied himself, Jacques pitied Rachel, who was in a state of constant grief, despite all his efforts to console her. Every few days he visited the offices of the Alliance Israelite Universelle, to see if there had been any progress on the matter of his certificate, and the scholarship he had been awarded. In the meantime he sat by himself in the libraries of universities, devouring the books that he found there, in no order and with no plan. Every book he came across he would read.

One day when he arrived at the Alliance Israelite Universelle office, the staff received him with more deference than was their wont. When he had visited that office on previous occasions, it had seemed to him that he was regarded as a nuisance. That day the secretary greeted him warmly, invited him to sit, offered him refreshments and said: "Monsieur Jacques, that business of yours has now been clarified. A telegram has been received from the director of the society, confirming that you are the rabbi's son from Aleppo, and that you placed first in all the examinations set by the society, and that you are a prodigy, destined for great things, and have been awarded a scholarship to study in Paris for five years." A number of clerks and secretaries were assembled in the room, and they surrounded him, handing him all kinds of papers, everyone eager to see him, smiling at him and asking after his health.

When a man is visited by one deliverance, its fellows are not far behind. When he returned to his home, Rachel came out to meet him. He wanted to tell her what had happened to him, but she forestalled him, telling him a merchant had brought them a letter that day from the De Piciotto textile company, containing a large sum of money sent them by her father.

Members of the society leased them a spacious and impressive apartment, and attended to all their business affairs. They arranged an appointment for Jacques with Professor Pierre, the professor of philosophy at the Sorbonne, who was to interview him and assess him, and determine the course of study that he should follow.

Although his material problems had been solved, Jacques' spirit was still troubled, and he walked about during this time as if he walked in a world that was not his. The land, its atmosphere, its people, its customs, all were alien. His imagination led him from pictures of Aleppo his hometown, to pictures of Paris, and the pictures were confused. He saw his father sitting and reading the *Mishnah* in his home in Paris, and the *hazan*, Hacham Alfiyah, chanting in the synagogue in the Troisième Quartier. Once when walking on the boulevard, he was convinced that he saw Monsieur Pinseau in front of him, and he ran to greet him, only to discover it was someone else, and he wondered how it had occurred to him that Monsieur Pinseau could be on a street in Paris.

It was only when he returned to Rachel his wife, that Jacques felt he was at home. Or when he sat in his study and read a page of the *Gemara*; then he knew he was in his world. Abbaye and Rabba, Rashi and Rabbenu Tam, the Alfas and Rabbenu Asher, with them he walked with confidence. He had known them since his boyhood, and they were his friends. What matter if the view from his window be an alleyway in Aleppo or an alleyway in Paris, so long as in spirit he was in the great seminaries of Sura and Neharde'a.

Professor Pierre was curious to meet him. In the report he had been given, it was said of Jacques that he was the son of a great Talmudic scholar. For a long time he had wanted to know the secret of this Talmud of the Jews. He had heard that the study of the Talmud is something special, and he had also been told that this Jacques came from the East, and it wasn't an everyday occurrence to meet a student from there, especially one who was reputedly a genius, keen of intelligence, profound of thought, and a lover of wisdom.

For his part, Jacques was excited at the prospect of meeting the professor. He already knew of his scholarship from his writings, and now he was to see him with his own eyes. That day, Jacques donned his Sabbath clothes. After walking along innumerable corridors, and asking directions from innumerable clerks, he found the office. When the door was opened to him, he entered hesitantly, and saw before him a mane of white hair, framing the head of a short man with dreamy eyes, and the ghost of a smile on his face. On seeing Jacques, Professor Pierre rose at once to greet him, slapped his shoulder cordially and said: "Ah, Monsieur Jacques, this isn't the way I imagined you would look. A man sketches the image of another in his heart, and when he sees him, the truth confronts him. And who knows what truth is, and perhaps what we see is nothing other than imagination, and truth is the truth in the heart. And who was it that said that the world appearing before our eyes is the world, and perhaps there are other worlds in the mind and in the heart, which are not seen. What is your opinion, Monsieur Jacques? Does the Talmud deal with this?"

He did not wait for an answer, but continued at once: "I have a young student who is destined for great things. My colleagues deride both myself and him, but believe me Monsieur, I know the qualities of students, and I say it is his destiny to shake the world to its foundations, but his fellows cannot fathom him. Such is the way of mortals that they want to hear only what the mind can cope with. He says, this student of mine, that there is a world of truth that exists within the self, and there is a world outside it, and all we have to do is join these worlds together. And this student also says that man is a free agent, he can do whatsoever he pleases and his destiny depends only on him. How this notion terrifies the foolish! Man finds it convenient to believe that his destiny is fixed from the day of his birth, and his actions are preordained, and his own choice is not a factor. What is your opinion, Monsieur Jacques? Does this not run counter to religion, which holds that only the Creator is a free agent, deciding the fate of man? What does the Talmud have to say about this?"

Jacques did indeed have an answer to give, and he would have liked to quote the words of the Rambam, that man has free choice, and that none can force him to take any particular path, other than he himself, but he did not want to interrupt the other's speech, this not being the way of wisdom, and Professor Pierre did not give him the opportunity to say a word, constantly asking him: "What is your opinion Jacques? Do you agree?" as he passed from one topic to the next.

Eventually Professor Pierre said: "I think it is right that the two of you study together, as both of you have a keen intellect, and your thoughts are not like those of other people, since the majority can think only what they have heard from others, while the wise man's thoughts are governed by his inner essence. I believe he will be glad of your company, and you will be glad of his. Oh, Monsieur, I beg your pardon, you are still standing. I didn't invite you to sit, and you a newcomer here, a guest in my office—are these French manners? Jacques, you are a philosopher, and I'm sure you will judge me with sympathy. You understand, when someone has a philosophical problem on his mind, it gives him no peace while he is troubled by it. Especially, when it's something that human lives depend on. Yesterday we were discussing an issue until after midnight, and I am still concerned about it."

When they were both seated, Professor Pierre seemed more at ease, and he invited Jacques to introduce himself, to tell him what he was studying, and what he proposed to study. Jacques spoke judiciously, telling him what he had learned from his teachers and what he had learned by himself, and which texts he had read when in Aleppo of those that had been sent from France. He also referred to articles that Professor Pierre had written.

As he was speaking, a tall man came into the room, neatly dressed and with a stern expression on his face. Professor Pierre turned to him, "Professor Mantour, I would like you to meet a new student from the East. He's a Jew and a Talmudist, and studying philosophy on his own account. He has already achieved a great deal, and I believe that his future achievements will be greater still."

A scornful smile flitted across Professor Mantour's face, as if he were saying to himself: This is just another of Professor Pierre's follies. He likes weird people. He despises those of our students who are conscientious in their work, repeating what their teachers have taught them, and writing things down exactly as they have been dictated, yet whom does he befriend? Foreigners, who have come to France from who knows where, saying all kinds of outlandish things.

Professor Pierre drew up a curriculum for Jacques, determining what he should study and with whom, and arranged times for his personal tuition. Before parting from him he shook his hand and said to him: "Monsieur Jacques, you are fortunate in that you need pay nothing. All has been paid in advance by the Alliance Israelite Universelle. Be sure that you don't waste their funds. Don't be like those students that fill our universities who repeat what their teachers tell them and have no ideas of their own. Don't be put off by the cynics, and don't be afraid to say what's in your heart and in your mind, even when your fellows don't agree with you. My heart tells me you have a great future before you. Welcome to France and welcome to the Sorbonne."

Then Professor Pierre sighed and added, "You have come to us in hard times. It seems the world will soon be at war. Who knows how many will perish in it? How foolish people are, destroying the world that they live in, and not knowing for what purpose. What is more, they are eager for the fight! Who knows if we will still have the heart to pursue philosophy?"

Then he sighed again and said: "My son has already been called up, and in a few days he will be taken away to serve in the army. My heart goes out to him."

From that day onward Jacques immersed himself in philosophy, studying as Professor Pierre advised him, and seeing that everything he said had been the truth, since that other student of whom he spoke became his mentor and his friend, someone to confide in before expressing his ideas to the world at large. They would sit together and examine an issue from every angle.

Although much of his energy was devoted to philosophy, Jacques did not neglect the Torah. In Aleppo he had been accustomed to rising with the dawn, as was the practice of the sages and the scholars, and even the merchants used to do the same. This habit served him well now in Paris, as all the rest of his day was spent in the study of philosophy, while this time was dedicated to the Torah. These hours when there was no one to disrupt his studies were precious to him, hours when the air was clear, the soul pure and unsullied, as if newly given from his Creator each morning. He used to go over the point at issue aloud, according to the rhythmic patterns of Aleppo, those he had inherited from his father, and he derived great pleasure from this.

It was not long before Jacques became acquainted with his surroundings, and accustomed to them. For Sabbath eve and for prayers at the close of the Sabbath, he assembled a prayer *minyan* in his own house, and he himself would lead the prayers, standing before the *tebah* and expounding on the scriptural passage of the week, to draw the congregation closer to love of the Torah. At first they were wary of him, being unused to lengthy services, but as they came to know him, recognizing him as a man of stature, a distinguished scholar with an easy manner of dealing with people, the *minyan* grew until there was no longer space for it in the house.

He also held classes in the *Mishnah*, and classes in the Rambam's *Sefer HaMitzvot*.

After a while he began gathering together the children of the neighborhood, and teaching them Hebrew and Rashi. Many of the young men were being recruited into the army, and he did his best to comfort their fathers, encouraging them to hope. Many who had strayed far from the Torah and from the *mitzvot* were brought back to the fold through his influence, as Jacques revealed its beauty to them.

In time, he produced a pamphlet of extracts from the Torah, accessible to all and written in the French language, with the title *Shema Israel*, and every week he wrote an exposition of a passage and a section from the liturgy, and so forth, and would distribute it among the members of his *minyan*.

In short, within a brief period Jacques had illumined the whole of his neighborhood with the splendor of the Torah. He gained a reputation for wisdom and understanding, as one who could explain the Torah with pleasantness. Many of our fellow Jews in France in those times were far from the Torah, and even faith itself was faltering in their hands, and the rabbis used to send these Jews to him. All kinds of strange and extraordinary people would come to him—all with their questions and doubts and demands. Jacques would distinguish between those who had come to make mischief, to whom he gave short shrift, and those whose aspirations were to the Heavens, between scholars and ignoramuses, and to each and every one he responded in the manner most befitting him.

Once they sent him a young priest, a man full of questions, seeking to know what is above and what below, what is before and what behind, and his soul filled with longings, yearnings for a living God. This young priest had gone from one source to another, consorting with Christian sages and philosophers, and now he would know no peace of mind until he had become acquainted with the wisdom of the Torah. Jacques shied away from him for obvious reasons, but the other would brook no refusal.

Day and night they used to debate over questions of faith, with the priest drinking in his words thirstily. Not content with what he learned, he asked that Jacques teach him Hebrew, so he could read the Torah for himself, and he studied it so well that he became an acknowledged expert in that language. Furthermore, he asked to be shown what worship is, and how a Jew stands before his Creator, and how he makes his peace with Him. And Jacques took him to witness the *Kal Nidre* prayer on the eve of *Yom Kippur*, and when the priest saw the sons of Israel standing at sunset wrapped in their *tallits*, after making peace with one another, and directing their hearts toward the Lord, his soul was cast into turmoil seeing the sons of Israel cleansing themselves like the Seraphim.

It is true, many have seen Israel at prayer, but not everyone has been privileged to see what he saw. Jacques was aware that a precious soul had come before him, truly seeking its repair, and aspiring toward Heaven, and yet when this priest asked him to arrange his conversion, Jacques rejected his appeal, explaining to him that his duty lay in his own world. Finally the priest approached a distinguished rabbi who advised him that rather than convert, he should be a Gentile who observes the seven commandments of the sons of Noah, and hence become one of the righteous Gentiles of the world. The priest heeded his advice, and rose to a position of eminence, always praising our Torah, and consorting with Jews and telling them of his experience, and expressing his admiration for this people.

All this time, neither Jacques nor Rachel forgot the homes of their fathers, or the rooms where their education began. Because this was a time of crisis, it was difficult to send letters from one place to another and from Paris to Aleppo was no exception. Only seldom did a letter arrive safely, and then it would take a long time, arriving by circuitous routes. Hacham Hiyyah wrote letters in the language of the sages, and at the end his wife would add a few tearful lines. These lines were filled with love and longing, written in a blend of Arabic and French and Hebrew, and all of it in the language of the heart.

At the end of the letter the wife of Senor Franco also added some words addressed to her young daughter, who had left scarcely a year after her marriage, and it was sealed with the blessings of brothers and sisters and aunts, all of them appending their names, and Jacques' mother returning and adding still more blessings, and recalling memories, and Rachel's mother also returning with a short postscript of her own.

The day the letter arrived was a festive day in their house. Rachel would read it, and read it again, poring over every word, how it was written and why it was written, and what it alluded to. She would even examine the form of the script, trying to see whether the letter had been written in joy or in sorrow, in a state of serenity or of oppression. And she used to imagine her mother weeping, handkerchief in hand and mumbling words of longing in the Arabic language, Rachel my daughter, may no harm befall you, may we see you well, and dipping her pen in tears. By this time the letter was awash with Rachel's tears, her tears mingling with the tears of her mother.

Rachel kept the letters as if they were holy things. She would open them again and again whenever she was alone, and read the words over and over, as if they were not mere words but precious pearls. Such is the way of the world, that when we are close, we know nothing of the value of words, and yet when we are far apart, it is as if we had never heard these words before.

When Jacques saw the letter, he would skip over his father's words and read the rest of the letter, saving the words of his esteemed father for the Holy Sabbath, a time of good will. After the prayer of *minha*, when all the world is serene, and Israel is professing the unity of God: *You are one, and your name is one, and who is like your people Israel, one nation upon the earth*, that was when he read his father's words, upholding with them the commandment: *And you shall call the Sabbath a delight.* And he would study and analyze every single one of his father's hints and allusions, interpreting them in numerous different ways.

When he wrote back to his father, out of his great respect for him he hardly mentioned Paris or philosophy. He knew his father, and knew what was precious to him, and there was one thing he knew he would appreciate. During those days he spent at the university, if he had time to spare he would approach the librarian, who would admit him to the department of Jewish manuscripts, taking out for him ancient manuscripts from the earliest times, and these Jacques copied in his own handwriting and sent to his father. There he found new versions of the Talmud, and commentaries that were quite unknown. There he found an extract from Rabbenu Hananel's commentary on the Talmud, and innovations on the part of the Ritba, and a fragment of the *Book of Creation*. And only once did he come across one of the dialogues of Plato, that addresses the relative merits of learning from a teacher or learning from books, and Jacques was so impressed by what he read there that he could not stop himself from copying out the whole passage and including it in one of his letters to his father.

A son and a daughter were born to Jacques and Rachel while they lived in Paris, children who were their joy and their consolation, and in every single letter that they wrote, they would describe their features and their mischief, and recount their activities. They called their firstborn son Hiyyah, and his nickname was Victor. He was a composed and happy child and he resembled Rachel's father, Senor Franco. They called their daughter Sophie, after Jacques' mother whose name was Shafi'a. Whenever they looked at her, it seemed to them that they were seeing the face of Hacham Hiyyah. Her eyes were black and deep, and her wits sharp. Her childhood was a difficult time for her mother; whatever instruction she was given, not only did she not obey it, she made a point of doing the opposite.

It was a source of great sadness to Rachel that her father and mother had not been present at the birth of her children. The night before they were due to admit their son Hiyyah into the covenant of Abraham our Patriarch at his *brit*, they resolved to perform a 'Zohar' after the tradition of Aleppo.

In Aleppo, on the eve of the ceremony of the *brit mila*, it was the custom that all the relatives and friends of the family gather together and read chapters from the Zohar relating to the covenant. Every one of the assembled company read one passage, the last being left to the father of the infant son. Then they would sing the hymn:

Bar Yohai, anointed and blessed, with every one of the cantors, the *hazanim*, displaying his skill. And when the hymn was finished they chanted *Kaddish*, and presented the infant. All those present who were *Cohanim* laid their hands on his head and gave him a priestly blessing. And then the grandmother brought in a big silver tray, bearing candles and garlanded with flowers and blossoms, known in Aleppo as the *soneya* of Elijah the Prophet. A small dish would also be brought in, and every one of those present would light a candle, set it on the tray, and put a few coins into the dish.

When all—men and women and children—had lit candles, and the tray was a blaze of light, and the dish full of coins, the most eminent guest would take the tray and announce: "The *soneya* of Elijah the Prophet, who wants to buy it?"

The assembled company made bids for the tray, since according to tradition it was firmly believed that the purchase of the tray was an act that boded well for the arrival of male children for the one who bought it. Whoever offered the highest price and succeeded in buying it took it in his hand, and the rabbi blessed him with many and various blessings, in particular the benediction predicting the birth of sons. The money pledged in the auction would be donated to rabbinical charities, and the small coins in the dish were kept by the purchaser, these being symbolic of wealth.

Throughout the ceremony, cantors were singing their anthems in honor of the father of the child, and in honor of the *sandak* and the *mohel*, and the women carried on serving the delicacies they had prepared, and everyone would be in high spirits and a beneficent mood. Such was the custom in Aleppo on the eve of the covenant. It was called 'the Zohar' and no inhabitant of Aleppo would even think of omitting it.

When Hiyyah was born in Paris, Jacques and Rachel set about inviting a number of the synagogue worshippers to their home. There was no one to prepare sweetmeats in the fashion of Aleppo, so Jacques bought cakes from the bakery. When the guests arrived after the evening prayer, they had no idea what they were supposed to do, as they had never seen this ceremony before. Jacques read all the passages from the *Zohar* himself, being the only one who knew how they should be read. He recited all the poetry and led the singing of *Bar Yohai*, as there was no one else there to officiate as a cantor, and when the tray was brought in with the candles, all were mystified. When the guests noticed the lateness of the hour, they simply wished them *mazal tov* and left one by one. Only Jacques and Rachel lit candles, and all the other candles were left lonely and aggrieved. This was a time when Jacques and Rachel remembered their home in Aleppo with particular longing, and were filled with yearning.

❧

In the seven years that Jacques lived in Paris, he hardly ever strolled in the squares or the markets, but made his rounds of the universities and the libraries, making the acquaintance of academicians, delving into their methods and debating with them, until he acquired a name for himself as a highly promising philosopher.

His fellow student also went from strength to strength, becoming a tutor at the university, and was praised by all. One night he came to Jacques' house, in an agitated state. He said to him: "Jacques my friend, I have given much thought to the way that the world is managed, the poor and the rich. Is this the decree of fate, or is it the actions of men? If it's the actions of men, what can we do to change the pattern of the world, make a world where the poor and the weak also have the right to live? Surely your people, the Jews, know about the soul of the outcast, and the oppression of the weak."

And so he talked on in this vein, of setting the world to rights, and of honesty and justice. All night long he talked to him of these matters, while Jacques sat and listened. Departing from his usual practice, he neither objected nor agreed, but only listened.

Never had he heard such ideas before. He knew there was a duty of charity, and a duty of assisting the poor, and of philanthropy, but his friend spoke of other things. And although no one could possibly disagree with the logic of these things, his mind could not accept them, and Jacques did not know why. It seemed to him he knew instinctively that they weren't to be accepted. These ideas, which in his case had fallen on deaf ears, were destined to shake the world to its foundations, and captivate the hearts of the young. Little did

Jacques know then that the outlook on the world, which his mind refused to accept, would one day hold his own son's heart in thrall.

Jacques was close to completing his studies at the university. Already he had written his long dissertation, and already Professor Pierre had hinted to him that his position for the future was secure. It was then that Professor Farreur summoned him to the office of the Alliance Israelite Universelle.

When Jacques arrived there, Farreur congratulated him on completing his studies, and on achieving such success, which had brought credit to the society. He said: "We knew what we were doing when we brought you here. Only once have we made a mistake. We brought a student to Paris from the east, and he neglected his studies, giving himself and us a bad name. But apart from that, our managers have made the right decisions, sending us conscientious scholars.

"As you know, the objective of our society is to disseminate scholarship in all the places where Jews live, and especially in the East. We believe that if the light of knowledge shines on them, they will be freed from barbarism, since knowledge is the mark of the truly free man. Furthermore, when the Gentiles acknowledge their merits, they will no longer hate them."

He went on to drop hints about sages in those countries, who did nothing to help their society but opposed them at every turn, fearing the loss of their own status.

Jacques was shocked at hearing this, and wanted to utter a vehement protest, but he restrained himself and spoke calmly, saying: "Professor Farreur, with respect, you are mistaken. Sitting here in Paris, you have no idea what life is like in those places. If you knew how much wisdom there is on one page of the Talmud, or in one chapter of the Rambam, you wouldn't say what you have said. You should know that if your teachers took more care, not despising the Torah and the Commandments, and not deriding the sages, they could instill in their pupils both the Torah and secular knowledge. What are the sages expected to do, when they see teachers belittling everything that is holy, and dragging the community toward neglect of the tradition of their fathers? It isn't their own status they are concerned about, but the status of our nation, since a nation exists only by virtue of its laws, and if people are taught to abandon the heritage of their fathers, in the end they will have neither Torah nor knowledge.

"Yet these very sages that your teachers deride are the ones who risk their lives for the community in times of crisis, and serve them with all their might.

"And the other thing you said, that if they have education the Gentiles will love them—that is mistaken too. Those Gentiles who hate us do not hate us because we have education or because we have no education; because we have money or we have no money; because we are dwelling in their land or we are dwelling in our own land."

Professor Farreur answered him: "I disagree with you in every respect, and in the end history will decide between us, but that is all the more reason why we want to send you, and you in particular, to Aleppo, to go back to your community, and the sages you are acquainted with, and to run our school there. You will be a leading light both in Torah and secular wisdom, so the sages will have no reason to oppose you, and you will disseminate the light of knowledge. That is why I have called you here. You should know that these times of ours are not like former times. The terrible war is over, and there is an air of peace and reconciliation in the air. Days of calm and brotherhood are coming, and reason will prevail, and people will be able to study in tranquility, and the world will know no more war. Aleppo has been placed under a French Mandate and I have heard there are many there who are eager to learn the French language and study French culture. And we need people like you to go there."

Jacques did not have to work too hard at persuading his wife. He knew she would be happy at the idea; although she had grown accustomed to living in Paris, and come to love many things there which she knew she would not find in Aleppo, still she longed for her father's house.

Chapter ten

It is a tradition among us Jews that Elijah does not visit on the eve of the Sabbath, not wishing to trouble the folk of Israel, and what is more, he does not come on the Sabbath. So it is after *Havdalah* that the Jews of Aleppo await his coming. Since at the close of every Sabbath Elijah has to record the merits of Israel, they are at pains to recite poems recalling his praises. The congregation of Aleppo observed this custom assiduously, prolonging the *Havdalah* and the poems of Elijah at the close of every Sabbath.

Ever since the day that the husband of my great aunt Senora Victoria died, she insisted I come to her at the close of every Sabbath, and recite the *Havdalah* for her. And although she had heard the *Havdalah* recited by Hacham Mansour, in the synagogue of the émigrés from Aleppo, who used to prolong it with decorous chant, praying that the week to come would be a good week for us, with good tidings in store, and he used to smile a little before the blessing over the wine, and all the congregation smiled with him, for a good omen—in spite of this she declared that she could not be satisfied until I had recited the *Havdalah* for her in her house. And she also insisted I sing all the tunes of Aleppo as her husband had sung them, and I was not allowed to skip anything. After the poems she would reward me with coffee and a fairy story.

At one such time I sought to hear from her additional material that I could use in telling the story of Hacham Hiyyah. And although I knew she was so sparing with words, I assumed that the return of Jacques and Rachel from Paris to Aleppo after the Great War must have made an impression on her, and that she would not only remember it but have a lot to tell me. But upon hearing my request, she replied dismissively: "What story is there to tell here? Trivialities! So they came back to Aleppo from Paris! What of it? Do you suppose that the whole of Aleppo was on its feet to greet them? In those days there were many people coming and going. My respected father arrived from Egypt, Hacham Attia and Hacham Dweck emigrated to *Eretz-Israel*, Senor Totah set sail for Mexico, and Madame Anteby Antavi for Brazil. If you saw someone standing up to read the Torah on the Sabbath and reciting *Birkat HaGomel*, the Blessing of Deliverance, you didn't know if he was a native of Aleppo who had recovered from a grave illness, or a newcomer from across the seas. And if you saw a woman being embraced by other women in the gallery, you didn't know if her daughter had given birth to a son, or she was on the verge of emigrating.

"But I do seem to remember that they said that as soon as he arrived, he went to our Teacher and Master and spoke with him. The rumor went that Jacques wanted to move the ancient manuscript of the Bible known as the 'Keter' to a different place, and the council of the congregation objected, and he backed down."

What was not revealed to me by Aunt Victoria was told to me by others. The Aleppo to which Jacques and Rachel returned was not the Aleppo that they had left. Since the day it had been placed under a French Mandate, a libertarian spirit had dominated the region.

Many of the tradesmen had profited during the war. As a result of the blockade, goods could not be imported from overseas, and anyone with any merchandise in hand could sell it for ten times the wholesale price. It was said that a certain merchant in the haberdashery trade, Aharon Safdieh by name, held a stockpile of needles and pins that he had bought for mere coppers before the war. Since the trade routes were cut, the value of the merchandise doubled with every passing day. Middlemen urged him to sell to them, offering a handsome profit, and warned him that by not selling he risked everything: if the trade routes were to be opened, the value of his goods would plummet—and yet he spurned them. It is said that every day he used to go to Hacham Salem after the dawn prayer and ask: "Shall I sell?" And the answer was: "Wait." Always the same: "Shall I sell?"—and: "Wait." Until one day Hacham Salem told him: "Sell!"

He made a huge profit on the deal. I heard that the wealth ensured by Hacham Salem's blessing was given in return for the loan of cash that Aharon Safadia had given Salem when he had been in financial straits. Others said he took care to sprinkle drops of *Havdalah* wine on his forehead and in his pocket—believed to be a specific charm for the acquisition of wealth.

These newly enriched merchants moved from the neighborhood of Bahsita to Jamaliya, where the streets are broad, the air pure, and the houses pleasant. Where there are wealthy people, there are people who aspire to be reckoned wealthy, and they too took to residing in Jamaliya. The French language was widely spoken there, by all, those who knew it and those who did not. Everywhere you could hear *Bonjour* and *Au revoir*, *Merci* and *Pardonnez-moi*, and other such pleasantries.

From day to day more and more clubs were opened, and there people used to congregate. In former times they had met in a club to hear lectures and read newspapers sent from Paris, whereas now they frittered away their time with games of cards and backgammon, and with dancing. Preachers protested in their sermons, asking: "What purpose is there in pleasure? When men and women consort together, the Devil too joins their company." But no one paid the preachers much heed.

Ladies took care over their *couture*, according to what seemed to them the spirit of the times, and as dictated by Paris. Whether the spirit of the times was comfortable with them, it is not for me to say; but the spirit of the sages most certainly was not. Many of the young people were sent to study at the Alliance Israelite Universelle School, while some continued to attend the state-sponsored school.

Three members of the congregation were studying medicine, and one of them went on to become an eminent physician. All kinds of societies were emerging from time to time, and not everyone knew what their purpose was. Many a pot was being stirred.

The congregation was still obedient to the sages, and held them in very high regard, seeking their favor and fearing their displeasure. But despite this, all sensed that the atmosphere had changed. Some of the most distinguished individuals emigrated to *Eretz-Israel*, others left for Egypt or set out across the seas, and although senior sages remained there, they were careful not to issue edicts that the majority of the population could not cope with. Thus, occasionally, they did not object to something to which in former times they would have objected, thereby upholding the dictum better to err inadvertently than to sin with intent. Even Hacham Hiyyah changed. He immersed himself almost entirely in study of the *Kabbalah*, devoting his attention to the arcane and to the lore of ethics, and neglecting philosophy. He also became more amenable to people; the edges of his pedantry were somewhat rounded out, he became more amenable and his colleagues began to find him agreeable.

In Paris, Jacques had often wondered what he would do when directing the school in Aleppo. Far from Aleppo, he had believed he could instill in his pupils love of the Torah and fear of Heaven, and teach them the ways of wisdom, and bind their hearts to the men of wisdom, and read poetry to them, and tell them of world affairs, and open before them the portals of light.

However, not everything man proposes to do is aided by Heaven. The teachers at the school were veterans and it was impossible to replace them. Some of them had never savored the true taste of philosophy, knowing only what they had read of it from second- and third-hand sources. Some were wearied of the task of teaching, seeing it as a tiresome labor and feeling no dedication to it. If you attempt to teach without dedicating your whole self to it, you will never succeed. And there were some who did their work in a half-hearted manner, as if it were an irksome duty to be fulfilled. Some of them derided the Torah and the sages, and this caused Jacques great distress; he was pained by contempt of the Torah, and was pained to hear people say Torah and secular education were not compatible, that it had to be one or the other.

His staff, for their part, were not overjoyed by his appointment, saying: Why have they imposed on us someone from Paris; is there no one among us better qualified than he, we who have toiled and given all our lives to this school?

Nor did the pupils regard him with equanimity. In former times, those who had come to learn had been impelled by the love of wisdom, and they studied with humility and with urgency, mortifying themselves in the tabernacle of the Torah, and sustaining it. In these times, however, most came because their parents wanted them to learn a little French, in accordance with the spirit of the time, rather than delve into the Torah, and the pupils themselves attended as if under duress, not so much interested in learning but only in receiving certificates to show that they had learned, and they wasted their time, and demonstrated no commitment whatsoever to their studies.

There was so much work for Jacques to do, that he was left with no time for his own study of Torah. Most of his day was spent in conversation—with a pupil whose performance was poor, or with a teacher who wanted to change classes, or with someone complaining to him over his salary. A whole year was spent in acrimonious dispute with a teacher whom Jacques wanted to transfer elsewhere, but could not, however hard he tried, as the man had powerful contacts in the group. Nor was there anyone with whom he could discuss philosophy, as there had been in France. As for the articles that Professor Pierre sent him—he had no time to devote to them.

Rachel was busy all day with the children, and even if she did find some free time, she no longer went to the club. After her years in Paris, she had little patience with the conversation of her friends, or with their attempts to speak French. At first she used to correct their grammar and their pronunciation, and tell them about Paris and its literary circles, and the delights of the Louvre. When she saw that they looked on her as one affecting superior airs, she let them be, and withdrew into herself.

Jacques had a few short hours of peace of mind, when he was in seclusion and writing chapters of the major article which he intended to send to Paris, to the Society for the Study of Living Oriental Languages. But these hours were few, snatched from his working day, and even then he felt anxiety: was he failing in his duty? Was he using piety as an excuse when he should be conversing with one of his students and trying to kindle his interest in philosophy?

Their two children delighted Jacques and Rachel, filling their hearts with gladness. They were as enchanted by Victor's cheerful spirits as by Sophie's acute senses. But many years had passed since their return from Paris, and they had not been blessed with more children. This weighed on Rachel, and became a great sadness to her, for she had grown up in a large family and had always dreamed of one for herself. She was still more grieved when she heard the gossips whispering that she had adopted Parisian ways, and was no longer interested in children. Such is the way of the peddlers of gossip, thinking that the worst they can imagine of their friends is the truth. Her mother treated her with all kinds of remedies, and her father made the rounds of the sages, and Jacques resorted to various medications, but to no avail.

It is said that a certain sage with knowledge of the *Kabbalah* told Rachel's father that he should not press the matter, nor pray to excess. These things have a purpose, and who knows why, and so forth.

One day Jacques received a long letter from an eminent committee of academics in a foreign country. The letter was as follows:

"To the highly respected and justly renowned headmaster, Monsieur Jacques Sapporta, son of the wondrous sage, the glory of sages and the beauty of rabbis, scion of a good and learned family.

"We know of you that you have walked in the ways of wisdom, and that from your childhood you have been destined for great things, and that you are a man of cordial relations with all people. Our scholars have agreed to turn to you with a question that is of the greatest importance to us, and the matter is in your hands.

"For fear lest the letter fall into the hands of strangers, we write to you only by way of allusion, being confident that a sage such as yourself will be capable of understanding one thing by means of another. The subject is the concealed delight that resides in Aleppo in a well-known

place, and she is bright as the sun and the graceful gazelle, the maidens
have seen her and blessed her, queens and concubines shall praise her.
For all men of wisdom are entranced by her and lust after her, and their
heart goes out to her, and all their thoughts are upon her, and they fear
for her life, since she is situated in a place of danger, and men of wisdom
cannot enjoy her, and who knows what the day will bring forth. Perhaps
this precious jewel will be forever lost, and who could ever replace her,
she who is not to be valued in gold?

"We are relying on you, that all the money that they ask of you
for her ransom, you will pay them at once, and we guarantee we shall
refund it to you to the very last copper. Furthermore we can give as an
indemnity, if they so desire, a great many books. Who knows if it was for
such a time as this that you came to Aleppo, and the Lord will be your
helper, and your reward paid from Heaven."

Jacques knew at once what the letter was referring to, and so he went
immediately to visit a member of the council who was his friend. He
wandered with him from topic to topic, before telling him, in the
style of a parable: "There is a girl, and she is imprisoned in a far-off
country, and her family and acquaintances are much aggrieved, and
their hearts go out to her. So they seek to perform the duty of ran-
soming captives on her behalf, and they are prepared to pay all the
money in the world to ransom her."

Jacques had not yet finished his speech, when the man rebuked
him: "Jacques my dear friend, I am surprised at you, a sage such as
you are, and a son of Aleppo as you are, talking with me of this matter. The case that you make does not conform to the evidence. You
say she is imprisoned? Is she not in her home, enthroned in regal
splendor, endowed with all the precious things of the world, arrayed
in garments of silver and gold, with all of her needs provided? For
she is the apple of our eye, and she is our glory, and how could she
possibly be snatched from her house?"

Jacques said to him: "I too know she is the glory of our congregation, but the beauty of wisdom is recognized only when its light
is seen, and why should her place be with us, is it not the essence of
the thing that she be properly preserved, and enjoyed, and studied?"

The man answered him: "I should be scolding you, but out of respect for you I shall speak calmly. Know this: many have desired her, and offered great sums of money as a bride-price, and there are those who have sought to seduce, and those who have sought to ravish, and the men of our congregation, may their God preserve and reward them, have stood in the breach, and repelled them with disdain."

Jacques answered him: "I know, my friend, I know, but this time they are not merchants enamored with profit, rather they are men of scholarship, and they want only to discover her secrets."

The man said to him: "And who is stopping them? Let them come here, and ask our Teacher and Master all their questions, and he will go alone into her presence, and give them an answer."

Jacques said to him: "That is well said, but we fear what will happen in days to come, as we are in exile here and her place is not secure."

That man answered him: "Is not all Israel in captivity? Who knows where she could be safe?" He went on to say: "You know I am your friend, and I ask you not to say anything more to me on the subject of the *Keter*, for we have already sworn a solemn oath, and vowed we will never let it be taken away from here. We have a tradition that it is a safeguard for our community, and it has mystic properties, and if it is taken from the congregation, then the whole congregation will be devastated, God forbid. And furthermore I ask you, let no one know you have spoken to me of this matter."

Jacques went on his way, disappointed.

He resolved that he would go and speak with our Teacher and Master and explain to him the danger of the affair. He did not know how our teacher would receive him, and many thoughts pursued him: How would the sages receive him? For since the day that Jacques had returned from Paris and had become headmaster of the school, he had sensed a certain coolness between him and the sages. Sometimes a man's fears are greater than reality itself; yet in spite of this he went to visit the great sage, who greeted him cordially enough.

Jacques said to him: "If Our Teacher will permit me, there is a matter I wish to raise with him."

He said to him: "Tell me."

Jacques said to him: "I appeal to your Honor, that he speak with members of the council with regard to the *Keter*."

The sage recoiled, and said to him: "You ask a difficult question. Why do you involve yourself in such trouble? Tell me what it is you seek."

Jacques explained to the sage, judiciously and lucidly, the importance of the *Keter* in the eyes of the scholars, and their fear lest it be lost.

Our teacher said to him: "I shall tell you what we have heard from impeccable sources. There were certain traders who traveled among the people of Yemen, going from village to village, and urging them to gather together bundles of ancient and priceless manuscripts, and giving them in exchange printed books, and afterward those traders went and sold them in European cities to universities and to wealthy collectors of manuscripts, making huge profits."

Jacques answered him: "I too have heard this, and it was a reprehensible thing on the part of those men, cheating people who trusted them. Certainly it was not decent behavior." But a moment later he added: "And yet, craving your honor's indulgence, if we examine the issue a second time, we will find that these same traders, unethical as they were, did more good than harm. After all, by whatever tortuous paths, in the end those manuscripts will make their way into the great libraries, and the learned will peruse them, and use them as the basis for new and revised editions, and scholars of the Torah will come and contemplate these books, and use these improved versions to solve any number of problems, and then the *poskim* would come, read the books and endorse the new versions, and be able to make a branch of a revitalized *Halacha* of them, and the whole world will be seen to benefit from these writings. And if they had remained in those villages in Yemen, what would have been their fate? It is true that our brethren there, sons of Israel, dearly love the Torah, but Gentiles rule over them, and shameful poverty prevails, and who knows what would have befallen them. Half of those rare manuscripts would have been eaten by moths, while the other half would have gathered dust in the *genizah* of some remote rural synagogue. And who could have studied them?

"With your honor's indulgence, I shall tell him one more thing, and I entreat him to believe me. We live peaceably in Aleppo today, and the French are our rulers, and they are respecters of knowledge, but hear, sir, what I was told by a certain venerable sheikh who teaches the Arabic language in our school. He told me this: 'I know you believe the French will rule over us forever, and you will live in peace. But I have heard our young people saying that soon they will take to the streets, to protest, and to rebel against the French, and they will drive them from their land, and already a number of groups have been set up to further these purposes, and there are secret meetings, and even the imams in our mosques are supporting them implicitly.'"

Jacques went on to say: "We could say that these are only dreams which neither increase nor diminish anything, and who can stand against the French? But who knows what time will bring forth? Can the French rule forever over a land that is not theirs? And who can say what the fate of our brothers of the House of Israel will be under the sway of the Arabs? There are those among them who love us, and there are those among them who love profit, but the majority of them hate us and are not open to bribery in either money or in words. How can we endanger the *Keter* and the treasures of wisdom stored in it—for which there can be no substitute?"

Our teacher answered him: "To scholars like yourself, the *Keter* is precious to you only on account of its antiquity, and the different versions that it comprises, but for us the *Keter* is precious on account of the depth of piety inherent in it. We are the custodians of holiness from generation to generation, and how are we to take one of our congregation's holiest things and put it into the hands of others? Who even knows if they are observers of the Torah or not?

"And you also need to know, the issue of the *Keter* is not entrusted to one sage alone, or to one member of the committee alone, and there is no one who can authorize its removal from here, and there are all kinds of prohibitions and oaths involved in the matter, including oaths of public consensus for which there is no absolution, not ever."

Jacques was silent. He knew he could not fulfill his mission.

For months now he had been anxious, both on account of what the sheikh had said, and on account of his own intuition. His heart told him that hard times were in store for Aleppo and that this tranquility was merely an illusion, and he was walking about like a mourner at a wedding feast.

Jacques knew that if the *Keter* remained in its place in Aleppo, it would be lost forever. He resolved to set aside the time for himself to copy out all the unique texts contained in it, and send them in to academic journals for publication, thus ensuring their survival. But not everything man proposes to do is aided by Heaven, and the pressure of work denied him the fulfillment of these wishes.

One way or another, the years rolled by. Such is the way of the world, the years do not stop to give man time to chart his course, but continue on their way, regardless.

The children Victor and Sophie grew up, and were the delight of their parents and grandparents. Victor was everyone's favorite, with his equable temperament, bright eyes, and the hint of a smile forever on his face; Sophie was shrewd and rebellious.

Since Jacques and Rachel lived in the Jamaliya neighborhood, close to Senor Franco's home, they dined at their house on Sabbaths. At festival times and on special Sabbaths they were the guests of Hacham Hiyyah in Bahsita, in Harat al Yahud, the Jewish Quarter. Although Senor Franco had offered to help Hacham Hiyyah transfer his domicile to Jamaliya, Hacham Hiyyah had declined. He told Franco: "My father Hacham Raphael lived here all his life, and I have lived here more than seventy years, so why should I leave the house that has served me, that was so pleasurable in my youth? Do you think it remarkable that a man should owe a debt of gratitude to wood and stone? There is a responsa of the eminent rabbi, Rabbi Yoseph Ibn Migash, where he writes of his great master, Rabbi Isaac Alfasi, of revered memory, who happened to fall sick, and went into the house of a certain man, and used the bath that was in his house, and he enjoyed the aforesaid bath, and stayed in that house until he recovered. As time passed, that man fell upon hard times, and his property was mortgaged and he owed money to creditors, and matters came to such a pass he was obliged to sell the aforesaid bath, to offset the debt to his creditors, and Rabbenu Isaac of revered memory said: 'I shall not formulate an opinion or pronounce judgment on the issue of this bath either in regard to sale or valuation or any other matter related to it, since I have personally availed myself of it.' And he, of revered memory, availed himself of it for only a short time; yet I, having lived in my house pleasurably all my days—shall I now leave it for no reason? Moreover, we are dwellers and residents in this land, and what is it to me if it be Jamaliya or Bahsita? Because the rich who think they will live forever have moved there, must I shift my domicile too?"

❧

In Senor Franco's home, the grandson, Victor, was a great favorite. They used to say he was theirs, since he resembled his mother's father both in features and in temperament. And when Jacques and Rachel came to her parents' house for Sabbath, they could not bear to let him go. As for Sophie, Hacham Hiyyah was especially fond of her, and in her childhood he used to play with her often. On Sabbath Eve, when they had finished chanting the *bakashot*, he sat her on the chair beside him and asked her questions, to test her knowledge, and she always gave him a pithy answer which he had not expected, much to his pleasure.

For the first few years Jacques sent his son Victor to the Talmud Torah, and the whole community was surprised that he had not sent him to the Alliance Israelite Universelle School. Some averred he had done this out of respect for his father, others said it was because he was the headmaster, and did not want his son studying there, but the truth was that Jacques and Rachel wanted Victor's education to begin with piety and love of the Torah; other subjects could be studied later. There is a difference between one whose foundation is in the Torah and who adds to it the other forms of knowledge, and one whose foundation is in the sciences of the Gentiles and who studies the Torah at a later stage.

Jacques tried to open his heart to philosophical matters, and often talked to him about the Torah, but the boy did his best to avoid it. Even though he greatly respected his father, and every time he was asked to sit and study with him he did so, he obeyed only out of deference, and his heart was not drawn to it. Jacques saw that he had no inclination toward study, and was pained, as he had thought he could raise this son of his according to his own lights, instilling in him Torah and philosophy alike. He tried and tried again, until he saw his efforts were bearing no fruit, and he feared that pressing him further would only drive him away, and he would learn nothing of importance.

At last, he felt more at ease about him, because Victor was assiduous in his observance of the commandments, and popular with people, setting time aside for the Torah and for ethics, and Jacques used to say to others, when they asked him about Victor: *Train the child in the way he is going.* But Rachel knew the sorrow in his heart. He had always hoped his son would be a lover of wisdom and a master of the Torah.

Victor did not want to make the Torah a regular part of his life, or immerse himself in philosophy. He preferred going to his grandfather's warehouse, the Franco and De Piciotto textile firm, and helping the salesmen there. From day to day he learned more about the business, and everything that he turned his hand to prospered—and earned a profit. Eventually he was hired as a cashier for the company, and was popular with everyone. From the day he was first employed there, the enterprise went from strength to strength.

His sister Sophie was not at all like him. From her infancy she loved learning, taking her father's books and reading them. They thought she was just turning the pages and not understanding anything; later, it emerged that she was a genius. One day she asked her father to teach her the Talmud. He found himself in a dilemma: in Aleppo it was not the custom to educate girls to any advanced level, and yet she was sharp-witted and astute, loving everything to do with knowledge. People used to mock her, suggesting she should learn to sew and cook and help her mother with the housework, but she did not care, and her sharp riposte was never long in coming: "Are domestic chores all that a woman is good for?"

When she had completed her studies at the Alliance Israelite Universelle School, she wanted to continue her education, and pleaded with her father to let her attend the Gentiles' school. And although he offered to bring tutors into the house, and promised to teach her philosophy himself, she was not deterred. Every day she spoke with him and with her mother of her desire to attend the school, until eventually they relented.

When Jacques used to visit his father on the Sabbath, he wanted to discuss with him the philosophy of the *Moreh*, and debate with him the fundamentals of faith, as he used to do in his youth, before going to France. But when he embarked on philosophy, his father would explain things to him on the basis of the arcane. He would ask about the literal meaning, while his father answered him with the lore of Isaac Luria, the celebrated Kabbalist.

Hacham Hiyyah saw his perplexity, and said to him: "My dear son, you should know that the questions you are asking, I also asked many years ago, and I tried to find an answer for everything on the basis of logic, by way of the Rambam. But today, as I am approaching old age, I see and I believe with all my soul that it is the arcane wisdom that opens before you the gates of light, and you are filled with light and the soul is bound to its source, and seeks to cleave to it, and what is unclear is clarified by itself. Hacham Khaski opened the gates of this wisdom before me, and set me on the way. For a whole year I studied with him, and there was light in my eyes."

These words made little impression on Jacques. He did not understand them, and did not even want to understand them. All his life he had sought to discover everything on the basis of the intellect. In Paris, he had given much thought to the time when he would come to his father, and discuss the *Moreh Nevukhim* with him on the basis of what he had learned of the new philosophy, and show him how many of the innovations introduced by the *Moreh*, which they had not understood in the past, were clarified now by reference to his study of modern trends in scholarship. He also sought to raise some new questions that were proving difficult for him, but he saw that his father had changed a great deal. To every philosophical question, he answered on the basis of the arcane, and to every assertion relating to matters of the moment, he responded with some precept from the literature of ethics.

Therefore, Jacques preferred not to discuss these things with his father, consulting him only in reference to *Halacha*; in this he always relied exclusively on his father's opinion. For Hacham Hiyyah would never blend the *Halacha* with anything drawn from the *Kabbalah*, but made every judgment on the basis of profound reasoning, and according to the Aleppo system of analysis, famed for its acuity, as was always his way.

Since Jacques was finding little satisfaction in his work, despite the fifteen years that he had devoted to it, and there was no one with whom to engage in philosophical debate, he began to entertain thoughts of returning to Paris, and he and Rachel mulled over the idea between them. On many occasions it was resolved and decided that they would go—they knew there was no other option—but it isn't easy for anyone to uproot himself, let alone a whole family, from his place of abode. So it was postponed from year to year. Once on account of Victor's work, and once because he had come of age and his mother was afraid of what might befall him in Paris, and wanted to find him a wife among the daughters of Aleppo, who are good to their husbands. Yet this proved a futile effort, for these days were not like the days of old. In former times the mother made the match for her son, and he would accept her choice, knowing that she understood him, and was acting in his best interest, and had made inquiries about the girl and found a suitable spouse for him. However, Victor wanted to choose a wife for himself, that being the custom of the new times. And although he was liked by all, and there were many who wanted him for their daughters, he was still seeking his love, and had not yet found her. Another time, they postponed the move because Sophie needed to complete her studies, and another, because Rachel's mother fell ill. And besides all this, Jacques did not know how he could leave his father in his old age.

The years passed, and the things told to Jacques by the sheikh, the teacher of Arabic, which had sounded strange at the time, were already plain for all to see. Many Arab youths were forming themselves into groups, and talking openly of expelling the French and taking over their land for themselves. There were some young Jews who supported them, but the majority of the community feared them and wanted French rule to continue. Rumors began to be heard about what was going on in other regions of Syria: leaders emerging, and the government arresting them, and a population on the verge of revolt.

Just as Jacques had forecast, so it was coming to pass: the tranquility in which they had been enfolded was disappearing; everywhere anxiety took its place. Members of the congregation began repeating rumors they had heard of attacks on Jewish shops, and others had still more lurid stories to tell, to grieve the mind still further. But the greatest concern was not knowing what would be. Newspapers from overseas reported developments in the politics of Europe, and there too the atmosphere was bleak.

One day the Jamaliya was filled by a crowd of demonstrators, stretching from the Sultani seminary to the Al Saddik mosque, yelling and shouting and waving flags. There were excited, hotheaded youths leading them, at their head the son of Hanenu, chief of the protest movement in Syria. The Jews of Aleppo knew him. He used to wander about all day long, and no one knew what he was doing, neither studying nor working, but thinking and brooding, his finger in every pie.

They were marching in a great throng, crying out in a loud voice: "Down with France!" and "Freedom for Syria!"

And although they said they had nothing against the Jews—on the contrary, they had approached Senor Faraji, one of the leaders of the congregation and suggested that the Jews might care to join them, as the people of one land—in spite of this the Jews were filled at this time with great fear. And they huddled together in their houses, and locked and bolted their doors, and added chests and tables and anything that might serve as a barricade, until the crisis should pass.

At the same time youths congregated in the Alliance Israelite Universelle school, and formed a group which they called 'Scouts,' and they went to the Al Padihi quarter, and pitched tents and hoisted ropes, and took it upon themselves to defend the Aleppo orphanage and the 'Charity and Healing' clinic, and they also took part in secret activities which not everyone was aware of.

In those days envoys began arriving in Aleppo to organize

groups of Zionists. In the past, the only people to travel from Aleppo to *Eretz-Israel* had been old men and a few pious individuals seeking the privilege of residing there. But these envoys spoke of other things. And their words, strange though they sounded to the ears of the congregation, strange and even alarming, took root in the hearts of many young men and young women. These people used to gather them together, and teach them songs, and tell them stories, and inform them of new things happening in *Eretz-Israel*, saying that every nation needs to reside upon its own land, and that we, the Jews, we too deserve to live in our land. The young people who listened to them drank up their words thirstily. One group called itself the 'Pioneers.' We have heard how a number of them, including the son of the eminent judge, emigrated to *Eretz-Israel* to take part in the great enterprise of establishing the country.

The sages were wary of them for several reasons. One essential reason was that elders of the community in *Eretz-Israel* had sent them word, warning them to beware of the envoys, since many of the pioneers were not devout followers of the Torah. On one occasion our Teacher and Master called on Jacques, and told him that a certain man whom he had engaged as a teacher at the school was secretly inciting unrest among the young, and he asked Jacques to speak with him. Jacques himself was unsure what to do. His mind, so orderly and lucid in everything else, was far from clear on this matter. Several times he talked things over with his father, but they came to no clear conclusion. They knew that the duty to live in *Eretz-Israel* outweighs all other precepts, and they knew of it as an agreeable as well as a sanctified obligation, but still their hearts were unsure. They themselves did not know why. Was it because they thought the time had not yet come, or were they afraid of the unrest among the nations, or were they afraid they would be leaving the Torah behind? *Eretz-Israel* as envisioned in their eyes was not the land described by these envoys. Not knowing how he should act, Jacques stood aside, neither helping nor hindering. When he was asked if a room in the school could be used for an afternoon meeting, he gave his cautious consent.

Hard times came upon the world and upon our brothers of the

House of Israel. Kingdoms tottered and the Gentiles were in ferment, nations giving no thought to the Lord and His anointed. Rumors reached them from diverse places, grieving the hearts of those who heard. A fearful war was raging in the world, but in Aleppo itself life went on almost as normal. The letters that Jacques received from France were full of hints as to what was happening there and in the rest of the world, but there was little communication. The Jews of Aleppo found themselves virtually cut off from events in Europe, and in the absence of solid news, Jacques was confused about what was really taking place there.

When the tide of war swelled and spread still further, and it was reported that German forces were approaching Egypt, only then were the Jews of Aleppo afraid. Every day brought its batch of stark rumors. Aleppo was under French mandate, and when it became known that Marshal Petain and his government in France had agreed to German demands and established a puppet-state with Vichy as its capital, the Jews of Aleppo were informed that the local administration had announced its loyalty to the Vichy government and acknowledged its authority. There was a well-founded rumor that letters and envoys had been sent by the British, urging the French authorities to change sides, but they spurned them contemptuously, saying their only loyalty was to their homeland and they would never betray it.

Among the teachers of the Alliance Israelite Universelle school there were many differences of opinion on this issue. Some said it was well done, and every man should be loyal to his homeland, and others said that man owes loyalty to morality and truth and not to those who have betrayed them, and the former speakers silenced them with a rebuke for calling the rulers of France traitors. And others said it was the duty of France to remain free, and everyone was relating what he had read and what he had heard and what others had told him.

Later, when Jacques was again in Paris, he told Professor Pierre that neither side had really known what it was talking about. And when he discovered the truth of what had been happening, he was amazed and ashamed of himself; he and others like him had made no attempt to explore the deeper significance of events, and continued with their lives as in normal times, and had done nothing. All he could remember was that they knew there was great fear in the world, and from day to day that fear came closer to them.

At first the directors of the Alliance Israelite Universelle in France had written to them, telling them not to neglect their studies and to carry on with the routine of learning and teaching, as they had no business meddling in politics. But after a while, they heard nothing more from them until the end of the war.

Professor Pierre told Jacques about differences of opinion that had arisen between himself and Professor Mantour: he, along with his student, Jacques' friend, had claimed that Petain's government had betrayed the people and sold them into the hands of the Germans, and that they must be resisted. Professor Mantour, on the other hand, had declared they had done well in saving the people and preserving peace, and furthermore, anyone opposing them was a traitor, as this was a legally constituted government, and no one had the right to question its actions. He had countered this with the argument that no one had the right to betray the freedom and the justice of France, and anyone doing so had to be opposed, that this was a moral imperative—and harsh words were exchanged between them.

During those days, when it seemed the gates of prayer were sealed, something happened in the home of Jacques and Rachel. A miracle befell them. Their prayers were heard by the One who hears prayers, and were answered. For a long time Rachel kept this miracle a secret from everyone, even from her mother, since the greatest blessing is in things concealed from view, especially with a miracle such as this. She knew that other people—just as she herself had been—would be amazed at this blessing after eighteen barren years—and she feared the evil eye. She knew her mother would be unable to resist telling her sister, and the sister would whisper it to a friend, and the friend to another friend, sworn to secrecy, and the other friend would tell her daughter without naming names, and that when the daughter asked, "Do you mean Rachel Sapporta?" she would reply: "You said that, and you did not hear it from me." Then, within an hour all Aleppo would be congratulating her, and there would be some indignation too, the women asking: "Why did you not tell *me* before it was common knowledge?"

There is no one who was in Aleppo in those days who does not remember the Zohar ceremony and the *Brit Mila* that was held to welcome the son of Jacques Sapporta's old age into the covenant. The *sandak* was Hacham Hiyyah, the *mohel* was the renowned and indefatigable Hacham Khaski, and the benediction was delivered by none other than our Teacher and Master in person. It is said that when Jacques said the *Shehehianu* blessing, tears welled in the eyes of the entire congregation. It was then that our Teacher and Master asked that the *mohel*, immediately after the circumcision, with the blood of the covenant still visible, should appoint someone to bless the entire congregation, including our brothers of the House of Israel in all places where they are subjected to oppression and captivity. He prayed that the Lord spare the remnant of his people and save them from all cruel decrees, and that the virtue of Elijah, angel of the covenant, protect them all, and the congregation of Aleppo in particular, and the dwellers in *Eretz-Israel* in their time of peril and strife, and he concluded that the blood of the covenant should soar to the heights of Heaven and halt the pestilence. All this time, while the *mohel* was making this blessing, our Teacher and Master stood with the infant in his arms, his eyes closed, and his heart toward Heaven.

After our Teacher and Master had blessed the wine, and named the child Raphael Menahem, he laid his hands on him and pronounced a priestly blessing, and added further blessings, that he might grow up in wisdom like his father, and his name be recorded among the great. Then one of the congregation rose to give a blessing, hoping that the infant would be as great a scholar as his father, a man of wisdom and renown, and more.

Hacham Hiyyah, who appeared to be dozing, started suddenly from his seat, took the child, laid his hand on his head, and vowed on his behalf that he would be God-fearing and as saintly as his grandfather, Hacham Raphael, and he added many other things in a whisper, and asked all the congregation to give the response with him, amen.

At the ceremonial meal, Jacques spoke judiciously and with good taste, citing references to the covenant in the Torah and the wisdom literature, and explaining its meaning in accordance with the writings of the *Moreh*.

Before the blessing of the food, Hacham Hiyyah preached, and his entire sermon was based on ideas of the arcane. He went on to clarify the obligations of the covenant according to the teaching of the Kabbalist Isaac Luria, and spoke of the migration of souls and the mending of worlds, explaining that we do not know which soul is sent into the world, for there are souls and there are souls, and there are some that are crafted in a higher place, and he concluded: *And the outcast will not be expelled by him.* Then once more he took the babe in his arms, and blessed him again, and repeated: *And the outcast will not be expelled by him,* and he kissed him on the forehead.

It was said that on that very same day the German armies were halted in the desert, at the battle of El Alamein.

Chapter eleven

W hen my grandfather of revered memory was old, when he sought relaxation, I used to read to him from the stories of Shmuel Yoseph Agnon. One of his stories is a short story with the title "We Shall Not Fail." Once I was reading it to him, and he said: "See how great is the power of the imagination, but before you tell me anything more that the writer has imagined, I shall tell you a story that truly happened."

That day I heard from him the story of Raphael Menahem, the son of Jacques Sapporta, who in Paris was known as Max Sapport. Grandfather gave me a shortened account, merely the bare bones of the story, and showed no sign of enthusiasm, but I am of a different nature entirely, and stories such as this fascinate me, and I shall tell the whole story as it was revealed to me.

From the moment Raphael Menahem was born, the entire attention of his father and mother was devoted to him, and he was their delight. They used to pamper him, and play with him, showing him all their love and longing. All that he asked of them they gave him at once, until Jacques' colleagues complained: "Since the day he was born it has been impossible to talk to Jacques about any philosophical subject in the world if little Raphael Menahem is in the vicinity." Instead, looking admiringly at every trifling thing his offspring did or said, Jacques would ask them: "Did you see what a clever thing our Raphael has just done?"

One elderly teacher at the school warned him a number of times: "Monsieur Jacques, you'll harm the lad if you don't let him be." Jacques knew something of the principles of education, and when he taught his pupils he was careful to repel with his left hand while enticing with his right, but with this son of his he behaved as if he had two right hands.

As Raphael grew up, they could tell he was very perceptive, capable of deducing one thing from another, and delving deeply. Rachel often warned Jacques to conceal this from the public, and not to boast of it. She was afraid of the evil eye, and although Jacques scorned the very notion of the evil eye, this son of his was so precious to him, that for his sake he was prepared to fear even things that his intellect did not believe in.

I have heard many exaggerations regarding the infancy of Raphael Menahem in Aleppo, such as the claim that he could take in at one glance a whole page of the Talmud along with the *Tosafot*, or the story they told of his response to our Teacher and our Teacher and Master over a problem in the Maharsha, at five years old, or the assertion that he read a whole book of animal fables, in French—but we don't deal with exaggerations, only with relating things as they really were.

That year, 1945, the eve of the festival of *Shavuot* was the occasion for double celebration, and in the Sapporta family there was threefold cause for jubilation: the world was glad that the war was now drawing to a close, Israel was glad to honor the day on which its laws were given, and Jacques and Rachel were overjoyed that, at three years old, their son Raphael Menahem was ready to take his first steps in the reading of the Bible.

The day arrived when Raphael Menahem went up a grade and was admitted to the Bible class. He was dressed in his Sabbath best, and his father asked that Raphael Menahem accompany his grandfather, Hacham Hiyyah, on his way to the *Beit Midrash*. That day they rose early, Rachel served them tea, and as the first light of dawn appeared, they went together to the house of Hacham Hiyyah.

Hacham Hiyyah was already wearing a *tallit* and was adorned with *tefillin*. The sage did not greet them, as it is not customary to utter greetings before the prayer, lest the respect paid to flesh and blood be seen to precede respect paid to the Lord, but he nodded to them. Hacham Hiyyah took the hand of little Raphael Menahem, and they walked to the *Beit Midrash*. Hacham Hiyyah was in the habit of starting to pray on the way, and his lips were mouthing the blessings of the dawn and the prayer of Hannah and the account of the binding of Isaac to the sacrificial altar. Raphael Menahem watched his grandfather as he made supplication before his Creator, as a son purifies himself from sin before his father, thanking Him for restoring to him a pure soul, and opening his eyes, and releasing the bound, and he prayed that he would always embrace the teaching of the Torah, and that his offspring engage in Torah for its own sake. Then he heard snatches of the prayer of Hannah, the first prayer in the liturgy, emerging from his grandfather's lips, every word accentuated as if these were pearls of song: *For a God of knowledge is the Lord, and by Him are deeds assessed… they that were full have hired themselves out for bread and the hungry have stopped… so the barren woman has born seven…* and he went on to intone: *And Isaac spoke to Abraham his father and said: Father. And he said: Here am I, my son. And he said: Behold the fire and the wood but where is the lamb for sacrifice… and they went both of them together…* The dawn is rising, the air of Aleppo is cool, and the world of the Almighty is pure, a great silence all around, and he holds his grandfather's hand tightly, and watches him as he prays. After the prayer Hacham Hiyyah went to bathe, and prepare himself anew for the holiness of the day.

All that night Hacham Hiyyah recited the *Tikkun* of the eve of *Shavuot*, and with the rising of the sun they stood for the festival prayer. They invited him to go up to the Torah and read the Ten Commandments. After he had read, he blessed the Torah: *who gave us his Torah, the Torah of truth, and planted in our midst eternal life,* and before he had time to finish the blessing, he went to his eternal rest.

ૐ

In those post-war years there was a proliferation of clubs in Aleppo, and envoys from *Eretz-Israel* were also coming in increasing numbers. Many young people emigrated to *Eretz-Israel*, because the envoys from there were inflaming the hearts of the young, and they followed them. There was one club in Aleppo founded by an envoy from Israel called the Organization of Religious Pioneers, and it was especially popular with the young. Because the envoy was a God-fearing man, there was no call to object to this. They used to gather together at night and sing songs about and from Israel, and every time they concluded the session by standing to chant *Hatikvah*.

Jewish soldiers of the British army, arriving after the Second World War, stirred the imagination of the young, telling them of the war of the Jews. Many of them envied the Syrian Arabs who were preparing to fight for a state of their own, and when they saw what they were doing, they said: "When shall we too have a homeland?" The envoys told them more of what was happening there, and of the heroism displayed by the people of Israel, saying they had villages of their own and were planting trees and sowing fields, and building cities, and seeking to establish their own state.

Among the Arabs too, much had changed since the war, as more and more young people aspired to independence for their land, and took to the streets in noisy demonstrations. At first the congregation came to no harm, either from the authorities or from the mob, and they lived in peace, until the frenzy and chaos of that bitter day…. The day that the United Nations declared the right of the Jews to establish a state for themselves in *Eretz-Israel*, was a day of rejoicing for the Jews in *Eretz-Israel* and all over the world. Everywhere they celebrated the miracle that had occurred.

That joyful day was a bitter one for the community of Aleppo, as young men gathered in the streets and rioted, shouting out slogans of hatred for the Jews and surging onward, toward the Bahsita Quarter, breaking into shops great and small, looting all kinds of goods, piling them up and setting them on fire.

That day the Lord punished our iniquities and dispensed justice, and a stern edict was decreed. It was an evil day for Israel in Aleppo, a day of sorrow and sighs. For the synagogues and centers of learning of Aleppo were set on fire—the synagogue of the Beit Nasi, the Beit Midrash of Hacham Ovadiah Harari, the Midrash of Hacham Moshe Dabah, and the Midrash of the Beit Ades, and the main buildings of the Talmud Torah, and even in the Jamaliya neighborhood the rioters burned the synagogue of Senor Silvera. As if all this was not devastating enough—alas indeed for the burning of the Torah, for close to one hundred scrolls were torched, including some precious collections, and thousands of printed books and manuscripts, parchment blazing and letters flying away—may woe befall the villains on the Day of Judgment. The decree did not pass until the accursed vandals had despoiled the ancient synagogue that dates back to the time of the Second Temple, the pride of Aleppo, and set it on fire together with the Torah scrolls stored there, and most tragically of all, the famous *Keter,* the apple of the community's eye.

At that time they said alas for the congregation that has lost its treasure, and if the guardian has gone, the congregation is doomed. But the Guardian of Israel does not rest; He vented His rage on wood and stone and books and scrolls, and the rioters injured nobody, save one youth who seemed intent on opposing them. After some time had elapsed the authorities decided the rioters posed a risk to them as well, and they dispersed the mob forcibly, and imposed order on the town.

All the time that the riots were raging Raphael Menahem was confined to his house, staring out of the window. The fires and the looting upset his innocent heart. He said to his father: "Daddy, why are the Gentiles burning our synagogues? Why can't we live in peace like any other nation?"

Jacques answered him with words of consolation such as those we find in the *Haggadah: For in every generation they stand against us to destroy us and The Holy One, Blessed be He, delivers us from their hand*, and similar such words, but Raphael Menahem was not satisfied, his mind was not eased. His heart was in ferment: Why are we different from every other nation on the earth? Was there no justice and no judge?

Jews are accustomed to decrees. They bow their heads like reeds in the wind, and wait for the storm to pass. When the city became quiet again they opened their shops, salvaged what they could salvage and went on living as before. Jacques was stunned when he heard of the burning of the *Keter*, and bitterly regretted not doing what he had meant to do for so long—make a copy of all the unique texts contained in it. He set himself to saving what was left of the scrolls, and he went from person to person in search of any relic that had survived. He took consolation in Raphael Menahem and in the pleasant times he spent with him.

Ever since Raphael Menahem learned to read, he had shown himself to be an avid reader, and as time passed he would not let go of any book that he had seen and not yet read. And he did not distinguish between one book and another; it could be a *Humash* or *Mishnah* or new interpretations of the Torah, or literature and poetry, or even the texts that his father wrote to be sent to Professor Pierre in France. It seemed he was swallowing and absorbing everything, whether he understood it or not.

When he studied in the Talmud Torah they passed him from one teacher to another, and everyone told his father there was nothing more he could be taught. After three years in the Talmud Torah, Jacques transferred him to the Alliance Israelite Universelle School, which was close at hand, so he could supervise his education, and for various other reasons. He wanted to fulfill in this son of his the kind of upbringing that he thought every man deserved. Heaven does not help everything man proposes.

From day to day the boy gained a reputation in Aleppo. The old folk of the town told his father that they saw in him his father and his grandfather and his great-grandfather. It is said that he had the love of wisdom of Jacques his father, the keen intellect of Hacham Hiyyah his grandfather, and the innocence of Hacham Raphael, his great-grandfather.

These were qualities inherited from his ancestors. There was another quality, which was not inherited from his ancestors. These ancestors were always inscrutable to their friends and their innermost thoughts were a mystery, whereas Raphael Menahem had the Heaven-sent gift that from his infancy onward, people were attracted to him. Wherever you saw him, you saw a group of friends surrounding him and listening.

He had the stature of his mother's father, and a fit, muscular body. One of the teachers told his father they were fortunate that the Torah was consuming his energy. Were it not so, who knows what he would have done.

It is the way of the wise that they are not innocent, but nothing is to be learned from generalities. Raphael Menahem, though wise, was an innocent. He too pursued justice and honesty with all his might. For this reason, the sons of the poor used to come to him whenever the son of someone wealthy was harassing them, and he would defend them. And so he continued to grow in knowledge of Torah and in wisdom, popular among his peers and loved by those older than him, while his father and mother delighted in him.

It is said that by the time he was ten, the age reached when children begin to learn *Mishneh*, he had already embarked on systematic inquiry. This pleased his father, who acknowledged his talent for intellectual research of what is above and what is below, accepting nothing unless it was scrutinized in the light of his intelligence. Raphael Menahem continued his studies and excelled. His teachers liked him and his friends all respected him, except of course those who were jealous of him. Such is the way of the world.

One day, when Raphael Menahem wanted a break from his studies, he went to visit his brother Victor at the Franco and De Piciotto textile warehouse. He met him in his office. Although Victor was very busy he was glad to see him. Raphael Menahem said to him: "What are those pieces of cloth on your desk?" He answered him: "These are samples of materials that we intend to trade."

"And where do these materials come from?" Raphael asked. Victor explained to him how these goods were imported by ship from overseas, some coming from Manchester, from textile merchants based there, from the Mizrahi family, some from Italy, and some from other places, and he explained to him the merits of each particular source, how the material from Manchester was pure wool and ideal for the tailoring of suits, while the Italian fabric was light and good for the sewing of *jallabias*, the white smocks which were the habitual clothing of the Syrian populace. He explained to him how the goods in transit were insured, and told him of some incidents that had occurred, to impress and amuse him, such as the story of the consignment that was saturated in sea-water, because of which they didn't know what to do with it and feared a big loss, until Victor had the novel idea of selling it to a certain agent who sold it to an Arab trader to make sails from it.

Victor loved the business and spoke of it with enthusiasm, like a precocious student proposing a new solution to a longstanding problem. Raphael Menahem asked him: "And what do you do with the textiles?"

Victor told him: "Some of them we sell through agents to small dealers."

He asked him: "And how much profit do you make on them?"

Victor looked around to be sure no ears were listening—such is the way of the merchants of Aleppo, not liking to tell of their profits, for fear of the evil eye—lowered his voice, and told him: "If we sell to a wholesaler, forty percent."

Raphael Menahem asked him: "And why don't those merchants buy it for themselves?"

Victor replied: "What kind of a question is that? They don't have the working capital to buy goods from Manchester."

He asked him: "So where do you get the working capital from?"

Victor said: "We take it from the De Piciotto finance company as a loan."

"Can't they borrow money from the same company?"

"If they borrowed it they'd have to pay forty percent interest, and they'd make no profit, whereas we, since we own the finance company, get the money for twenty percent interest, and because we're the sole importers of these goods, we can sell them at whatever price we choose."

Little Raphael didn't understand, if the finance company was theirs, why they needed to borrow from themselves, but he pretended to understand and went on: "So we can say you couldn't make a profit if you didn't have money to start with?"

"Yes," replied Victor.

Raphael continued: "So as you earn more, you have more money, and you buy more goods, and make more profit, and does that mean that anyone with a lot of money in hand can go on to make a fortune?" Victor said gladly: "Absolutely right! You've learned your first lesson in business."

Raphael Menahem looked out of the window, and saw spools of material stacked in the open space down below. He turned to his brother and asked him: "What do you do with the materials that you don't sell to middlemen?" Victor answered him: "We employ twenty machinists who sit in their homes in Bahsita and sew white *jallabias*, which a merchant from Orpal in Turkey has been buying from us for years. We hear he makes a handsome profit selling them to civil servants there. A number of poor widows make a living from working for us, and we mark every festival by giving them the left-over materials, so they can make clothes for their families, and very grateful they are."

"And how much do they earn?"

Victor answered him: "Seven pounds and fifty kirsh per month. We pay them a reasonable wage. The work isn't easy, they work from morning to evening, hunched over our sewing machines, but they make a decent living, and they don't need any support from charity or community funds."

"And how much do you make on the *jallabias*?" Raphael Menahem went on to ask.

Victor smiled and said: "On every *jallabia* we make fifty kirsh (it was the custom in Aleppo to round all figures up to multiples of five—a precaution against the evil eye), and on every spool we make a profit of fifteen pounds, which we exchange for French francs, after all, who knows what's going to happen. A nice profit, don't you think?

From this sum we have to deduct commission for the agent who introduced us to that merchant from Orpal, and of the remainder a tenth goes to charity. That was the practice laid down by the great De Piciotto, son of the founder of the company, that of all profits a tenth should be earmarked for charity. He used to say: 'The partner's share is not to be neglected.' So Franco and De Piciotto Inc. know how business works, and they're generous benefactors too. Wouldn't you agree, brother?" Victor concluded, on a note of triumph.

Raphael was silent for a moment, gazing around him with his dreamy eyes, and then said: "That's right Victor, you're making a fine profit, and yet I have one problem with it. Why is it that those poor widows who toil all day making *jallabias*, earn a pittance which is barely enough to live on, while everyone else—the buyers ordering the textiles from Manchester or Italy, and the porters who carry the spools, and give them to someone else who cuts them into strips and gives them to the machinists, and the merchant from Orpal who comes and takes the *jallabias*, and you sitting in your big office while the money just rolls in—everyone else is earning so much more than they are? After all, they're the ones who make the things!"

He paused for a moment to think and added: "If all the seamstresses in Bahsita refused to work unless you doubled their wages, you'd be forced to accept their demands. If not, what would you do with all the materials?"

Victor was shocked, not knowing if his brother was asking in all innocence, or making a joke at his expense. After a moment he recovered his composure and replied: "That might be a nice idea to bring up in a debate between seminary students, but it's never going to happen. We could leave those textiles untouched for a whole year, and there would still be the income from our other interests, enough to survive on and to keep us trading in profit. As for those women—one month without work and they'd starve to death. We're doing them a favor, supporting their families. It's a pity you haven't seen the gratitude they express to us every month, when our cashier pays them their wages."

Raphael Menahem went on to say, thinking aloud in the cadences of a *yeshiva* student: "If they were to bring in the textiles themselves, they could make a lot of money, and if as you say, they don't have the capital, they could join together in a collective, and the community would lend them what they need, or the Mizrahis of Manchester would give them credit and supply the goods, and working for themselves, in the fullness of time, they'd make enough to pay off their debts in cash and order more merchandise from Manchester."

Victor laughed at his little brother's naivety and said: "And who do you think experienced traders like the Mizrahi family in Manchester would rather trust and give credit to, a bunch of impoverished widows in Bahsita or a distinguished firm like Franco and De Piciotto, who have a worldwide reputation dating back more than a hundred years?"

So Victor's young brother left him to deal with the work piling up on his desk and returned to his studies.

॰

Raphael Menahem was taught by every teacher in the school. He was especially fond of one teacher in particular; he felt close to him, and studied with him day and night. This teacher, who was new to the school, was a specialist in the teaching of French literature and poetry, and had been sent by the office in Paris after the war. This teacher also loved him dearly, in a manner recalling a phrase from the Proverbs of Solomon, *As face reflects face in the water, so is the heart of one man to another.* The teacher was shrewd and had a sensitive heart, and was attuned to the hidden thoughts of students. Loving Raphael Menahem as he did, he knew the depth of his feelings and could read him like an open book. When he recited poetry to him and interpreted it for him, Raphael Menahem sat before him with blank face and dreamy eyes wandering in the air. The teacher knew he was not dreaming at all, but listening to every word. Only he knew how misleading Raphael Menahem's blank face was, and only he was aware of the intensity of the force concealed behind it.

So close were they, that Raphael Menahem used to tell the teacher what was in his heart—things he was reluctant to share with his father. In any case, for as long as he could remember he had felt a

171

distance from his father. He himself could not explain why he trusted this teacher more than his father. Though he held his father in the very highest regard, and knew that his father's love for him was profound, yet he would only reveal to his teacher the things that were concealed in his heart. Who knows the ways of the soul? Often he felt his father would not have understood what he was trying to say.

Jacques admired the work of this teacher, but did not warm to him, perceiving that like other new teachers from Paris he knew nothing of the Torah and disdained the commandments and the sages. How often did he hear him telling his pupils that a new world was opening up, and they no longer needed what we used to have in the old world. Once he even hinted that they should abandon their present course altogether. For this reason Jacques was not pleased to see Raphael Menahem choosing such a man to be his mentor, but he never made his objections known, on account of his love for his son, and on account of the tolerance and humility with which he treated all men, and the scholarly in particular. Raphael Menahem also tried to set his father's mind at ease whenever this teacher's name was mentioned, telling him of his erudition and good nature.

One day they were reading a book by one of the great modern French writers. The story revolved around the rich and the poor, and reform of the world and the new society. The teacher was inspired and the pupil was inspired, and they discussed the matter at length.

As the conversation continued, the teacher said to Raphael Menahem: "Can you keep a secret? I shall tell you something which you must not divulge under any circumstances, even to your esteemed father."

Raphael Menahem listened with yearning, and promised him none of his words would ever be heard from his lips. The teacher told him about a group of world-reformers in Paris, to which he belonged; how they met at regular intervals and discussed how society could be changed, and how one of the great philosophers of Paris was their mentor. He was fulsome in his praise of this philosopher, who was a famous writer and thinker, and a defender of the weak. And he also told him how during the war the philosopher had fought the Germans as a partisan. And people were constantly coming and going at his house, hearing his learned discourse and then considering what could be done. Most of their activities were secret. Already there were groups of workers in the cities who they were in contact with, and one big union in particular to which hundreds of thousands of workers belonged; if the union told them black was white and white was black, they would still be unswerving in their loyalty. He went on to tell him more, and Raphael Menahem listened, with innocent eyes and an alert heart. That day they talked from the time of the afternoon prayer until two hours after sunset. Raphael wanted to hear more, but the teacher urged him to return to his home, lest his parents worry about him. The conversation had lasted so long that Raphael missed the afternoon prayer that day, and prayed the evening prayer by himself.

Before he went, the teacher told him that from this day onward he would call him neither Raphael nor Menahem, but Max, after the hero of a story they had read, who was courageous and a valiant fighter for justice and truth. Raphael Menahem was glad. For some time now he had felt his name weighing heavily on him, and henceforth he began calling himself Max. At first only the teacher used the new name, but then his fellow pupils began using it too, and it was not long before the old name had almost fallen into disuse, since the shorter the word, the less effort is required of people. The only exceptions were his father, who always called him Raphael Menahem, and his mother, who continued to call him by his childhood pet name. Some time later the teacher took him to a house where a group of world reformers used to gather, and the teacher addressed them. Max took to attending their meetings regularly, but no one outside this circle knew of it. Some said it could be dangerous if the authorities became aware of their activities. Not long after joining the group, Max became its leader, and whenever he spoke his mind, the others fell silent and listened.

His mother was aware that he was coming home late at night, and seemed preoccupied, but since there were a number of clubs in the vicinity, she assumed he was going to one of these. She thought he had joined the Religious Pioneers group set up by one of the envoys from *Eretz-Israel*, and for this reason she said nothing to Jacques. She knew he did not approve of them, but she really admired the envoy and admired what he was doing—enticing the hearts of the young toward *Eretz-Israel*. Once, without her husband's knowledge, she even went to hear him speak, and found that she agreed with every word the envoy said, even his saying that before the young people of the community thought of traveling all over the world, they should go to their own land and help to build it.

Jacques also sensed that Raphael had changed, but he was busy writing the long article that he intended to send to Paris, and he thought all that had happened was that Raphael had reached adolescence, and was thinking the same kind of thoughts he had himself experienced years before.

It was at about this time that something happened to Max. I have heard a number of versions regarding the drastic change that came over him, and no two of them are alike. Some said that one who was close beside him during prayers, noticed he was standing still and not moving his lips to the prayer, and he went and reported it. Others said that one day he stopped studying the *Hok le-Yisrael* after prayers. The first time this happened, they thought he had some urgent appointment he had to keep, but when his behavior was repeated, this too was reported. Some even made the exaggerated claim that they had seen him strolling with his teacher on the Sabbath, carrying something even though there was no *eruv*.

All these accounts have one feature in common: the whole community knew what had befallen Max, except for his father and his mother, love being blind. Yet no one told them anything, and out of respect for their feelings, in their presence he behaved as normal.

When the affair became known to Hacham Ades, the very eldest of the Aleppo sages—who had yet merited during his childhood to have beheld the light of the face of our Teacher and Crowning Glory, he said: "The scorpion sting of our Teacher and Teacher and Master was unleashed in defense of Hacham Raphael two generations ago."

Hacham Ades went on to say to his pupils: "Who knows what Raphael Menahem will do now with the awesome powers Heaven has bestowed upon him? Previously it was his privilege to find in the Torah his elixir of life, and now, who knows?"

And the sages said, "What hope is there for those who have not had this privilege?"

Since the day Raphael Menahem was born, Jacques and Rachel had not even spoken of leaving Aleppo and returning to Paris. When Raphael had grown older and had almost completed his studies, Jacques had said to Rachel: "Do you remember what we used to discuss in the past, and how we said that there was nothing to keep us here in Aleppo? Now my father is long departed and my mother followed him just two years after. Your parents are living in your sister's house. Our Sophie is studying in Paris, and Raphael is growing up and he also wants to study in Paris."

She did not answer. She wished she could tell him that she wanted to go to *Eretz-Israel*. Since the day of her miracle and the birth of Raphael Menahem, she had wanted to thank the Redeemer of good debtors and go there. She, too, believed the right place for the people of Israel was in *Eretz-Israel*, and she had heard the envoy say: "Jews will never find ease in any other place than their own land, especially now, with their success in establishing a state of their own."

But she knew the time was not right. Jacques would not agree, and she had never spoken out against her husband. She remained silent.

At about this time there arrived in Aleppo an emissary from *Sha'are Zion*, the congregation of Aleppo émigrés in New York, looking for somebody to set up a high school for the youths of their community. The emissary wanted to know if there was anyone in Aleppo who had experience in education and was well-thought of by the sages. They all told him: "There is one such person among us, Monsieur Jacques Sapporta."

The emissary went to Jacques and offered him the post. The thought of going to New York had never occurred to Jacques; he had always assumed he would be returning to Paris, and he rejected the offer out of hand. However, there is a maxim to the effect that a good emissary does not fail in his mission, and this emissary too, had not the slightest intention of failing, especially since people from New York are not accustomed to taking "No" for an answer, being affluent and aggressive by nature, and the committee of the congregation had authorized him to offer whatever fee was required, and to spare no effort in bringing them what they sought: a sage from their home town of Aram Zova, a scholar and a linguist, a God-fearing man and a pleasant person.

So the emissary told him about the congregation in New York, which practiced all the customs of Aleppo, in its prayers, poetry, festivals and diet, and although their sharpness was a little dulled through blending with the ambient American culture, they were still unmistakably of Aleppo, especially in the kind of commerce in which they invested all their acumen.

They were reasonable people, according great respect to scholars, and setting aside times for the Torah, even if they didn't show as much dedication to it as did the residents of Aleppo. And they gave generously to charity, and they had succeeded in their commerce and become rich. As the wealth increased, so the respect accorded to people of wealth had also increased, and because the acquisition of wealth was seen by all to be respectable, no one wanted a career as a teacher, and all of them, from the least to the greatest, became businessmen, or affected the ways of businessmen. They feared that if good teachers were not brought in from outside, their children would become estranged from the Torah. They had imported teachers from the *Ashkenazi* community but this proved unsatisfactory, for one whose roots are in Aleppo can only feel comfortable with another like himself, and they saw these teachers were incapable of teaching the tradition of Aleppo. So they resolved to bring in a scholar from Aleppo, someone versed in both the Torah and the secular sciences, and pay him a salary for his services, and give him all the help he might ask for, just so long as he would construct a school according to their requirements. And they set up a committee, and the committee elected an action committee, and they appointed a president to supervise them until such time as they should find what they were looking for. Jacques agonized over the decision, thinking long and hard. In the end, he agreed.

For several months now, Max had been asking his father to let him go to Paris to study. And now Sophie wrote to them from Paris, saying she had taken a job in the offices of the Alliance Israelite

Universelle. Jacques said, let Raphael go and study there as I studied, and Sophie will keep an eye on him.

Jacques wrote a letter to Professor Pierre, asking him to keep an eye on his son too, and wrote another letter to his Parisian friend of long ago, his opponent in philosophical debate; Professor Pierre told him how the man had risen to great eminence in the academic world of Paris, and mentioned him often in his letters. Then Jacques summoned his son and said many things to him, some of which he heard, and some which he pretended to hear, but his heart was far removed from them. Finally his father said to him: "When you get to Paris, I wouldn't like you to have the hard time that I had at first. I arrived there knowing nobody. But I made many acquaintances there, and I had a good name, and they treated me with respect. Give these letters to two esteemed friends of mine, and I'm sure they will remember their obligations and help you on your way."

Max took the letters and looked at the names written on them. He saw on one of the letters the name of the philosopher with whom his father said he used to argue in his younger days, and he was astonished. Was this philosopher not the same man the teacher of French literature had told him about, saying he was the leader and mentor of a group of world-reformers in Paris, the philosopher to whom the teacher had also written a letter introducing his pupil and given it to him? He compared the two letters, and found they were both addressed to the same man. One from his father and one from his teacher. Max smiled and said to himself: "If only Father knew what his former friend was mixed up in, I doubt he'd be sending me to him."

With tears in their eyes, his mother and father accompanied Max to the railway station, to take the train to Beirut. He kissed his father's hands and his father put his hands on his head and blessed him. His mother kissed him and wept. She was weeping so much she could not say any of the things she had meant to say to him. His brother Victor carried his luggage and boarded the train with him, traveling with him as far as the port, and Max embarked alone on the ship bound for Marseilles. Max was in good spirits. He felt absolutely no sorrow at the parting from his parents. On the contrary, he had felt for a long time that his father's love was stifling him, and he craved freedom. He had also long tired of the routine of the community, especially as everyone knew everyone else's business. There were many things in the community which seemed false to him, and there was no one he could discuss them with, because in Aleppo they were all so proud of the way things were done, and lavish in their praise of the systems they knew. He wanted absolute freedom for himself.

He went up on deck as the ship put to sea; it was a fine day and the sea calm. He looked at the blue water, and felt freedom flowing through all his limbs. He had brought a lot of books to read on the way, to pass the time and to improve his French, and he became engrossed in them.

When he arrived in Paris Sophie met him, and greeted him very warmly. She wanted to hear all the news about their father and mother and about Victor and Aleppo, and he wanted her to show him the sights of Paris. For a long time he had been eager to encounter the new world, and here it was before him.

He stayed with her for a few days, and asked her to help him rent a room near the Sorbonne. She pleaded with him to lodge somewhere closer to her, as her mother had made her promise she wouldn't let him out of her sight, but this he definitely did not want. Freedom was what he sought, absolute freedom from everything he had known before. He had a list of names of people given him by the teacher and he went to visit them. He was made welcome by a number of students, who did everything they could to make him feel at home. When he had gained a little more confidence, he decided it was time to call on the philosopher.

The philosopher read the letters he gave him and said: "So, you are Jacques' son! If it wasn't written here, I would not have believed it. He was so unlike you when he came to Paris. Your father had some very fine qualities, and especially a passion for the truth, which he never deviated from. I remember in my youth I would often expound my ideas to people, immature ideas as they sometimes were, and they would all nod their heads at me. Your father was the only one who took up the challenge and refuted my arguments, which made me all the more keen to back them up. It was a good way of clearing the air!"

Then he turned his attention to Max, and discussed a few philosophical issues with him to test his mettle. The conversation was short, and it left Max disappointed. Having heard such glowing reports of the man, he had expected to pick up all kinds of knowledge from him all at once, but he seemed more interested in telling him about his father. Was it to hear about his father that he had come to Paris?

In time he came to know the philosopher better, associating with him closely and learning from his ways. For ten years Max studied in Paris, like one snatching everything that came to hand—philosophy and poetry and literature and art. He made the acquaintance of the new painters, and poets, and was a regular houseguest in literary circles. No one would have believed he was a Jew, and of eastern origin, and he made no effort to advertise himself as such. The first few Sabbaths he prayed in the synagogue, and then stopped. Henceforward he only attended the synagogue on the Sabbath when he was Sophie's guest. His income was meager but this did not concern him. He had always despised those enslaved to money, and it was of no interest to him whether he was going to eat the following day or not. He upheld the precept: *Content yourself with bread and salt*, and everything else the *Mishnah* has to say on the subject. When money ran out and he was short of funds, even by his standards, he tutored students for their exams.

For much of the time he was silent, and yet, whenever he spoke, everyone listened intently. Even the philosopher himself, whose opinion he relied on in everything, spurning the advice given to him by others—even he wanted to hear what Max had to say. And in every argument he always took the side of the weak; the plight of the impoverished workers of Paris affected him deeply. His thoughts on the subject of world reform were not in his case an axe with which to hack out a role in politics or in the labor unions, as they were for some of his colleagues, but came from the very depths of his heart. When he addressed audiences on the subject, they believed him, knowing that he spoke from the heart, and every single word he said was hewn from the quarry of truth, something to be taken to their own hearts. As the years passed, he became a member of a number of societies, some clandestine, and whenever he attended them many came to hear him speak.

He no longer mentioned his hometown of Aleppo and his father's house; a new world had opened before him and he was besotted with its charms. The arts fuelled his spirits, notions of justice and equality filled his thoughts, and his frenetic activity in the clubs consumed his creative energy; he was not left with a free moment to consider where he came from and where he was going.

Sophie was now in her mid-thirties and part of a very distinguished circle of Jewish intellectuals. For some reason she had veered away from marriage proposals, perhaps fearing that this was a state that would infringe upon her fierce independence. Yet she remained loyal to her family and her religious upbringing, and still wrote to her father at regular intervals. Now and then she would make brief references to Max, saying he was studying and making good progress and had many friends, that he liked Paris and Paris seemed to like him, and other such pleasantries. However, one day a long letter from Sophie arrived, densely written and all of it concerned with Max. After the customary salutations she wrote:

My father, dearest to me of all men,
I have been agonizing over this, whether to write or not to write. Writing is hard for me but silence is harder still. I'm sorry, but I don't know what has happened to Max. It seems he has turned his back on everything. He wants no contact with me or with his family. They say he's involved with all kinds of students, people I know nothing about, and hanging around in clubs, and engaged in activities that I just can't fathom, but I feel that they are dangerous. You know how naïve he is, and who knows who is exploiting his naiveté?
I've heard that for a long time he hasn't been putting on tefillin, or even keeping the Sabbath. I know that no one knows what is in the heart of another, and who knows how the fate of a person unfolds, but I could not do other than inform you, and you must do as you see fit, although I don't think there's anything that can be done. A number of times I've tried to talk to him about this. He began by avoiding me, and then rebuffed me, out of hand. Lately, I haven't been seeing him at all. I

wish I could give you better news, but I'm afraid I can't, although I hear he's very well thought of by his teachers and colleagues, and considered something of an idealist.

I think it's best you don't tell Mummy about this. It would break her heart.

Sophie.

Sophie didn't know that her mother had sensed for some time that all was not as it should be with Raphael Menahem. Even before he left home, she had had her suspicions, but had been reluctant to speak out.

The letter was a grievous blow to Jacques. He read it and reread it, and said not a word. His heart ached; he, the perceptive one, had never suspected anything was amiss. He uttered a sigh, and was silent. He held his head in his hands and sank into contemplation.

The years passed and Max carried on as before. One day the news broke that the State of Israel was in danger. Enemies had risen up against it, intent on destroying it. Opinions were divided in the universities as to what the outcome was likely to be. Max began grabbing newspapers, eager to read whatever was being written about events in the East. He had never before felt the slightest interest in the State of Israel, but now he could not relax until he had read every available scrap of news. One day the Foreign Minister of the State of Israel visited Paris, and students came out to demonstrate in his support. Max found himself drawn to this demonstration. He had no intention of participating in it, and he stood to the side, but he felt something happening to him. He wanted to shout: "The State of Israel must not be destroyed! This isn't fair and it isn't just. The world cannot be silent, France cannot be silent!"

A few days later it was known that Israel had struck suddenly at all her enemies, and was out of danger; her armies had proved their worth on the battlefield, and Jews had returned to the Western Wall. The Jews of Paris gathered together to celebrate, waking up to their people and their land, and Max, estranged as he was, was surprised by himself, realizing he wanted to join them. He even went to one such meeting.

Another turn of the wheel: this meeting had been organized by Sophie, and she was one of the main speakers. She had the impression she saw him in the crowd, and tried to catch up with him, but before she could reach him he had slipped away. The people he met there were not to his taste, and the things they said were not to his taste. He got up and left.

The days that followed and the dramatic events unfolding in Paris made him forget this entire episode. The students were angry and discontented, the workers had grievances against the French government, and all the things he had been talking about in the clubs for years were about to become actual and visible. The leaders of the students were regular visitors to him, discussing issues far into the night, and everyone wanted to hear what he had to say. Activists from the unions used to confer with him too, and then one day matters came to a head.

The students announced they were striking from their studies. For a long time they had been demanding changes in the curriculum. They wanted the freedom to choose, rather than be told what to study and how to study it. There can be no education without freedom, they insisted. The authorities were in no mood to yield, and rejected all their demands. The young are afraid of hard work, and education depends on hard and persistent work. There are no shortcuts. That was their response.

Max called a meeting, and made an inflammatory speech. Almost all the students were in agreement, and toward evening they went out to demonstrate. The streets were filled with students who brought everything to a standstill. The police arrived and could do nothing. Cars hooted and sirens blared, but all traffic was halted. When the event was repeated, police arrived in greater and greater numbers, and still they could do nothing. The students formed a solid mass, and could not be moved. One of Max's friends, Danny, was at the head of the marchers, and all followed his lead. The demonstration continued through the night, and early the next morning special forces arrived, the C.R.S.—enough of them to fill several buses—and their appearance was intimidating: they wore flak jackets and steel helmets, and carried clubs and shields. Some were armed with rifles designed to fire gas grenades. Within minutes the street was a battlefield. The police stood in tight ranks and advanced slowly toward the students, as the students shouted and threw paving stones torn up from the roadway; the police, as if unperturbed by the onslaught, continued their steady advance, step by step. And suddenly they were charging at the students, shoving, lashing out with their clubs, seizing the ringleaders and bundling them into vans. The students were not to be silenced, hurling iron bars and stones. One of the riot police fell, and was caught and severely beaten. His comrades tried to extricate him, and when this failed, the sound of a gunshot was suddenly heard, and students began fleeing in all directions with eyes streaming, and the street was filled with the reek of tear gas.

Max stood his ground, ignoring the gas, waving his arms and shouting defiantly at the police. His comrades saw this and they all returned to the street. They picked up the lids of garbage cans to ward off the clubs, wrapped clothing round their heads as a defense against gas, and went on shouting and hurling everything they found at the police lines, and the rioting resumed. Pitched battles continued day and night.

There was panic in Paris. Shops were closed, business suspended, and no one left their home unless it was absolutely necessary. Within a few days, groups of workers had joined the fray. Many thousands of union members went on strike, accusing the government of oppressing the workers and favoring the moneyed classes. The workers took to the streets, and the rioting grew ever more intense. The ranks of the protesters were further swelled by drunken revelers and lovers of riots, the kind who see a brawl in progress and have to join in, whether they know what it's about or not, seeing it as an opportunity not to be missed. Nor were the political parties idle, and radical deputies sent their underlings to inflame hearts and foment sedition. Rumors chased rumors, and no one knew whom to believe. It was said that the President had fled, and no one knew where he was, and everyone assumed the government was about to fall. The chaos continued for weeks throughout France, and in Paris in particular. Cars were over-turned, streets were blocked by barricades of bricks and scrap iron, and there was a scent of danger in the air.

All this time Max rushed from place to place, encouraging and supporting and supervising, and wherever he was seen students set out to follow him, and he never retreated from confrontation with the police. Every night, four of the leading world-reformers used to meet in a different place to consider what was to be done the next day. Max favored carrying on with the demonstrations until the government was overthrown. Others disagreed with him, saying they should negotiate a compromise with the authorities, since they had achieved all they could hope to achieve, but he would have none of it.

One day a student handed him a note, which read simply: *Max, I need to see you.* Max recognized the handwriting as that of his teacher and mentor, the philosopher. He went to see him. Straightaway and without any salutations, he said to him: "Max, was it to destroy France that you came here? You've done enough."

A few days later, they reached a compromise with the authorities.

Most of the students were satisfied, feeling they had won, and the workers too had achievements to celebrate. But Max was disappointed by the compromise. He had wanted to go all the way; he had wanted to overthrow this corrupt government and set up a new regime, which would do justice for the poor and take from the rich. He had waited a long time for days such as these—it had taken more than thirteen years of raising consciousness, preparing the hearts and minds of his comrades for this, and now, when they were almost there, when they had almost achieved what they set out to do, his comrades were calling a halt. He was at a loss.

Max decided he must get away from everyone to think matters over. Suddenly he realized he had time to spare. For thirteen years his activities had left him no space for leisure, and now there were no demands on his time, and when a man has some leisure many thoughts occur to him. Now all kinds of thoughts arose in Max's mind, and when he tried to dispel them, they simply dug themselves in deeper and rose up again. Such is the way of thoughts; you may try to uproot them, but they grow stronger than before.

Chapter twelve

A few weeks after this episode the great philosopher, the teacher and mentor of the whole group, fell ill, and his eyes were heavy with age. It was hard for him to read for himself. Since the life of a scholar who cannot read is little better than death, he asked some of his students to read to him. In the past, the philosopher had concerned himself with the writings of the moderns, but now he turned toward the works of the ancient philosophers, which he had long neglected. The students were glad of the opportunity to serve their master, thinking they might hear words of wisdom from him, or even simply an anecdote. Every day a different student would minister to him and read to him.

There had been a time when the philosopher used to read the Rambam's book *Moreh Nevukhim*, comparing the translations. Now he ordered a copy of the *Moreh Nevukhim* in Hebrew, from the university library, and asked if there was anyone familiar with this language, who could read to him the treatise of Maimonides. Max told his friends: "I'll read it." They looked at him in surprise, wondering how he came to know Hebrew. He didn't explain.

He stood and read to him, the philosopher stretched out on

his bed, listening. One day, the philosopher asked Max to read him the master's comments at the end of the third section. Max opened the *Moreh* and read:

> *Philosophers throughout the ages have shown that the per-
> fections available to mankind are of four kinds. The first,
> which is the least of them, is that upon which the people of
> the world consume their days, the perfection of acquisition,
> meaning: what is available to man in terms of wealth and
> garments and instruments and slaves and the ownership
> of land and so forth—and even if the man be a great king,
> it is of this kind he seeks, and it is a perfection wherein
> there is no adhesion between it and the man, only a con-
> nection. And most of its pleasure is sheer delusion. And
> the philosophers have shown, that whosoever devotes his
> efforts and his toil to this kind of perfection, is striving for
> nothing other than sheer delusion.*

The philosopher asked Max to read this passage again, and he complied.

He then went on to read:

> *And the second kind is more dependent on human nature
> than the first, and that is the perfection of the structure
> and the state of the body, and this kind of perfection is
> not to be made an objective, since it is physical perfection,
> and man has it not because he is human, but because he
> is animal. It is a physical benefit, but spiritual benefit is
> absent from this kind.*
>
> *And the third kind is the perfection of degrees of
> virtue, requiring that the qualities of this man aspire
> always toward the summit of virtue. And most of the
> commandments are aimed solely toward the attainment
> of this kind of perfection. And this kind is nothing other
> than an extension of another and is not an object of inten-
> tion in itself.*

*And the fourth kind is the true human perfec-
tion, whereby the man of enlightened qualities learns
truthful perceptions of the divine from them, and this is
the ultimate objective, and it perfects the man with true
perfection, and it is his alone, and through serving it he
will earn eternal life, and with it man is man. And therefore it is fitting that you strive to attain what it is that
remains yours, and pay no heed to others.* Lest you give
your glory to others and your years are devoured by the
world's cruelty. *The Prophet Jeremiah said of these four
perfections:* Let not the wise man glory in his wisdom,
neither let the mighty man glory in his might, let not
the rich man glory in his riches, but let the one who
glories glory in this, that he understands and knows
me, that I am the Lord, doing kindness and justice
and righteousness on the earth, for in these things is
my delight. *He did not say in this passage that perception
of the Blessed One alone is the most honored of the perfections, because if this was his intention he would have said:*
he understands and knows me, *and finished there. But
he said there should be no boasting except in perception of
me and knowledge of my ways and my nature, meaning
his acts, which are kindness and justice and righteousness
on the earth.*

Then Max read what the Rambam had concluded: "This is
what I sought to express in this piece, considering it to be most
efficacious… and it shall gain for us, together with all the House of
Israel what we were foretold: *Then the eyes of the blind will be opened
and the ears of the deaf unstopped.*"

The *Moreh* sealed the passage with these lyrical lines:
*Our God is close to those who call, if they truly call and do not
lie.*
*All seekers will find their desire, if they walk the straight way and
do not stray.*

Max finished reading and the philosopher asked him: "Max, what is your opinion of the sayings of Maimonides?" He smiled without waiting for Max's reply, and continued, "You know, Max, how many times did I argue about them with Jacques, your father! Fifty years have passed since then. We were both young, and much has happened to us. You are young in years and innocent, and you should know, many true thoughts are at odds with what man sees in his life…"

The philosopher went on talking with Max, but it was as if Max couldn't hear him. He was in a different world, eyes staring into the void before him, hands gripping the book of the *Moreh*, as if dreaming.

He was back in Aleppo, a small child, and he and his grown-up brother Victor were sitting at the Sabbath table, and their sister Sophie was sitting and listening from the other side of the room. And he remembered his father discussing a chapter of the *Moreh* with his brother Victor. Of the text itself, he recalled nothing; what he recalled was the light in his father's face as he read the text.

And the words of the Rambam pounded in his head like a hammer. "*Lest you give your glory to others … All seekers will find their desire, if they walk the straight way and do not stray…*" What does it mean, to stray, and what is perfection, and is there perfection for man? And is there another world? He was perplexed and confused. Things that had been clear to him were now blurred in his eyes, childhood memories rising to his mind's eye with ever greater intensity, the image of his father appearing ever more often.

His head felt very heavy. He asked the philosopher to excuse him and left. He went to his room and lay on his bed, picking up the *Moreh* and trying to read it in order. The letters were jumbled before his eyes, and he didn't understand many of the words, let alone their meaning. He put the book down, picked up another book of philosophy. He read a little of it, put it down again. He closed his eyes and slept. His sleep was fitful.

When he awoke he decided to go to the museum. Whenever he felt preoccupied or troubled he used to go to the Louvre and look at the wonderful pictures until his spirits were soothed. That day he went at an early hour, and the museum was almost empty. The attendants recognized him and greeted him. He replied in a more subdued manner than was his wont, and began wandering in the halls, yet he found that he had little patience today for the pictures that usually calmed his spirits. He was on edge, his body trembling. He moved restlessly from room to room, until he found a sign pointing the way to a special exhibition of Jewish art. He went from exhibit to exhibit, and saw nothing out of the ordinary, until he came across a glass case containing a *menorah*, which according to the catalogue was of a very rare and almost unique type. What was so special about it? It had nine branches and an auxiliary, rather than eight and an auxiliary, which is the universal form of the *Hanukkah* lamp. The catalogue referred to the Jewish *Hanukkah* ritual, adding that there was a Jewish congregation in the East where it was the custom on the first day of *Hanukkah* to light two candles and an auxiliary.

Max felt drawn toward this menorah and he examined it closely. He saw it was engraved with worn Hebrew letters and the motif of a ship. He made an effort to read the script and fit the letters together, until he had it: *Sapporta*. Max's face turned pale, his heart pounded, and he thought he was losing his mind. Finding his family name engraved on a *Hanukkah* lamp in Paris of all places, was something Max could never have envisaged. How did this *menorah* come to be in Paris? And how did he come to see it? Max took it upon himself to find out who acquired the *menorah* for the museum, and where it was acquired, and from whom, and so establish the facts, but he was beginning to wonder what was happening to him: the image of his father appearing to him every day, the Rambam that he read to the philosopher, and now this *menorah*.

He had never known his heart to beat so hard, with longings and memories and thoughts and musings, with the days of his life passing before his eyes like a procession as he looked on. He found the official who had organized the exhibition and asked where the *menorah* had come from, and who had authenticated it. Could it be a forgery?

The official was shocked, and angry: "A forgery at the Louvre? Perish the thought! Nothing is put on show at the Louvre until we have checked it, not once, not twice, but three times. We have never been taken in by a forgery." He searched in his files, took out a card, and read the details aloud: The *menorah* was purchased from a certain dealer who bought it from a certain person (it was not customary to reveal the names of dealers) who visited the township of Aleppo in Syria to collect ancient *menorahs* from synagogues and elderly people, and this was bought from a pair of scrap-metal traders named Franco and De Piciotto. And here is the certificate of provenance. I quote: This is to certify that this *menorah* has been in the possession of my family for several generations, and I am selling it willingly to the holder of this document. I confirm that this is a legal sale. Signed: Raphael Sapporta.

You see! The man brandished the cards triumphantly. When Max heard the name Raphael Sapporta, he sprang to his feet and asked to read the documents himself. He had no idea what was happening to him. For some days following that incident Max was in a state of utter confusion, not knowing what the future held for him, and feeling his destiny was hanging in the balance. A week later, one of his friends approached him and told him that a group of them were planning a trip to Israel and Jerusalem, and would he like to join them. Max was delighted by the invitation, which he felt had come at just the right time, and he readily accepted. It was a group of twenty young people, eight of whom he knew well. None of them had ever visited Israel before, and Max was looking forward to it with great excitement. He decided that on arriving in the country, his first destination would be the Western Wall.

Throughout the plane trip, Max sat immersed deeply in his own thoughts. His friends chatted among themselves and laughed, but he was enveloped in a great silence. His face was tense, his eyes closed, his mind preoccupied. His friends were used to him, they knew he was schooled in the art of silence, and this was not the first time they had seen him like this, so they didn't think anything of it. Only when the announcement was heard that Israel had come into view did Max sit up and peer through the window. He saw the sea and the shore, and inland there were villages and fields and towns. Once again memories of his childhood arose. He remembered how, long ago, he had strayed by chance into the religious pioneers' club, and heard the envoy from Israel describing the kibbutz and the moshav movements; he had also described how the sun beat down on golden sands, and the sea and the blue waves. At the time these words had meant nothing to him, but now they affected him strongly. What he saw through the window was like a picture in the Louvre, unconnected with the reality of his life.

When they arrived they were met by the guide they had hired, and he took them to a hotel in Jerusalem. He advised them to rest, as they had a busy schedule planned for the next day. He wanted them up early to watch the sunrise from Mount Scopus, and then they would be going on to the Dead Sea. In the morning, Max asked the guide if they could visit the Western Wall. His friends objected, preferring Mount Scopus and the sunrise, so he decided to leave the group and make his own way to the Wall. They accompanied him as far as the Jaffa Gate.

The precinct before the gate was almost empty. There was only one Arab boy with a green cart, offering bagels with sesame seeds, and hard-boiled eggs and herbs in paper bags, and an old man stooping beneath the weight of a polished brass kettle, carrying a tray of coffee cups. The guide showed Max the lane leading to the Wall. At that moment an old man was walking in the same direction, wearing a *tallit* and adorned with *tefillin*. The guide assumed that this man was making his way to the Wall to pray the dawn prayer, and he asked him to take Max along with him, so he wouldn't get lost. The old man did not reply. His lips were murmuring the dawn blessing. He took Max by the hand, nodded to him, and went with him.

The air of Jerusalem was chilly and pure, the Tower of David standing to the right erect as a sentinel, with the old city wall surrounding it. The old man was wrapped in a white *tallit*, and the dawn was breaking with pale light. Max was in a trance. The old man was walking and blessing and chanting *bakashot* in the tuneful prayer style of Aleppo, being purified from sin as a son is purified before his father, and every word spoken with intent: *Who restores souls to the dead...opens the eyes of the blind... supports those who have fallen... And make pleasant, we pray, the words of Your Torah in our mouths...who preaches Torah to his people Israel...* Max looked at the old man and felt his whole body shaking. What did all this mean to him?

Distant memories from another world arise in him. He feels he has heard this once before, the same man and the same voice and the same litany. This is his first time ever in Jerusalem, he is sure of that, so how can he have seen this man before? Perhaps he is dreaming, or this might be the kind of sight that a man sees and feels he has already seen before; deja vous, a quirk of the mind. Such things have happened to him before. But this time he *knows* that he has heard this voice, or perhaps the truth is that his soul has heard it. Is there a world of souls? And the old man continues: "*And Hannah prayed... Make broad my mouth upon my enemies... And Isaac spoke to Abraham his father, and said, Father...*" And suddenly Max recoils. Now everything is clear to him. This is no dream, no world of souls. Suddenly the dim memory is awakened in him of Aleppo, his hometown, of walking with his grandfather at daybreak to the *Beit Midrash*, his grandfather holding his hand. But... what has happened here, and how has grandfather turned up in this place?

The reader has surely realized that it was quite impossible for this old man to have been Hacham Hiyyah, since Hacham Hiyyah had passed on to the life of the world hereafter a quarter of a century previously. This old man was in fact Hacham David Muhadeb, beloved in Jerusalem, son of the saintly sage and judge Ribi Menashe Muhadeb, son of Hacham Nissim Muhadeb. And every morning as the dawn broke he would pray at the Wall in the *minyan* of émigrés from Aleppo, and I too have had the privilege of praying with him, when I was studying at *Yeshivat HaKotel*, the yeshiva of the Western Wall in the Jewish Quarter.

They came to the Wall. Max looked around in the pleasant, early summer breeze. A man came over and asked to put *tefillin* on him. He offered him a big cap made of paper, and laid it on his head. The man took the *tefillin* and tried to bind them on Max's arm. Max's eyes filled with tears. He said to the man: Let me. Max wound the *tefillin* for himself, on his arm and on his forehead, then made three bindings around his finger, his mouth intoning automatically: *And I have betrothed you to me forever.* He moved his hand to touch the *batim* of the *tefillin*, put the hand to his lips, and kissed it. The man gave him a piece of paper, and asked him to recite with him the *Shema Yisrael*. Max raised his hand, a sign that he wanted to be left alone. He approached the Wall, stood facing it and wept. He listened to the wondrous chanting of Hacham Muhadeb, and the cooing of the doves. It was a Monday of the week of *Shavuot*, and they read from the Torah. They invited him to come forward. They asked him his name. He said, Max son of Jacques, and hurriedly corrected himself: Raphael Menahem son of Jacob. His eyes streamed with tears and his heart was in ferment; it was some seven years since he had put on *tefillin*, seven years since he came forward to read the Torah, seven years since anyone had called him Raphael Menahem.

He spoke the blessing over the Torah: *Who gave us His Torah, a Torah of truth, and planted eternal life among us.* He could scarcely finish the blessing, for the tears were streaming down his face. Hacham Muhadeb looked at him with love, and finished it with him. Raphael Menahem kissed the hand of Hacham Muhadeb, as he used to kiss the hand of his grandfather Hacham Hiyyah, and asked him to perform a *hashkavah*. Hacham Muhadeb began with a brief exordium, like that which is spoken over a simple person: *The One who is merciful to all his creatures, He will save and forgive and have mercy upon the soul of*… and he listened intently to hear the name, whispered to him by Raphael Menahem: the soul of my late lamented grandfather, Hacham Hiyyah son of Hacham Raphael, the anniversary of whose passing fell that week. Hacham Muhadeb started, and almost shouted: Sapporta? Raphael Menahem nodded his head, and his long hair swung from side to side. Hacham Muhadeb gripped his hand firmly and repeated the *hashkavah*, in the way it is said in Aleppo on behalf of the greatest of the great: *Whence then comes wisdom, and where is the place of understanding… how great is Your goodness, which You have laid up for those that fear You*…. for the soul of the righteous and most excellent judge, knowledgeable in all matters, the complete and the consummate sage, of unfailing humility, Hacham Hiyyah…

Raphael Menahem heard no more. He buried his face in the *siddur* and made his way to the Wall. It was said that he stood by the Wall without moving or stirring for three full hours. Hacham

Muhadeb waited for him all this time, while reading the *Hok le-Yisrael*. He then approached him, took his hand and led him away.

Later Raphael Menahem was to say: "I had many troubling questions, and many real doubts, but with every blessing spoken by the sage on the way to the Western Wall, I felt as if another doubt was dissolved, and by the time I reached the Wall, and came to bless the Torah, I felt that I had no more questions."

Broken Tablets

Chapter one

My grandfather of blessed memory was one of the sages of Aram Zova. Aram Zova was a city of sages and scribes. Every one of its sages could be told apart by his clothing and was set apart by his title. A sage of Aram Zova never wrapped himself in a cloak not appropriate to his status. The caftan of a *Beit Midrash* sage was not the same as the caftan of a pedagogue, just as the turban of a head of the *Beit Din* did not resemble the turban of a *Bashi* sage, and even an expert observer could distinguish between the sash of a storyteller and the sash of a scholar of Jewish law. The turbans, the caftans, the cloaks and the sashes were distinguished by their fabrics, their colors, their embellishments, their tassels and buttons, the threads hanging from them and the pleats into which they were folded.

Just as the clothing of sages was not the same, so their titles differed. There were many titles of sages there. And although there was no official designation of titles, each and every one was known by a title that fitted him. One was called an 'Elder of the Law', another was called 'A Champion of the People,' another was called a 'Chief of Aram Zova,' another an 'Elder of the Yeshiva,' and so on and so forth. Those engaged in *Kabbalah* were known as workers of miracles, but workers of miracles or otherwise, they did not stray from the norm of the sages of Aram Zova, being sharp-witted and fond of jests. Such was the story told by the eminent rabbi, Rabbi Mordechai Attia, may the memory of a *tzaddik* be blessed, he who penned the books *Artzot HaHaim*, *Mahseh VaOz* and other compositions.

"Once there was a gathering in my house of a number of writers of scrolls, and we discussed the business of writing scrolls. I told them a certain man had an ailment of the eye. He went to the rabbi, and the rabbi said to him, bring me the *mezuzot* from your home. He brought them. The rabbi examined the scrolls and found that on the *mezuzah* of the outer door, in the verse: *And you shall see it and remember,* the words *And you shall see* were blotted out. All the scribes were impressed by the miracle. I said to them, you call yourselves scribes? Ignoramuses that you are! The verse, *And you shall see it and remember* is said in the ordinance of the *tzizit*, and the ordinance of the *tzizit* is never quoted in the *mezuzah*."

Hacham Mordechai went on to say: "So you may see how miracles are beloved of Israel. Many times I have told this story, and I have not known anyone who was not amazed by the miracle, until I reminded him that this verse is not mentioned anywhere on the *mezuzah*. Will you find any man of Israel who doesn't know that the ordinance of the *tzizit* does not appear in a *mezuzah*? But so beloved of Israel are miracles that they forget their learning."

Yet there were also sages endowed with a title to be spoken with a shudder—'The Punitive Judge' or 'The Killer by Decree.' A sage who earned this title cast terror upon the congregation, and even the Ishmaelites feared him. Hacham Avraham Anteby, may the memory of a *tzaddik* be blessed, was widely known as such. We heard the following from the pupil of one of the elderly sages of Aram Zova:

Hacham Avraham Anteby used to hold classes in *Halacha* for a select group of pupils, all of them erudite students but yet to be ordained. He was a very old man, and he dozed off in one of his classes. The pupils began talking among themselves. One of them said: "When our teacher goes to his eternal rest, I shall deliver his funeral oration." Another said: "That's not right! The person who'll deliver it will be me!" All of them said this about themselves. Suddenly, the rabbi awoke and said severely: "I vow, upon your lives, that the person who will be doing the eulogizing will be me—over all of *you!*"

Men in authority should beware of such rash oaths: not one of those pupils lived out the year. He was one of those of whom it was said: Their bite is the bite of a snake, and their sting, the sting of the scorpion, and all their words are like burning coals.

And there was another title that was highly regarded in Aram Zova: *Hacham Me'ayen*, or 'The Contemplative Sage.' Anyone who earned this title was highly regarded among the sages. My grandfather of blessed memory was called a contemplative and, having earned the title he was no longer among those who debated in the *Beit Midrash*, but sat in his regular place, head supported by his right hand, his eyes closed, sitting in silence. And when all the sages of the *Beit Midrash* had finished asking and replying, raising difficulties and proposing solutions, ascending to the Heavens and descending to the lower depths, the problem still weighing heavy on their hands, he would open his eyes, move his hand in a slight upward motion, as if asking permission to reply and suddenly—the *Beit Midrash* would be silent. A moment before there had been the roar and tumult of students vying with one another on issues of *Halacha* until the walls seemed about to cave in, and all at once there was silence, all pursing their lips at one another and straining their ears to hear the words of the contemplative sage. Grandfather would set out the whole issue as if he had not heard any of the pretexts that had been put forward, as if he were not responding to any of the difficult questions raised, but through his quietly spoken words all problems were resolved, all pretexts refuted, and all was clear as crystal. And no one had any response to make to him, because once he had explained something, there was no other explanation. Sometimes he alluded to the words of one of the sages of the *Beit Midrash* and should he praise him, then his prestige among his colleagues would soar and his words made that sage's day.

A few years later grandfather was awarded a further distinction, and dubbed a *Me'ayen Pashtan*, a 'Contemplative Exponent.' He prided himself on his ability to teach the whole science of Talmudic analysis with a page and a half drawn from the Talmud tractate *Baba*

Metzia. And his pupils feared him. They knew that anyone who held an opinion without deep analysis was worth nothing to him, however much he had read and studied.

There was a story of one pupil who had held his own opinion and debated with him for some years, and he was planning to go to *Eretz-Israel,* and wanted to hear his teacher's opinion of him. He asked him: "Rabbi, what am I?" My grandfather moved his head lightly from right to left. The student understood and asked for the second time: "A grain of incense?" And again my grandfather shook his head and said not a word. "Half a grain?"—he asked in trepidation, and the sage repeated the same movement. "A drop of honey?"—he persisted, and the sage kept his silence. Unable to restrain himself further he finally asked: "Rabbi, what am I worth?" "Nothing at all," grandfather replied, and returned to his studies.

Even in his childhood my grandfather of blessed memory was known for his asperity. A certain old man told me an interesting story about his schooldays. He said: "When your grandfather started attending the *kuttab,* for the study of Talmud Torah, he was three years old, and already very astute. In the *kuttab* they were teaching the letters of the alphabet. The teacher taught them the letter *aleph* and called on every pupil by name to say *aleph* after him. The first one to be called said *aleph,* the second said *aleph,* and so the third, and so all of them. When it was your grandfather's turn, he said nothing. The teacher came to him and said: 'Say *aleph.*'

"He said to him: 'I don't want to say it.'

"The teacher said: 'Why don't you want to say *aleph?*'

"He told him: 'Because I don't want to.'

"The teacher spoke to him kindly: 'You're going to be a great scholar one day, why don't you learn a few letters?' And he still refused. He scolded him, and he refused. Made him stand in the corner of the *kuttab,* and he refused. Made him lie on the bench and lashed him with a little whip—nine and thirty strokes for the thirty-nine letters in the verse beginning, *And he the merciful...* and still he refused. The teacher summoned his father. His father was a great sage, and he wrapped himself in his cloak and came to him. He said to him: 'You're a clever boy, so what's the reason for this nonsense? Is it not easier to say *aleph* than suffer all these humiliations, scoldings and beatings? Say *aleph* and be done with it.'

"Your grandfather answered him: 'Father, everything you say is the truth. It would be easier to say *aleph*, but if I give in and say *aleph*, he's going to tell me to say *bet* and then *gimel* and *dalet*, and then it will be the Bible and the *Mishnah* and the Talmud, and there will be no end of hard work; if I don't say *aleph* I'll have to put up with scolding and beatings, but I won't have to do all that studying.'"

What the sages have told us, that the Torah preserves man from all evil in his youth, was fulfilled in grandfather's case. As to what is taught in the supplement to the *Mishnah*: *Giving him a future and hope in his old age*—that is the basis of the story unfolding before us here.

Chapter two

In keeping with the ways of many of the sages of Aram Zova, my grandfather did not make a living from the Torah. He was a trader in fabrics, spending a few hours in his shop and the rest of the day at his studies. What would have been surprising in *Eretz-Israel* was considered normal in Aram Zova, where they were avid disciples of the Rambam and were loath to depend on the Torah for their livelihood. Once, a certain scholar came from *Eretz-Israel* to collect funds to publish a book of *Halacha* that he had written. He was a very distinguished scholar, from Hebron. He went into the *Beit Midrash*, and asked the sages about a *halachic* ruling that was the object of dispute in *Eretz-Israel*: the regulation concerning the washing of hands before a meal—whether it should be three times continuously, or with intervals between. They could not answer him. They told him: "We have no answer, but there is a sage among us, a contemplative sage; perhaps he can answer your question." He asked them: "And where is he studying?" They told him: "In the textile market." He went to the market and found him grappling with rolls of satin fabric, a variety of glossy silk of which the Arabs of the countryside were especially fond, buying large quantities of it to give to their wives as festival gifts. He asked him: "Is it possible you have knowledge of such a *Halacha*?" The contemplative sage gave him the answer. The scholar from *Eretz-Israel* said to him: "What is your source for this?" He said to him: "Wait for me, I have a transaction to complete with this roll of fabric, and then I shall tell you." He went to wherever he went, sold whatever he sold, and returned to his shop. He took the scholar from Israel by the hand, went with him to the *Beit Midrash*, climbed up to the dais, took from the bookcase a copy of *Nehar Shalom*, showed him the reference, and returned to his shop. The scholar returned to the *Beit Midrash*, and said to them: "Have you taken leave of your senses, Heaven forbid? You have such a treasure in your midst, and yet you let him waste his time among spools of fabric?"

As we have said, what was surprising to a scholar from *Eretz-Israel* was nothing unusual in their eyes. Our teaching has always been that it is a fine thing when Talmud Torah is combined with secular employment, since success in both fields discourages any inclination to defect from the straight and narrow.

When he shut up his shop, grandfather would return to his studies and sit among the sages of the *Beit Midrash*. For questions of divorce and desertion, he was chosen to serve in the *Beit Din*, and the rest of the day he would teach Talmud, following the analytic method. Whenever an envoy came from *Eretz-Israel*, he would be sent to grandfather, who debated with him on matters spiritual and matters temporal, and soon had the measure of him. Then grandfather would send them the allusive message, "The lion that you spoke of has become a fox," or "How fortunate is the Holy Land, that even those who derive no benefit from the Torah gain the benefit of dwelling there…" and other hints in a similar vein.

But my grandfather's essential fame was as a preacher, a *darshan*; not a preacher in the style of the preachers of today who, due to their inadequacies, have lost the spark of preaching that used to be so popular, but a preacher like those of whom the sages said that scholars of the *Mishnah* and students of *Halacha* left and flocked to hear them—to hear sermons such as made the Torah dear to Israel, instilling in the people faith and the fear of God, sustaining them in times of violence, and slaking their thirst with the expectation of deliverance. Such a preacher was my grandfather of blessed memory, besides being one of the elite, since he was a contemplative. When he gave a sermon, it was neither a lecture, nor a story, nor a conversation, nor an oration. It was a sermon.

The time he used to preach was on a Sabbath that heralded the start of a new month, after the *Minha* prayers. People would flock to hear the address, erudite sages and astute scholars, tradesmen and artisans—all of them thirstily drinking in his words. His manner of preaching was to begin with a passage from the weekly Torah portion. He would then pile upon it any number of questions relating to language, style and content, then introduce a verse from the *Haftarah*, raising all kinds of problems there as well, until it seemed that in all these verses there was not a single letter that was straightforward. He would then set these verses aside, and start the sermon again with an idea drawn from the works of the Rambam or the Ramban in his commentary on the Torah, or from the Book of Principles or from Duties of the Heart, and would quote them in their own language, word for word. This was a congregation that demanded rigorous standards from its preachers, insisting that everything be quoted word for word and by heart; it was considered ignorance to consult a book in the course of a sermon.

A certain Hasidic rabbi had a story to tell: when he arrived in *Eretz-Israel* he was invited, as a special honor, to preach before a *Sepharadi* congregation. He was told what the congregation would expect of him and so he sat up all night, learning the verses and the *midrashic* references by heart and repeating them aloud—until he lost his voice and was unable to preach at all. My grandfather of blessed memory would preach using reams of *midrashic* texts and whole chapters from the Rambam, and he could recite them by heart. He would proceed to accentuate the notion he had raised with references to legend and stories drawn from the Talmud, blending them with the current events of that week. At this point in the sermon he would resort to the Arabic language or to French, depending on his audience, with a little humor for seasoning, then revert to Hebrew and prove that all the problems he had raised had solved themselves, and all the verses explained themselves—and having rounded off the sermon with a return to the start, he would conclude with the invocation of our righteous Messiah, may he come and deliver us, and gather in our exiles, and rebuild our Temple, quickly and in our time, so our eyes might see and our hearts be glad, amen and amen. Grandfather never needed parables or the numerology of *Gematria* to underscore his meaning, but his words were like a taste of the World to Come, in which the congregation used to savor all kinds of Sabbath delights. His words sparkled like diamonds, his sentences flowed like pure water, *Midrash* and legend were poetry, and the sayings of the Rambam were song. And he, too, derived much pleasure from preaching, and he would keep a keen watch on his congregation to see what kind of an impression he had made. And although he used to say he didn't prepare a sermon before seeing the faces of his public, this was not entirely accurate, for I personally saw him polishing and honing every notion and every word that he was going to preach. After the sermon, as grandfather would walk from the synagogue to his home, he would be treated with great respect. The entire congregation stood in two rows, bowing their heads deferentially and taking his hands to kiss them. He would place his hand on their heads in blessing; happy is the eye that has beheld these things. In my childhood, when I read in the tractate *Yoma* of the respect accorded to the High Priest on *Yom Kippur* when he emerged safely from the Holy of Holies in the Temple, this was how I saw grandfather, leaving the synagogue after his sermon.

There was one old man who made a point of hearing every one of grandfather's sermons. Once he told us he had studied with grandfather in the *kuttab*, and there he had heard his first sermon. The occasion had been the death of a bird that the children of the *kuttab* used to play with. All the children were terribly upset, mourning the death of their pet. As an expression of their love and grief, they conducted a funeral and a burial service for their pet bird. Grandfather, who was four years old at the time, stood on a wooden crate, and preached over the deceased in a melancholy voice and in the traditional style of mourners, beginning with the verse: *Balak, son of Zippor, king of Moab in those days...* And this old man also told us of grandfather's speeches in honor of government ministers who used to come to visit the community, and in honor of the *Gaonim,* the outstanding scholars, when they were appointed chiefs of Aram Zova, on the day of their investiture.

When a great sage and pillar of the *Beit Din* passed away, grandfather would be invited to preach at the funeral, and he always began with a verse appropriate to the occasion. Once he struck a bitter note in his oration. It was for a sage departed in his prime, and so he began with the verse: *Do not delay me, the Lord has prospered my path, send me and I shall go to my master...* and all the congregation broke down in tears. So it was that grandfather's reputation preceded him, and he was the pride of the congregation of Aram Zova.

Love of Zion and expectation of salvation filled all the chambers of grandfather's heart, and he felt real pangs of yearning for *Eretz-Israel.* This love and longing overflowed from him, diffusing through the entire house. Envoys from all over the land stirred his affection; when the lights of salvation began to flicker in *Eretz-Israel,* and our exiles were gathered in by the grace of the Lord, and when the grace of the Almighty prevailed for us, we too gained the right to go to the land of our delight.

Every house built in *Eretz-Israel,* and every tree planted there, was a joyous sight for grandfather. A few days after our arrival, I went for a stroll with him in the streets of Jerusalem. He stopped suddenly and watched two children playing, heard one saying something to the other. Grandfather was thrilled to hear children in *Eretz-Israel* speaking Hebrew among themselves. The Holy Tongue was very dear to him, and in Aleppo it was spoken only by erudite scholars and patricians. Excited, he called to the child and said: "What did you say, my son? Repeat it, so I may hear." The little boy looked up and said at once: "What's that to you?" Pedant that he was, grandfather smiled.

Chapter three

When we had been living in Jerusalem for a few weeks, my grandfather wanted to find a place for regular worship. There were a number of synagogues in the Beit Mazmil neighborhood, some of them *Ashkenazi* and some of them *Sepharadi*. The *Ashkenazi* synagogues belonged to Hasidim and the opponents of the Hasidim, the *Mitnaggedim*. But the Hasidim were not Hasidic, and the *Mitnaggedim* didn't seem to be opposing anything. The difference between a synagogue of the Hasidim and a synagogue of the *Mitnaggedim* seemed to be that all the Hasidim used to drink a glass of brandy after the service, and on the anniversaries of their masters and teachers they didn't say the *Tahanun*, whereas among the *Mitnaggedim* it was not the custom to drink a glass of brandy after the service, and on the anniversaries of their masters and teachers they *did* say the *Tahanun*. As for the *Sepharadi* congregations, there were synagogues of Babylonians, and of Moroccans from Meknes, and Moroccans from Fez, and Moroccans from the High Atlas, and Tunisians, and immigrants from Algiers, and immigrants from Tangiers and Libyans—and there were even some from Jerusalem—not to mention the Yemenites, who constituted a community in their own right.

These synagogues had attractive names: Memorial to the Saints, Fellowship of Brothers, Hand of Brothers, Love and Fraternity, Sweet Discourse, Comfort and Refuge, Song for David, Psalm for David, Scholars for David, Lilies for David—and yet they were not known by these names, but by the names of those worshipping there, Moroccans, Tunisians, and so on. Although every synagogue was named after a certain place, all the synagogues had a jumble of traditions: sometimes they chanted a certain hymn, and sometimes not. Some prayed with *tefillin* on the Ninth of Av, following the custom of Jerusalem, and according to the opinion of the *Gaonim*, some put them on at home as is the custom of the *Sepharadi* congregations abroad, some put them on at *Minha;* some with bare palm fronds, others adorned them with tassels and colored threads; some recited the poems of Rabbi David Hassin, and others chanted the *bakashot* of Rabbi Israel Najara. In short, all the synagogues were a mixture of all the communities gathered in the country. There were Moroccans worshipping in the synagogue of the Babylonians, and Babylonians in the synagogue of the Tunisians, and so on. Add to them immigrants from Shushan and Mashhad, and the Bukharians, and Turks, and Greeks, and Italians, who did not have their own specific synagogues in our neighborhood, and used to pray in any of the synagogues. And on top of all this, everyone arrived with a copy of the liturgy in his hand. A liturgy printed by Sasson in Baghdad, and a liturgy printed in Livorno, and another in the Italian style printed in Venice, and one printed in Marrakesh, and one in Istanbul by authority of our sovereign the Sultan Abdul Hamid, may his glorious name be ever exalted, and in Cairo at the press of the printer Yoseph Yehezkiel, and at the press of the Heder brothers in Djerba, and so on and on. Each community had its own tradition—sometimes one tradition taking precedence, and sometimes that of a rival had the better of them. And the versions were confused, and the poems mixed, and the tunes intertwined, and the synagogues became a morass of interpretations and counter-interpretations, traditions and counter-traditions, schisms and dissensions.

Some stand while others sit, some whisper while others chant. All shout and all argue; yet all declare that their thoughts are directed toward the Heavens. As everyone believes that the tradition of his community is superior to that of another, he strives to put it in its proper place, each keeping in mind: *Do not forsake the law of your mother.* The unifying factor in *Sepharadi* synagogues is that their Torah scrolls are kept in cases, not wrapped in velvet, as is the *Ashkenazi* practice. Wealthy congregations make them of silver and gold; the poorer ones make them of wood. And furthermore, they recite the prayer about the ingredients of incense before *Minha*, and the poems of Rabbi Judah Halevi and Rabbi Solomon Ibn Gavirol on *Rosh Hashanah* and *Yom Kippur,* and they do not talk during the reading of the Torah.

Grandfather was used to the traditions of Aram Zova, and meticulous in the application of these traditions, so it was very hard for him to settle on a place of worship in any of these other synagogues. Every Sabbath we went to a different place, different synagogues which were usually not to his taste, while they, for their part, didn't know him, and didn't make him feel welcome, let alone invite him to preach. Because he wasn't invited, he kept his sermons to himself and resisted the urge to preach. You could tell from the look on his face how much of an effort it was for him to keep his sermons to himself. On Sabbath afternoons he would still prepare his sermon, polishing his style, as had been his habit over many years. When the hour of *Minha* arrived and there was no sermon to follow it, and worshippers came out to talk trivia until it was time for the third meal at the close of Sabbath, we knew that his mind was brimming with memories of Aram Zova and how he used to stand before the ark, pondering a few moments in silence, and how the sermon would then flow from his lips. He would be silent while we accompanied him from the synagogue to his home.

Many Sabbaths we wandered between synagogues, until we settled on a place of worship in the Heaven's Gate synagogue, in a transit-camp, the 'Asbestos Camp.' There is a story behind why we chose this as our place of prayer, but first a few words of explanation regarding this transit-camp.

As the tide of immigrants to *Eretz-Israel* swelled, may the Lord increase their numbers still more, the neighborhood of Beit Mazmil was filled to capacity. The practical solution was to build flimsy shacks of asbestos on the riverbed at the foot of the hill. It was assumed that the immigrants would stay there only a short time before moving to proper accommodation. This being the theory, the place was called a transit-camp, and its inhabitants were called 'Asbestonians.'

Those arriving in the transit-camp were immigrants from Hungary, from Rumania, from Fez, from the High Atlas, from Meknes, from Tunis and from Algiers. Wherever there is peace upon Israel and some Jews are to be found, there has to be a prayer house. Two shacks were set aside, each adorned with an seven-branched *menorah*, thus creating two synagogues—one in the *Ashkenazi* style, and one in the *Sepharadi*. Worshippers in the *Ashkenazi* style were immigrants from Hungary and Rumania, and with them was a Hasidic rabbi from Nadvorna, who used to have a number of disciples in Rumania. It was the custom there to provide a *tisch* for the Hasidim after the service. They would set out the *tisch*, sample whatever delicacies the rabbi decided he could spare, drink toasts and sing songs. The Teacher and Master recited words of Torah, while his Hasidim danced. When the rabbi arrived in this land and settled in the transit-camp, he wanted to continue these practices, but his followers numbered only five or six, and four of them were his relations—his son, his brother-in-law, his uncle and a cousin. Every Sabbath Eve he would look for another four, to make up a *minyan*. The worshippers knew his ways, knew how he used to draw out meals at the *tisch* with pronouncements from the Torah and with music, and they tended to avoid him. For this reason, he tried appealing to the *Sepharadim*. A number of times I found myself helping to make up his *minyan*, and although it was sometimes irksome, and I didn't understand his words of the Torah, (since he spoke in Yiddish, a language with which I am not familiar)—in spite of this, I couldn't bear to see his distress so I would join him to help out. I did not know then that in the cycle of events to come, the path of this Hasidic rabbi and that of my grandfather of blessed memory were destined to cross.

Chapter four

The *Sepharadi* synagogue where immigrants from Fez and Meknes and Casablanca gathered was called 'Heaven's Gate,' and we wouldn't have known how to tell them apart were it not for what happened.

The episode occurred on *Yom Kippur*, and that *Yom Kippur* we too happened to be praying there. Why we were praying there revolved around an issue of law. And this is how it revolved: As is the way of treasurers, those responsible for Heaven's Gate sought to embellish the synagogue in honor of the Days of Awe. Money was gathered from donations given by those going up to read from the Torah and from the Feast of Rabbi Shimon Bar Yohai. The way in which donations were given by those going up to the podium to read from the Torah on the Sabbath was as follows: for each man who went up to the Torah on the Sabbath, the cantor would say the blessing, *Mi Sheberach*, over the Torah. And when, as the Aleppans used to do, he had blessed him and his family with healthy children, wealth and prosperity, and had recited the blessing of Elijah the Prophet, he would add: "May God speedily send him full healing from the Heavens for all his bodily parts and all his bodily sinews. Heal him

Lord, heal him, and may the merit of Rabbi Shimon defend him."
He would add an entire parcel of blessings, inasmuch as the hand
of the Lord had dealt kindly with him, and according to whatever
occurred to his mind at that moment. And when all the blessings
were done the cantor would bow his head toward the one called up,
saying in a whisper that could be heard the length and breadth of the
synagogue, that he had offered the sum of... and the one going up
would say what he had to say, willingly or unwillingly. The generous
give generously, and the misers give in a stingy fashion—it entirely
depends on the one giving the blessing and the one being blessed, to
say nothing of the order of precedence of his being called up to the
Torah. If the cantor has been generous with his blessings—he in turn
is generous with his cash. If, on the other hand, he feels resentment
against him or against the treasurer, because he has been called fifth
out of seven readers and is not to conclude the reading—he is miserly.
And if this is a happy time for him, he declares in the musical tones
of the Torah reading: "A certain sum to the synagogue," and after a
short pause for emphasis he says: "A certain sum to the reader of the
Torah," and another pause and he says: "A certain sum to the Talmud
Torah, and more cash for discreet charity, and more for the *shamash*."
If the donation is meager, the cantor discloses it in a whisper, and
if it is worthy of celebration, he declares it in a loud voice. And the
congregation responds with approbation. The modest among them are
reluctant to use up all their privileges in their lifetime, and when the
cantor proclaims: "He has contributed," the congregation responds,
"What he can afford." And when those ambitious for honor saw this,
they too began saying: "What he can afford," as the modest do, since it
is the nature of those ambitious for honor that money and respect are
not enough; they are not satisfied until they have also been awarded
the honor of being seen by the world to recoil from honor.

We shall yet tell of the schism that arose on account of a
bar-mitzvah donation, and how my grandfather of blessed memory
abolished this practice when he was appointed rabbi over them. And
how was money obtained from the Feast of Rabbi Shimon? It was
the custom at the Heaven's Gate Synagogue to celebrate the honor of
Rabbi Shimon Bar Yohai on the eve of *Lag BaOmer*. For people from

Morocco the celebration of Rabbi Shimon is extremely important: they light many candles in honor of Rabbi Shimon and of his son Rabbi Elazar, and in honor of Rabbi Meir the Miracle Worker, and in honor of the saints of all the generations, and in honor of the saints of Morocco: the saintly Rabbi Jacob Abouhatzeira, and the saintly Rabbi Amram Diwan, and the saintly Rabbi Haim Pinto who wrote the book *Shenot Haim,* and the saintly Rabbi David Ben Baruch Mazru, and Rabbi David Moshe. And between each candle and the next they sing songs and chant the praises of Rabbi Shimon, who established the reputation of the most celebrated of all the poets of Morocco, Rabbi David Hassin in the book *Psalm for David* which he printed in Amsterdam, and his brother-in-law Rabbi Aharon Hassin, who reprinted it in Casablanca. They make toasts, drinking arak that immigrants from Morocco have brought with them. And they eat a kind of pancake called an *ejjah,* made from meat and eggs and oil, and sugar cakes with coconut and honey, molded into shapes like towers. Because they drink, they are happy, and once they are happy, they drink more. And because they drink more, they become even happier, and they eat various kinds of strong pickles which make them thirsty, so they drink some more, singing a song of friendship for the beloved saints, the thirteen saints in particular, in Moroccan Arabic. The song translates as: *I went to visit my brother, I told the tzaddik what happened, I returned with joy in my heart, my prayer is accepted in Wazan, by the beloved Rabbi Amram Ben Diwan.*

Presiding over the repast is Madame Farha Buzaglo from Wazan, serving food and drinks and saying, "Alas for the feast of Rabbi Shimon! Do they call this a meal? In Wazan, when we laid on a meal—you should have seen it! We did it properly."

This feast had been given by the Buzaglo family for the past seven generations, ever since a miracle had been granted the matriarch of the family. Back then, when the entire family had gone to Wazan to visit the tomb of Ribi Amram and they were walking in the desert, Arabs attacked them on the way, stole all their money and absconded with the matriarch of the family. She cried out: "May the merit of Ribi Shimon and Ribi Amram defend me!" and repeated the name of Ribi Shimon numerous times. Then she slipped from the back of the donkey; none of the Arabs saw her, and she was able to make her escape. This was why the family had taken upon themselves the responsibility for and expenses for this feast. Madame Farha Buzaglo used to slaughter seventeen sheep and open a barrel of arak in honor of the celebration, while in the transit-camp she served omelettes and cakes. There, three hundred men and women sat down to dine, and here there are barely three *minyans*—less than thirty men. Besides, all this festivity is in honor of our Teacher and Master Rabbi Shimon who subsisted on a diet of roots and spring water for the thirteen years that he hid in a cave.

The celebrants read from the *Book of the Zohar,* which is renowned for its special quality of enlightening whoever reads it, even if he does not understand it. And sages preach to the diners on the subjects of numerology and the miraculous deeds of saints of yore, such as the story of Nahum Ish Gamzu, or of Rabbi Israel Abou-hatzeira who crossed a river on a mat when his enemies rose against him, and other tales of the saints. And all offer contributions with an open hand and a happy heart, since lighting a candle in honor of a *tzaddik* is a talisman for healthy sons and livelihood. Then finally the cantor declares before the entire congregation: "Praise the Lord for He is good, His grace will defend us, we and our brothers, the children of Israel."

So, one way or another, money came into the hands of the treasurers and they set about embellishing the synagogue. They bought white plaster and coated the interior walls of the hut, bought new benches, and repaired the holy ark, which was completely decrepit, fitting it with new wooden panels. On the ark were twin panels, made of wood and shaped to resemble the tablets of the covenant, with the Ten Commandments inscribed on them in abbreviated form and in pairs; *I am the Lord thy God* facing *Thou Shalt Not Kill,* since the shedding of blood is akin to contempt of the *Shekhinah*; *Thou Shalt Not Make Graven Images* facing *Thou Shalt Not Commit Adultery,* since idolatry is tantamount to being unfaithful to the *Shekhinah*; *Thou Shalt Not Take God's Name in Vain* facing *Thou Shalt Not Steal,* since the thief is fated to lie on oath, and this is blasphemy; *Remember the Sabbath Day to Keep it Holy* facing *Thou Shalt Not Bear False Wit-*

ness, since to profane the Sabbath is false witness against Creation; *Honor thy Father and thy Mother* facing *Thou Shalt Not Covet*, since the result of covetousness is the begetting of a son who does not honor his father.

The ark was old, and its decorative tablets were also old, their edges chipped, the letters on them blurred and the script worn. The treasurers replaced them with handsome new tablets, showing the text of the Commandments in letters of gleaming bronze. One person raised the question about what was to be done with the old broken tablets. Some said that since they were sacred artifacts they should be stored in a *genizah*; others said they had been designed for aesthetic purposes only and thus required no such storage. There was no one they could ask. Not that there was any shortage of erudite scholars in the transit-camp, as Ribi Aharon Hassin was there, and the revered father of the *Beit Din* in Mugador was there, and the great grandson of Ribi David Hassin was there, and Ribi Jacob Bardugo was there, and Ribi David Sabbagh, but having been removed from their places and uprooted from their abodes they were not recognized as sages worthy of consultation, for distance traveled diminishes respect. You find the same in the case of our father Abraham; when he went to *Eretz-Israel*, he was promised by the Holy One, Blessed be He: *I shall magnify your name*, as the distance traveled had diminished his name. He who has earned a blessing—his name shall be magnified, and he who has not earned a blessing—his name shall not be magnified. Regarding the old saying, that a sage that comes to *Eretz-Israel* is worth two sages who stay abroad, this means only that his wisdom will increase, not his reputation, for it is an everyday occurrence to see sages who used to be great men in their communities overseas coming to Jerusalem and finding their esteem dwindling away to nothing.

The treasurers did not know whom they could ask, but among them there was one who had heard of my grandfather as an arbiter on matters of *Halacha*. He told them: "Go to him."

So the two treasurers came to see grandfather. I opened the door to them and admitted them. After the customary courtesies and salutations, my grandfather asked them, "How can I be of assistance, gentlemen?"

They answered him: "We are the treasurers of the Heaven's Gate synagogue, and there is a question of *Halacha* that we need to ask. We hope that your honor will instruct us and give us a true judgment."

My grandfather's face lit up. In Aram Zova he had adjudicated in cases of divorce and desertion, levirate marriage and *halitzah*, inheritance and partnership, whereas in Israel not a single question had been put to him, not on the *Halacha* of mourning, nor even in the case of a dairy knife falling into a meat dish. And here at last there was an issue for his adjudication.

He wrapped himself in his cloak and said to them: "Ask your question, gentlemen." They said to him: "Broken tablets that were made for decorative purposes and are old, what is to be done with them?"

He answered them in a flash, "Nothing needs to be done with them, but put them beside the new tablets."

He assured them that the Talmud recommends that tablets and broken tablets alike should be kept in the ark. The treasurers were amazed, and were voluble in their approbation and respect. And they added, "Your honor is invited to worship with us on *Yom Kippur*," and they went away in peace.

After I had seen them on their way, I returned to my grandfather, and he said to me: "For a question like this they need a rabbi? In Aram Zova, a lad in the *kuttab* who had studied a few pages of Rashi could have answered them." Then he continued, his voice taking on a pedantic lilt: "They could have objected that tablets of the covenant are not the same as tablets made for decorative purposes, and the law of the ark of Testimony does not apply to the holy ark of the synagogue, and I then would have answered them according to the law, saying this is not a valid precedent, and furthermore I would have shown them that these tablets are not subject to the same regulations as the *parochet*, of which the *Shulhan Arukh* says that it must be hidden away securely, seeing that the Latter Prophets have already told us that this *parochet* was used for the wrapping of Torah scrolls, but these tablets are for ornamentation only, and because they are not attached to the ark they are not governed by the same rules, and thus they need no special treatment. But by way of allusion, I brought it about that the broken tablets are to be placed alongside the new tablets. And they could have objected that this being the case, why did I say they should be put in the ark, since the verdict of *Halacha* is that damaged parchments should not be placed in the ark, lest its sanctity be impaired. Because they did not press me on this point I did not answer them, and I led them in the direction to which their minds were inclined. Here, if no one asks then no one will answer."

In the end, because they had invited him so respectfully to worship with them, he accepted, since all synagogues were the same as far as he was concerned—equally distasteful in fact, as they did not worship in the style of Aram Zova. This is especially true during the Days of Awe when everyone longs for prayers after the fashion of his community and takes pleasure in no other tradition. Only the music of your father's house can awaken in you the spirit of repentance.

And thus it turned out that we were among the worshippers at the Heaven's Gate synagogue on that eventful day. It was between the silent prayer and the repetition of the *Mussaf* that the event occurred.

Chapter five

The Heaven's Gate synagogue was filled to capacity on *Yom Kippur*. There was no inhabitant of the transit-camp who did not come to pray—men and women, old and young. Most came to pray throughout the day, while a minority came only for the *Kal Nidre* and the closing prayer. People stood closely packed together, and were fasting, and yet no one complained of discomfort. The organizers had brought benches from the youth club and from the Yeshurun school, and chairs from the subsidized housing section and the health clinic section and every place where chairs were to be found, and put them between the rows, yet still there were not enough places. Early arrivals had the seats, and latecomers were forced to stand. Everyone was dressed in white and wrapped in white, since the worship of the day requires white clothing. The synagogue was filled with white *jallabias,* white suits, shoes of white canvas, and white caps, and even the stripes on the *tallits* were white and not black, so as not to detract from the purity and holiness of the day. Those who could read the text did so, and those who could not followed the cantor; and all chanted their responses in a loud and melodious voice in the tradition of Morocco. The cantor intones a verse, and they reply:

Amen. When he says: *Lord, open my lips,* they respond: *My mouth shall declare your praise;* when he says: *The God of Abraham and God of Isaac and God of Jacob,* they answer after him: *Peace be with them.* And the cantor chants the morning prayer with a wondrously tuneful lilt, and when he reaches the penitential prayers he switches to a penitential tone, since the strains of confession are mournful, and there is sorrow in them, blended with grief for the *Shekhinah* and the grief of exile and the grief of sin, but there is no despair in them. The tunes descend to the depths of the heart, and share in its dejection, and rise to musings of repentance, and trill to the rhythm of self-appraisal, before glowing once more with the spark of hope. As with the tunes of penitence, so it is with the poems of penitence. They begin with sorrow and gloom, and they end with forgiveness and conciliation. A somber spirit takes possession of the congregation, as they answer: *Amen, the Lord of Heaven is great* with all their might, in order to rescind the harsh decree, and recite once again, as if counting out gold coins: *Blessed be He and praised be He, may He be glorified and exalted, may He be raised up and adored, may He ascend and He be worshipped,* and they are not content until they have said: *His holy name be blessed.* And they bow their heads to confess, and beat their breasts with their fists: *We are guilty, we have betrayed, we have stolen,* and they recall their transgressions with a sigh and with a broken heart, and all weep. Some weep for the pains of the body and its infirmities, some weep for the torments of the soul and its wickedness. Some sigh for the grief of the *Shekhinah,* cast down into the dust by our iniquities, and some hear others weeping and begin to weep with them. For such is the nature of weeping, that it draws others to weep as well, as we have read in the tale of Rabban Gamliel, in whose vicinity a certain woman lived whose son died, and she would weep for him every night, and Rabban Gamliel heard her weeping, and he remembered the destruction of the Holy Temple and he cried bitterly too. The old men in the synagogue were like him, tears falling into their white beards and hanging there, glittering like jewels suspended on a thread.

And from the gallery, too, the sound of the keening of devout women may be heard. One stands in the corner and moans; in another corner one is whimpering. Old women among them sigh over their transgressions and ask for a painless, easy death, the middle-aged among them weep for their daughters who are unmarried, and the young girls among them weep because they see their mothers weeping. Such is the way of children, seeing their fathers and mothers weeping, and weeping in their turn. And babies cry, because it is time for them to eat and no one is paying attention to them, and seeing them cry their mothers silence them with a rebuke, and hearing their mothers scold them, they raise their voices and howl ever more loudly.

And the cantor proclaims with cantillaton: *And the Lord passed by him*, and the congregation bows its head in reverence, and when the cantor completes the verse and says: *And he cried*—at once they all feel their spirits revived and they cry aloud, as one man with one heart: *Lord, Lord, God compassionate and merciful*, and they count off the thirteen degrees of mercy, and it is a sound to cleave hearts asunder. And after the penitential prayers they all sing in a tone of conciliation, as if pardon is guaranteed: *For on that day he shall make atonement for you to cleanse you, that you may be cleansed before the Lord of all your sins*, and the word *cleansed* they sing in a loud voice, and prolong it. The perceptive among them find their attention drawn to the words of Rabbi Akiva in the *Mishnah*: *Blessed are you, O Israel. Before whom are you made clean and who makes you clean? Your Father in Heaven, as it is said: The Lord is the hope* [mikveh] *of Israel. As the ritual bath* [mikveh] *cleanses the unclean, so does the Holy One, Blessed Be He, Blessed Be He, cleanse Israel.* And those who do not know how to pray with intent direct their prayers with those who pray with intent. And this verse they repeat twenty-six times on *Yom Kippur*, twenty-six being the numerical equivalent of the ineffable name of God. And then they chant songs set to pleasant melodies, each according to the custom of his communities.

The people of Fez, of Meknes and of the Atlas have different customs and songs, but on *Rosh Hashanah* and *Yom Kippur* they recite the same penitential songs. And the folk of Morocco are filled with love of the Almighty, and love of the Torah, and love of Israel, and they are fired by enthusiasm and emotion. And when they sing, they sing with all their might, and when they sigh and weep, they sigh with all their heart, and when they are contented and happy, they are happy with their whole being. Show me the heart that will not melt like water on this day of awe. Who will not bow down and seek reconciliation with his Father who is in Heaven?

After the silent prayer of the *Mussaf* and before the repetition was when it happened, as the *hazan* was about to recite in tremulous tones the hymn *Lord I have heard your report and I am afraid*, which was written in piety and in purity, and which all the *Sepharadi* congregations recite on *Yom Kippur* before the repetition—except those of Aram Zova, who do not pause for anything between the whispered prayer and the Repetition.

Similar to this hymn is another composed by Ribi David Hassin. We have already mentioned that Ribi David Hassin was the greatest liturgical poet of Morocco and that he composed a great tome of songs, entitled *Psalm to David*. And every one of the songs was filled with blazing fire and holy reverence, love of the Name and love of *Eretz-Israel*. He also wrote songs relating to Shimon Bar Yohai, and Tiberias, and to Jerusalem the Holy City, all of them composed in rhyming verse. It used to be said of Ribi David Hassin that all his speeches, whether sacred or profane, were in verse. It was also said of him that never in his life did he hold a secular conversation on the Sabbath, nor from the start of the month of *Elul* to *Yom Kippur*. It was he who composed the well-known hymn, so full of yearning: *I hope day by day and I wonder, my soul always awaiting, when shall I come and see, the holy ground of Tiberias*. And it was he who composed the delightful hymn for the rite of circumcision: *Praise shall be my utterance*. People of his town said he lived in abject poverty but was an outstanding scholar, and that he knew by heart all the *Halachic* regulations concerning the ritual slaughter of animals. He had wanted to be appointed a slaughterer, but this was not allowed, as the business was held as a prerogative by three families. As they caused him sorrow, we do not mention them by name, and he, who was a lover of peace and a seeker of peace, did not argue with them. What did he do in his poverty and gloom? He sat down night after night in the *Beit Midrash* and put all the regulations regarding slaughter and uncleanness into verse. The house of Ribi Raphael Bardugo, the *Av* or head of the *Beit Din*, (whose nickname was Angel Raphael), was near the *Beit Midrash*. He heard the poetry and was amazed. He immediately appointed him supervisor of the slaughterers. In time, Ribi David added this hymn to his *Psalm to David.*

This was the Ribi David Hassin whose reputation stretched from one end of Morocco to the other, and he who composed an awesome hymn, which a few of the congregations used to recite on *Yom Kippur.* And it was on account of this hymn that the synagogue was in such an uproar.

Chapter six

Before the repetition, the cantor began intoning the hymn *'Lord I heard your report and I was afraid.'* When he came to declaim the first line and said: *Lord I have heard and I was perturbed, the day you visited me I feared the day whereon you would judge me*—a member of the congregation leapt forward and quoted a line from the hymn of Ribi David Hassin. The cantor was stunned into silence. Straight away someone else sprang up to oppose him, saying: "Cantor, cantor, open your lips and let your words shine forth!"

Then two of the leading members of the congregation stood up, thumping their prayer books. "Honor! Honor the sanctity of this place, good people!"

Then three more rose in their turn to confront them, throwing their prayer books down and exclaiming, "Honor Ribi David Hassin!"

Others stood up and yelled: "In Meknes, this is how they read!"

Others answered them with mockery: "In the royal city of Fez they don't say that."

Another member of the congregation rose, put his right hand

to his ear and began to trill the hymn of Ribi David Hassin. Others followed his example. The cantor standing by the ark was utterly at a loss, while all around there were cries of: "Cantor, cantor! The *Mussaf* please, the *Mussaf*! Gentlemen! Gentlemen!"

Some were standing and others sitting, some stamping their feet and others calling out, some yelling and others demanding silence, until the synagogue was all strife and contention. The cantor knocked on the ark with his fist and announced the start of *Mussaf* while others were still shouting out the words of the hymn. Every voice was raised. One man said to his neighbor, "My hometown is far more important than yours," and the other answered him, "Not at all, my hometown is more important than yours."

One of them clutched at the clothing of another, someone knocked the cap from someone else's head; soon there were all the makings of a brawl.

While all this was happening, one old man was standing by himself, elegantly dressed in white and of fine stature, with a long white beard and eyes that were big and blue, beautiful and kind. Everything about him bespoke dignity. During the fracas he was shaking his head from side to side. Standing close to him, I heard him murmur: Ribi David, why not Ribi David?

I was new to this synagogue, and did not know him either. The congregation was a mix of communities and émigrés from different lands, and for this reason there were others who did not know him. One worshipper heard him, and thought he was saying: Who is this Ribi David?—and he silenced him with a stern rebuke, saying: "Who are you to speak so of the sweetest singer of Israel?"

The worshipper was not satisfied until he had jostled the man with his elbow. The impetuous one did not know that in his zeal for Ribi David he had insulted a most distinguished old man, and on *Yom Kippur* as well. Such is the way of zeal, that it drives a man out of his senses. The old man was Ribi Aharon Hassin, son of Ribi Raphael Hassin, son of Ribi Avraham Hassin, son of none other than the renowned versifier Ribi David Hassin, composer of the *Psalm to David*.

Throughout the fracas I was sitting beside my grandfather of revered memory. In Aram Zova he had been accustomed to guiding his congregation with a firm hand. I watched him to see what he would do here. He seemed to be stunned. He said nothing. To be sure, even in Aram Zova harmony did not always prevail. If the cantor made a mistake in grammar or in pronunciation when reading from the Torah, or transposed the initial letters of words, the congregation would correct him, and scold him severely. And he would repeat his recitation exactly as before, especially if his text was one of the psalms. As if saying: You mind your business and I shall mind mine. And there were times when a certain member of the congregation admired his own voice rather more than the world admired it, and he would unleash it at full volume in the responses to the penitential prayers, and others would silence him with a stern rebuke. There were a number of such instances of friction. But we never witnessed disputes in the time between the *shaharit* and *mussaf* prayers on *Yom Kippur*. Until that moment we had been moved by the prayers, and even though we didn't recognize the songs and the tunes, and it is not human nature to be affected by melodies other than those of one's father's house, the prayers that we heard nevertheless struck a chord in our hearts—and then suddenly all was bluster and mayhem and sanctity was forgotten.

All this time grandfather was sitting in silence, until Ribi Aharon Hassin was jostled. At that moment he said to me: "Surely that is Ribi Aharon!" And he rose from his seat and made his way to the ark. His gait was proud and resolute, and made an impression in the synagogue. All at once there was silence. Grandfather stood before the ark, facing the congregation, thinking for a few moments as he used to do before preaching, and then looked all around with his black and penetrating eyes. When he began to speak, there were tears in those eyes:

"*Blessed are you, O Israel. Before whom are you made clean and who makes you pure, your Father who is in Heaven. As it is written: And I shall sprinkle clean water upon you and you shall be pure. And it is written: The Lord is the hope of Israel.* My brothers and my friends, never in my life have I paused between the silent prayer and the repetition of the *Mussaf*, not even for songs, less for banalities. And never have I reproached the congregation on *Yom Kippur,* since on *Yom Kippur* all Israel is sanctified like the seraphim, and it is forbidden to mention their transgressions, but one must rather present their merits before the Lord. However, for the sake of peace I am prepared to change my ways. So great is peace, it is one of the names by which the Almighty is called."

And so grandfather began speaking to them, words of reproof and words of conciliation, words hard as sinews and sayings gentle and mellifluous. The congregation were all truly God-fearing, and although the devil of contention had danced before them, on this day even his power was flagging—and they accepted his strictures. Scholars say that in numerology the letters for 'Satan' are equivalent to 364—the days of the year aside from the one day of *Yom Kippur,* when the devil does not prevail. I don't know if these things were said by way of parable, or to uncover an esoteric meaning, which is not our concern. It seems to me, he was seen dancing on *Yom Kippur* too. Numerology stands still, while Satan goes his own way. At all events, his strength is diminished on this day.

Grandfather went to Ribi Aharon Hassin, and invited him to come up and sit beside the holy ark. The man who had disdained him now approached, took his hands and kissed them. In the congregation too there was kissing and reconciliation between opponents, and this is to the great credit of the Jews of Morocco, who do not bear grudges and, however indignant they may become with one another, always make peace in the end and remain firm and loving friends. Grandfather stepped forward and said: *Hazan,* the *Mussaf* if you please! All stood for the *Mussaf* and the service returned to its normal course.

After the service I kissed grandfather's hands, and then I went on to kiss the hands of Ribi Aharon Hassin. He laid his hand on my head and blessed me, kissed my forehead, and invited me to visit him. From that time onward, steadfast friendship was forged between grandfather and Ribi Aharon Hassin. Every Sabbath after the service they used to discuss matters of Torah, and Ribi Aharon would tell my grandfather of the judgments he made when he was the *Av,* or head of the *Beit Din* for the Alcazar district, and grandfather used to debate against him, and tell him of the sermons he had preached in Aram Zova.

At the close of *Yom Kippur,* the treasurers of the synagogue asked grandfather to serve as their rabbi. Rabbi of the Heaven's Gate synagogue. He agreed, on the condition that Ribi Aharon Hassin sit with him. Grandfather held him in the very highest regard, although on account of his age and the rigors of his travels, he had forgotten some of his learning. They asked grandfather to preach to them every Sabbath after *Minha,* and he agreed, on condition that Ribi Aharon be invited to preach one Sabbath out of every four. So from that time onward, my grandfather of revered memory had his regular place of worship in the Heaven's Gate synagogue, in the Asbestonia transit-camp. Some new habits he instilled in them, and some aberrations he corrected. He pronounced judgment on essential questions, such as what is to be done if mistakes are found in a text of the Torah as it is being read; most rabbis are nervous of questions such as these, since an immediate decision is required, and the whole congregation is waiting and the Torah is laid open. And there are some mistakes which require the provision of an alternative Torah scroll, and some which do not, and mistakes which one shows to a child to see if he can read it, and some mistakes for which one must recite the blessing again over the second scroll.

He introduced some of the practices of Aram Zova, and they accepted them, such as the practice of not pausing for a hymn between the silent prayer and the repetition, and to sing songs after the repetition. And he also abolished the practice of selling the right to the highest bidder to read from the Torah. There was a youth who had been preparing himself for months to read the *Haftorah* on the Sabbath that he came of age, but he had a competitor who also wanted to read it. Reading the *Haftorah* is especially beloved of worshippers for a number of reasons, some of them worthy and some not. The father of the youth offered a larger donation so his son would not be disappointed, and his rival also increased his bid. In the end, the youth's father succeeded in buying the right to read the *Haftorah* for a considerable sum of money—far more than he could afford. After the Sabbath, my grandfather of blessed memory summoned the man and told him: "You don't need to donate any more than you offered in the first place." The treasurers protested this decision, claiming the synagogue's resources would suffer as a result. Grandfather, as resolute and determined as only a sage of Aram Zova could be, told them: "This is an issue of *Halacha*, and I decide on issues of *Halacha* in this synagogue—you do not." However, they insisted: "It's an issue of finance, and we are responsible for community funds." Still, grandfather would not budge. He was so irate that he refused to preach, and when a number of Sabbaths had passed without sermons, all the treasurers came to visit him in his home, and the quarrel was resolved. Henceforward, the practice of selling rights in the synagogue was discontinued.

The Chief Rabbi of *Eretz-Israel*, Rabbi Isaac Halevi Herzog, may the memory of a *tzaddik* be blessed, was a *Gaon* and a man of sensitive heart. He dearly loved all the people of Israel, and had a special fondness for scholars. Envoys coming from Aram Zova to *Eretz-Israel* used to tell the chief rabbi about grandfather and his erudition. Grandfather used to send him questions and the chief rabbi would respond, and firm bonds of friendship were forged between them. Yet when we arrived in *Eretz-Israel*, grandfather was so occupied with his other concerns that it never occurred to him to visit the chief rabbi.

In the year 5718, (1959) Rabbi Herzog died. A pall of gloom descended on the rabbinical world, and a solemn funeral service was held for him in Jerusalem. It was announced that the memorial eulogies would be delivered at Hechal Shlomo, the Great Synagogue in the center of Jerusalem. Grandfather heard where it would be held and wanted to go. I went with him. We stood with crowds of mourners coming to pay their respects.

Grandfather pointed to a certain distinguished looking man and said to me: "Go over to him and tell him that I would like to say a few words as a tribute to the chief rabbi. Tell him that there are things he said to me that are not generally known, and that I feel I should reveal them now, in honor of his memory."

The man that he pointed out to me had one of the finest intellects in all Jerusalem; an admirer of sages, he was himself a scholar of great erudition, and one of the few who became acquainted with grandfather when he arrived in the country and knew of his merits. He supervised a number of agencies dealing with immigration to *Eretz-Israel*. I passed on grandfather's message, and he said to me: "So you are the sage's grandson? Your grandfather is a great man, and a phenomenal preacher, but here his merits are not recognized. There are so many famous rabbis giving eulogies here, that I can't ask the organizers to allow one who is unknown to participate."

I went back to report to grandfather, and found him amid a crowd of people who had come in honor of the deceased, hemmed in on every side. When I told him what the dignitary had said, he was silent. I could see how hurt he was, but he said nothing, and listened to the speeches of the rabbis on the podium. Later he told me:

"All the rabbis and yeshiva teachers in *Eretz-Israel* were there that day. If they had given me just two minutes to speak…"

He had more to say, but was silent.

Chapter seven

Fr a long time I had wanted to visit Ribi Aharon Hassin. I was eager to hear about Meknes and Mugador and Ziaro and other cities of Morocco where there were large communities, each with its *Beit Din* and *yeshiva* and Talmud Torah. And I had another reason, which I kept to myself. I knew Ribi Aharon was the great grandson of the marvelous poet Ribi David Hassin, and I knew he had manuscripts of Ribi David that had never been published. As a lover of liturgical poetry, I wanted to see them.

One day grandfather called me, handed me a book entitled *Ketzot Hahoshen* and said to me: "Go to Ribi Aharon Hassin in the transit-camp, and give him this book. He wants to read it and he can't find a copy."

I was glad of this mission, and I made my way to the camp. The shacks that made up the camp stood on square slabs of concrete, and some of them were painted in garish shades of blue and pink. In winter the camp was a muddy morass, with rainwater flowing down from the hills and accumulating there. Rubble and planks were strewn about in the mud, and you had to jump over these obstacles to gain access to the shacks. Each shack was divided into two apartments, and in each of these there was one large room and one small. The small room contained a sink and a stove. The larger room served both as a living and sleeping quarters, with mattresses and blankets spread out at night and rolled up and folded away by day. Ribi Aharon's shack was close to the synagogue. I clambered over boulders and arrived there.

Ribi Aharon opened the door to me, his eyes as bright and playful as ever. He wore a black oval turban and was wrapped in a white gown with a broad blue sash, and over his shoulders was a bright red silk shawl of the kind known as a *sudra*, all of which was typical garb of the sages of Morocco. He kissed me on the head and cried: *"Blessed is he who comes in the name of the Lord, we have blessed you from the house of the Lord."*

I entered. On the walls I saw a drawing of Ribi Shimon Bar Yohai, and a drawing of the Rambam, and two gleaming brass plates. I also saw a very fine carpet, a checkered pattern in green and red, and woven into it in letters of gold was the verse: *So he has anointed you with the oil of gladness above your fellows.* In a corner of the room was a shelf, and on it silver candlesticks and a brass *Hanukkah* lamp, and against the wall leaned a carved wooden walking stick topped with a silver knob. Ribi Aharon saw me looking at the stick and he said: Pick it up, take a closer look. I picked up the stick and turned it over in my hands, and saw a verse inscribed on it: *They shall go from strength to strength and appear before the Lord in Zion.*

He told me, with a musical, sing-song lilt to his voice: "The people of Alcazar are lovers of the Torah, and the day I was informed, the day I was included, in the number of those who would go up to Zion, to see its light, they gave me this mighty staff, may the Lord remember their kindness, and save and preserve their congregation."

He took my hand in his and went on to say: "And this carpet that you behold, with the verse inscribed upon it, was woven for me by the good folk of my congregation, the congregation of Mugador-the-Fair. It was made to honor me on reaching my sixtieth year, safe at last from the threat of untimely death, and entering old age, may they be rewarded with a good ending. And that *Hanukkah* lamp that you see, with the eight branches, is more precious to me than any treasure, for it is a memorial to and an inheritance from my forefathers. I got it from my father, whose memory I cherish, who inherited it from his father, and his father from the splendor and the glory of Judah, the sweetest singer and poet of Israel, the wondrous versifier, his name be ever great, Ribi David Hassin. He was a very poor man, wandering among the communities in search of livelihood, and dipping his bread in tears. He sought a printer for his books and anthems, and the quest took him to Amsterdam, where the prince of philanthropists, Sabbagh, chanced to discover him, and Ribi Hassin and his wonder are revealed to us in his book—all praise to the one who stands before the throne of glory with ministering angels by his side."

He took an ornate silver snuff-box from his pocket, and offering me snuff, said: "And this was presented to me by my master and my teacher and my close friend, Haim Bardugo, may the memory of a *tzaddik* be blessed—the delver into deep waters, and scholar of the Talmud and so knowledgeable on the decisions of the rabbis—for in his presence I studied the *Arba'ah Turim, The Four Columns,* and we were as cubs before the lion, and when he laid his hand on me in mercy—I with lesser intelligence than an ant—he gave me this as a gift, as a souvenir and a comfort in our time of distress."

Again he said: *"Blessed is he who comes in the name of the Lord."* And then: *"My beloved shall come to his garden and eat his delicious fruit."* He set out before me pastry cakes with coconut and little colored sweets strewn on them, and almonds in date paste. I said to him: "My grandfather asked me to bring you this book, sir."

He took the book and opened it at random, and then said: "Be so kind as to excuse me," and rose from his seat and then returned with a wooden box. Carefully, he opened the box and took out a locked metal case. There was a key hanging from a string about his neck, and he leaned over, and unlocked the case with it, taking from it a bundle that was all wrapped and tied up. Removing the outer wrapping and untying the knots, he revealed spools wrapped in brown paper and bound with red ribbons. He untied them carefully, and then spread out a paper scroll before me. He showed me where it was written: '*Zevah Todah*—Thanksgiving Feast—Responsa and Novel *Halachic* Rulings on the Four Sections of the *Shulhan Arukh,* by the distinguished scholar Aharon Ben Hassin.' Then he showed me the response where he referred to the *Ketzot Hahoshen*. He took out another bundle of writings and I knew these were songs of Ribi David Hassin that had never been published. I became very excited. All this time he wanted to show me the innovations and responsa that he had produced, and I wanted to see his great-grandfather's hymns. What we want to see people don't show us, and what they show us we don't look at.

He told me: "In Meknes I was a judge, and in Alcazar I was the head of the *Beit Din*. My expertise was in the *Halacha* of slaughter and the laws of *Kashrut*, and no one declared an animal unkosher in that city until I had been consulted, and every slaughterer had to show me his knife. I also debated in the *yeshiva* of the sages over the novellae of Ribi Raphael Bardugo, until we were content, and everything as joyful and luminous as if it had been given from Sinai. After the *Shaharit* prayer we would sit down to engage in the study of *Halacha*, and we dissected the problem until we had reached a practical solution, having recourse to the Talmud and the medieval authorities, former Prophets, *Beit Yoseph* and legal precedents."

His face brightened still further and he said: "I had a large book printed in Meknes, and I called it *Aharon's Staff*, after my name, and it contains the responsa literature and insights into the *Shulhan Arukh*, the *Yoreh De'ah*, a section concerning things permitted and prohibited, and also a great deal drawn from the works of that angel Raphael Bardugo."

His face, which had brightened, dimmed a little and his kindly eyes filled with tears, and he said: "I have another bundle of writings, amendments to the *Halacha* of slaughter—the *Zevah Todah* is the name that I gave it. This, too, I would dearly like to see in print, but there is no one who will help me."

He went on to say: "Believe me, young sir, I am old and I am gray, but still I have the power in my loins to go forth and fight the battles of the Torah. As my strength was then, so it is now. But my books are not here, and there are no erudite scholars here with whom to discuss *Halacha*, as this camp is a mixture of so many communities from so many lands, some of them without work and some of them with too much work. Those who work are anxious for their livelihood, and those who don't work are anxious because they're not working; and mothers, who toil all day, and age, their faces turn gray between oven and sink; … and our sages who go unrecognized—may the Merciful One have pity on all of them. Our teachers used to say: Three gifts the Almighty gave to Israel, all of them attainable only through pain: *Eretz-Israel*, the Torah, and the World to Come. Look at Hacham Zorfati, who taught *Halacha* in the synagogue of the artisans in Mugador, and here he has become a digger of holes in the hills. They say they are going to plant trees there to enrich *Eretz-Israel* with their fruit. He is hard at work from sunrise to sunset. Or Hacham Peretz Attia, who used to preach in Mugador, and is now an assistant clerk in at the local health clinic. But many are His mercies, in that we have been granted the right to breathe the air of *Eretz-Israel* and to see the beauty of Jerusalem."

He went on to say: "Every night when the members of the household are asleep I take out the text of *Zevah Todah*, copying and checking, improving and amending as far as I am able. I am sure that the moment the book appears, the greatest scholars of *Eretz-Israel* will see it and will take me away from this camp, and they will appoint me a judge in one of the cities of Israel, and once again I shall be busy with new interpretations of the Torah, and teaching to the best of my ability. I do not seek honor for myself, as I am already old and gray, and I have seen that honor is vanity of vanities, but it is my ardent wish to learn and to teach, to arbitrate and to innovate, to repair all the parts of my soul. And as Rabbi Haim David Azoulai has written, a man has not repaired all the parts of his soul until he has published all the innovations that he has produced."

I asked him to lend me the hymns of Ribi David, or let me copy them, and he refused. He told me: "Important people from the university in Jerusalem have already been here in the camp, and they asked me to give them the writings of my esteemed great-grandfather, so they can publish them. I told them: 'By all means, by all means, gentlemen. I shall be delighted to see the works of Ribi David published, bringing light to the world.' But I made one condition with them. Together with the songs they should also publish the book

Zevah Todah, which I wrote in my penury. They argued with me, saying their funds were limited and the needs of the university many, and books of rabbinical responsa are not in demand just now. I answered them that *Halachic* guidance is precisely what this generation needs, and furthermore, it would do the songs of Ribi David credit to be published together with judgments and precepts; in Morocco, sages who conduct arbitration are also composers of hymns, as hymns are praise to the Creator may He be blessed, and are a delight to God and to man, while refined and revised verdicts are the finest fruit of all man's labor, as has been said of them: *The statutes of the Lord are right and they bring joy to the heart.* They gave whatever answer they gave. I once again presented my reasoned and logical argument, adducing persuasive testimony from the Bible and from *Midrash*. In the end, they said they would discuss the matter at the next meeting of the university council, and would tell me of their decision. So, I am not letting this bundle out of my hands. And whenever I feel distressed, I open the songs of Ribi David, and read his praises of *Eretz-Israel*. For all its sorrows, this is still the finest of all lands."

He began to recite to me one of the longer songs, opening as follows: *I David Ben Hassin declare, I shall set out a song and an anthem, for the glory of a pure and precious land, in sacral tunes and lucid tongue... How pleasant is her dwelling, how broad, at the very hub of the universe, a city high and fortified, wondrous is her love for the very holiness of her, her air gives increase of wisdom and reason. Gather in our dispersion and as I leave Meknes behind, grant me a miracle, and quickly restore the crown to its place."*

So he continued reciting the hymn. He was moved, and tears streamed from his eyes for the love of *Eretz-Israel*. I too was moved. I kissed his hand and parted from him in peace.

Chapter eight

On the eve of the holy Sabbath where the Torah portion that was read was: *For you shall lift up the head of the Children of Israel*, the Hasidic rabbi from Nadvorna died. It is the norm in Jerusalem that the dead are not kept there overnight on account of the sanctity of the place, and so the funeral had to be held before the Sabbath.

Outside the shack that was the synagogue, five or six of his followers were gathered, including his son and his brother-in-law and his uncle and his cousin, intending to pay their respects. Not only was it the Sabbath Eve, but the day was overcast, and frantic efforts were made to gather a congregation together to honor the deceased. I was in the habit of completing the *minyan* at his Sabbath table, and when they summoned me to attend, I went there. The rabbi's wife saw me, and she wept bitter tears and moaned, crying: "A rabbi who had thousands of loyal disciples in Rumania—but here there's not even a *minyan* to bury him. Who knows him here? Who knows his reverend fathers? Who knows of his deeds? His reverend fathers in the Garden of Eden will come and attend him at his funeral. They will testify to his deeds."

So she wept inconsolably, on and on.

There was no one to deliver his eulogy. I told them: "I shall call my grandfather and he will do it. My grandfather is an outstanding preacher, and whenever a minister or senior official died in Aram Zova, he would preach for him, he and no other." I ran to call grandfather. At the time he was sitting reading the *Targum* with the Ramban's commentary, as was his wont every Sabbath eve. I asked him to come and deliver the eulogy for the Teacher and Master from Nadvorna. He consented.

He rose and dressed in his most solemn garb, meticulous about his clothing as always. He found a matching suit and tie and hat, and put a shine on his shoes. He took up a pair of scissors and trimmed his beard. He wrapped a scarf around his neck, and then noticed the scarf was gray while the suit was black, so he changed into another suit. Now the hat did not match, so he was obliged to change that too. He saw a speck of dust on his hat, so that had to be brushed away. And every item of attire, before it was put on, had to be checked to be sure it was unblemished; for, as it is written in the Talmud: *Any scholar seen with a flaw in his clothing deserved the death penalty.* I pressed him, telling him time was short, but he was not to be hurried. He saw a crease in the hat, so that was changed yet again. Eventually he wrapped himself in his cloak and accompanied me to the transit-camp. We stood outside the synagogue shack, as the rain began to fall. The *minyan* of Hasidim had been swelled by a handful of elderly local residents, who had come to pay their respects to the deceased. You could tell they were impatient to get on with the business of the Sabbath, and that honoring the dead was an impediment to their routine.

Since the day he had arrived in *Eretz-Israel*, grandfather had not officiated at a single funeral. Now he stood and began in a tearful voice: "Pay heed to an old man who has forgotten his learning, and I will explain why tablets and broken tablets are placed in the ark. Once there was a king who found a flaw in one of the jewels in his crown, and asked his craftsmen to repair it. All the most skilled craftsmen came, but could do nothing, and then a layman came and repaired it. The king asked his viziers: 'How can it be that all these craftsmen worked on the jewel and failed, while this layman succeeded?' They told him: 'The craftsmen are aware of the king's majesty and the value of the jewel, and they feared lest they damage the king's crown, but the layman saw only a stone that needed repairing.' And the moral of this fable: For the Teacher and Master (he did not refer to the name of his city, for fear of mispronouncing it), there are many wise men qualified to preach over him, yet they called upon the layman who can do no harm. The jewel that is lost, wherever it is—is still a jewel, it is lost only to its owner, so wherever the Teacher and Master is, his teaching remains with him. He is lost only to us."

His accent was *Sepharadi*, and his speech almost unintelligible to the rabbi's wife and most of the Hasidim, but his words moved them all the same. As the eulogy proceeded, he turned, with renewed warmth, to extolling the merits of *Eretz-Israel*: "The greatest of the sages would embrace the boundaries of *Eretz-Israel* and kiss its stones and wallow in its dust, as it is said, *For your servants take pleasure in her stones and favor her dust.* Even those who have come down from the high status that used to be theirs in other lands would rather sit in the dust of *Eretz-Israel.* The Teacher and Master, he had so many disciples in Rumania, and there he was enthroned on high. Our sages have told us that every dweller in *Eretz-Israel* will be forgiven his sins, for merely taking four paces on its soil is enough to merit life in the world hereafter. And everyone buried therein will be absolved, as it has been said, *He shall make expiation for his land and his people.* And his reception in life is not the same as his reception after death, and yet the greatest of sages used to bring their dead there, as you may learn from Jacob our father and from Joseph the righteous.

"And now to the main point (thus the preachers of Aleppo used to say when broaching the main theme of the sermon): Pay heed to an old man who has forgotten his learning, the reason why tablets and broken tablets are both placed in the ark. The Torah tells us: *There is not in the ark only two tablets of stone.* 'Not' is written and 'only' is written—two negatives which constitute an affirmation. And what is affirmed, if not the broken tablets which are likewise stored in the ark. And here is a surprise. We find, that when the Almighty commended Moses our teacher, peace be with him, he said: *And there arose in Israel no prophet the equal of Moses, whom the Lord knew face to face, in all the signs and the wonders which the Lord sent him to do…* and in conclusion, *And in all that mighty hand and in the great terror which Moses showed in the sight of all Israel,* and our teachers have interpreted this as meaning, that he broke the tablets before them. And the Lord condoned his act, saying: *The tablets that you broke, you have done well in breaking them.* And here is a surprise: what possessed Moses our teacher, peace be with him, to break tablets which were the work of God? Twenty-six generations on from the Day of Creation, and the entire universe in great suspense, awaiting his utterance and the giving of the law, and Moses *breaks* them? The Almighty said to him: *Go, go down, for your people are corrupted, and they have made for themselves a molten calf,* and yet despite this He gave him the tablets and did not tell him to break them, so why did Moses stop and break them? But if you peruse the text you will see it says: *And so it was, when he came near to the camp and he saw the calf and the dancing, the wrath of Moses was kindled and he cast down the tablets from his hand and smashed them beneath the mountain.* Moses knew that they were worshipping the calf—God had told him so—but it was when he saw them dancing before the idol that he stopped and smashed the tablets, and God allowed this act to take place. And this being the case, our teachers of blessed memory have told us, tablets and broken tablets are stored in the ark, and these fragments are surely there to remind us of our transgression.

"And furthermore I ask you, my friends, the people of Israel who in that generation were worthy to receive Torah from the mouth of the Almighty, and were like prophets, and said, *we shall do and we shall hear,* to the extent that the ministering angels placed two crowns on the head of every one of them—how did they fall from the greatest height to the deepest depth, brought down by the sin of the calf, *While the king sits at his table and my spikenard gives forth its fragrance*? Our teachers expound that when Israel came out of Egypt they were steeped in forty-nine stages of uncleanness, and day by day they came out from a stage of uncleanness and entered a stage of purity, until they attained forty-nine stages of purity and received the Torah from Sinai. This ascent was beyond the scope of nature: for how can a man leap from forty-nine stages of uncleanness to forty-nine stages of purity in forty-nine days? As is said in the Book of Ezekiel: *And I passed by you and I saw your time was the time of love, and I spread my wing over you and covered your nakedness, and I swore to you, and entered into a covenant with you, says the Lord, and you became mine, and I washed you with water, washed the blood from upon you and anointed you with oil. And I clothed you with robes of brocade and shod you in badger-hide and girdled you with fine linen and covered you with silk, and adorned you with ornaments and put bracelets on your hands and a chain on your neck, and a ring for your nose, and pendants for your ears, and a beautiful crown on your head. You were decked in gold and silver, and your clothing was fine linen and silk and brocade, and you had flour and honey and oil to eat and you were very lovely and you prospered, you were a queen.* And because this ascent was beyond the scope of nature, the people fell from it. For what a man earns without toil and trouble does not remain in his possession. And that is why Israel failed and needed forty years of toil and repair before they rose once more to their proper station. And this matter is hinted at in the tablets. The first tablets were broken when the People of Israel fell from their station, and the second tablets, of which it was said *Fashion for yourself,* and on which Moses labored—they are the ones that remain with them.

"And if you say, if this be the case, what was the point of the first tablets which were so important, if they are broken, and for what purpose did the Almighty raise them to forty-nine stages of purity if they fell from them?—our teachers have shown us by way of allusion that the unborn child in his mother's womb is taught the Torah in its entirety, as it is said: *Who will give back to me the moons of old, the days when God watched over me and his candle shone above my head, and by his light I walked through the darkness.* Yet as soon as the unborn child emerges into the light of the world, an angel strikes him on the chin and makes him forget. And all his life he has to strive to regain what he has forgotten. And here, too, the question may be asked: What is the point in learning Torah if you forget it? But the Almighty delights in the good of Israel, and he brought them to their high degree in forty-nine stages of purity, and although they were destined to fall from it, all their days they would long to rise to it again. For it is not a new thing to them. For this reason the Torah has commanded that tablets and broken tablets be kept in the ark, so that Israel shall know of the degree of purity before the sin and long to return to it. So—pay heed to an old man who has forgotten his learning—this is why tablets and broken tablets are placed in the ark."

The crowd was becoming restive, gesturing to him that it was time to draw to a close, but he carried on preaching in his own particular style. It seemed he was no longer in the transit-camp, but in the precincts of the synagogue of Ezra the Scribe in Aram Zova, and there were not six or seven Hasidim listening to him, but a great crowd. When the sermon was finished he said to me: "Did I preach well? We have paid our respects to the deceased, and accompanied him on his last journey."

₫

After the funeral grandfather said to me: "Since we are in the camp, come with me to visit Ribi Aharon Hassin. I have heard he is unwell."

We went to his house, and found him lying on his bed reading Psalms. When he saw grandfather, he sat up. He was clearly very weak, but within moments the two of them were debating an issue of *Halacha* and his face lit up. They passed from the Bible to the *Mishnah* and from the *Mishnah* to the Talmud and from the Talmud to the arbiters of the law, and all their discourse was illuminating. Ribi Aharon Hassin rose to his feet with an effort, and said: "This is an issue that I have not considered for some thirty years, and I remember the phrasing of it as clearly as if I had heard it today. Thirty-two years ago a difficult question concerning *Halacha* came before us in the *Beit Din* at Alcazar, and all the dialecticians labored over it. For seven weeks they weighed and scoured it, until the Lord gave light to my eyes and I was graced with a profound reevaluation of the whole issue of levirate marriage. And all the sages rejoiced and accorded me great respect. There were even scholars in Jerusalem who heard of it and sent me commendations. That day I began writing my thesis entitled *Zevah Todah*, and gathering together all the innovations I had made in the field of *Halacha*. I don't know if I will still see it in print within my own lifetime, but I do know for a fact that one day students in the *Beit Midrash* will find it indispensable."

He began outlining the reevaluation to grandfather. Grandfather responded with examples drawn from another context and countered his argument in the style of the Rambam. Grandfather said: "In Aram Zova the students knew that if they had a question to ask about the Rambam, they should turn to me. There are many who consider themselves authorities on the Rambam, but they tend to go astray. The language of the Rambam was a language of gold—he never added a syllable that was not needed, or omitted a single letter from its proper place. And when I read to them from the Rambam in the way that it should be read, some difficulties were already resolved for them, and after a few words of explanation every problem was as clear as day."

Ribi Aharon had to make strenuous efforts, but he replied to him and it was a happy occasion, like a gift from Sinai. At that moment I saw their faces lit up by the light of the Torah. Since the day grandfather had arrived in *Eretz-Israel*, I hadn't seen his face as bright and his eyes as happy as they were then. During the conversation Ribi Aharon turned to me again and asked for my help with the publishing of his book, so that even if this were not granted to him in life, it would be granted after his death. And he said that his sons had promised to lend their efforts to the enterprise. I asked him about his great-grandfather's songs and he replied with some asperity: "It is my resolute intention that whosoever will publish my book will publish Ribi David's songs at the same time."

We were about to take our leave of him. Grandfather told him of the Hasidic rabbi who had died, and the funeral oration that he had preached for him, and how he had begun with the words, "Pay heed to an old man who has forgotten his learning, the reason why tablets and broken tablets are placed in the ark."

Ribi Aharon Hassin sighed and said: "Indeed it is so, tablets and broken tablets are placed in the ark." He was referring to the Hasidic teacher and master who had passed away.

The hour was late and Sabbath approaching. I began pressing

grandfather to leave. He answered me: "Let me take my leave of Ribi Aharon, who knows when I shall see him again, and where I shall see him."

When he had taken his leave of Ribi Aharon, grandfather sighed and said: "So it is, tablets and broken tablets are placed in the ark." And he was referring to Ribi Aharon.

We left the camp, climbing the hill in a heavy silence. Grandfather was worn out by the journey and by the sermon, but most of all by emotion. When we arrived at our house it was almost time for the lighting of the candles. A number of our relatives were already there to celebrate the Sabbath with us. Grandfather asked me to tell them about the sermon he had preached in honor of the Teacher and Master, and I began with the words: "Pay heed to an old man who has forgotten his learning—the reason that the tablets together with the broken tablets are placed together in the ark—"

I wanted to continue with the sermon, but grandfather made a sign, indicating he felt unwell. We took him to his bed. That same week we accompanied my grandfather of revered memory to his eternal rest.

Glossary

Abbaye—a Talmudic sage

Aggadah—refers to non-legal material in the Talmud.

Aguna—(pl., *agunot*) a woman who can't be divorced because he husband has disappeared, or refused to divorce her.

Alfas—Rabbi Yizhak Alfasi, North African and Spanish eleventh-century codifier of Jewish law.

Alliance Israelite Universelle—a French-Jewish organization set up to improve the welfare of impoverished and persecuted Jewish communities in French-speaking countries. It disseminated French culture in those communities.

Amidah—('standing'); refers to the central prayer in the daily services. Also known as 'the Eighteen Benedictions'.

Aram Zova—also Aram Zoba; the biblical name for the city of Aleppo, Syria.

Arba'ah Turim—see Turim

Ark—the cabinet containing the Torah scrolls in the synagogue. It is placed in the front of the sanctuary.

Ashkenazi—a loose term for all Jews from Western Europe, or Jews not of oriental or Sepharadic descent.

Ashre—the first word in Psalm 84 verse 5. "Happy are those who…" It is the initial word in a prayer, formed from three chapters of the Psalms, which is recited thrice daily.

Av—the eleventh month of the Jewish year. The destruction of the Temple took place on the Ninth of Av.

Av Beit Din—head of a rabbinical court of law.

Bar Mitzvah—the stage at which a young man undertakes the religious responsibilities of adulthood, and also the religious ceremony when the boy turns thirteen.

Bartenura—(more accurately, Bertinora) Rabbi Ovadya of Bartenura the late fifteenth and early sixteenth century rabbi, known for his commentary on the *Mishnah*.

Bashi—sage; an honorary title in the Ottoman Empire, given to the chief rabbi.

Batim of the tefillin—literally 'houses'; the small boxes containing scriptural verses that are strapped on the head and arm during morning prayer.

Bavli—(refers to the Talmud Bavli, or the Babylonian Talmud.) A collection of Jewish oral law, the base of which is the interpretation and the elaboration of the *Mishnah*. The Babylonian Talmud, and not the Jerusalem Talmud, is the one which is commonly studied.

Beit Dayan—literally, 'the house of Dayan', or the Dayan family, which traces its lineage back to King David. Another name for members of this family were the Beit Nasi family, or 'the family house of the president.'

Beit Din—a court of Jewish law

Beit Midrash—a 'house of study', a place where students learn Torah.

Beit Nasi—literally 'the house of the president', but here simply the name of a synagogue in Aleppo.

Beit Yoseph—the classic encyclopedic commentary on the *Tur*, (a thirteenth-century code) written by the great sixteenth-century legal authority, frequently referred to as a 'Marram' (our master) Rabbi Yoseph Caro, or after this work, Marram Beit Yoseph.

Ben-Asher, Aharon—a famous tenth-century *ba'al massora*—a group of experts who determined the proper spelling and pronunciation of the biblical text.

Birkat HaGomel—a blessing said by someone who has been in a life-threatening situation.

Book of Creation—(*Sefer Hayetzira*) an early work of Jewish mysticism.

Book of Supplications—(*Sefer Habakashot*) a book of liturgical poetry written and compiled by the sages of Aleppo in the course of many generations, but completed around two hundred and fifty years ago. It is customary in the communities of Aleppo to read from the *Book of Supplications* from after midnight on the eve of the Sabbath till dawn on the Sabbath morning. The tunes for these 'supplications' have become famous within the community of Aleppo and spread over many Sepharadi communities. This custom, mainly confined to the winter months when the Sabbath eve is long, continues to this day.

Book of the Zohar—the classic work of Jewish mysticism, attributed to the Mishnaic sage, Rabbi Shimon Bar Yochai, in the third century, during the Roman period.

Brit (Brit Mila)—the circumcision ceremony

Citrons—a citrus fruit, resembling a lemon, used on the festival of Succot, (*etrog* in Hebrew).

Cohanim—the Jewish priests who served in the Temple, descendents of Aaron, the brother of Moses. Members of the priestly family.

c.r.s.—Compagnie Republicaine de Sécurité, the anti-riot squad of the French police force.

Eighteen Benedictions—see *Shmoneh Esreh*

Eretz-Israel—the Land of Israel

Feast of Tabernacles—see festival of *Succot*

Gaon—('genius'); loose term for any intellectual giant, also used for Babylonian academics from the sixth to the eleventh centuries c.e.

Gaon Yehoshua—see *Pne'ai Yehoshua*

Gemara—the Talmud, the basis for Jewish law, which offers interpretations and expansions to the *Mishnah*.

Gematria—a form of numerology where each letter of the alphabet is assigned a numerical value and one explains a word according to the numerical value of the letters.

Genizah—(Heb. 'hidden'); storeroom (usually in a synagogue) where discarded Torah scrolls, parchments, old prayer books and other sacred texts and even non-sacred texts written in Hebrew letters. They cannot be destroyed since they contain the name of God.

Gr'a—Hebrew initials for Rabbi Eliahu, the eighteenth-century 'Gaon (genius) of Vilna' from Lithuania; here standing for the synagogue named after him, a well-known synagogue in central Jerusalem.

Hacham—('wise one'); term of respect for a sage, or the leader or rabbi of a community.

Hacham Me'ayen—('contemplative sage'), referring to the method of study that plumbs the depth of a Talmudic text, analyzing its latent layers of meaning.

Haftarah—weekly reading from the prophets on the Sabbath and holidays, following the main Torah reading. Its theme amplifies the weekly Torah reading.

Haggadahs—(pl. of *Haggadah*); the book from which the story of the Exodus from Egypt is read every Passover Seder night.

Halacha, halachic—('the way, path'); collectively, the laws and ordinances of Judaism.

Halitza—a ceremony involving a widow who has no children from her late husband, and performed by her brother-in-law.

Hallel—'praise' selection from the Book of Psalms, which are recited on various holy days.

Hanukkah—('dedication'); eight-day celebration commemorating the victory of the Maccabees over the Greek and Syrian forces that occupied the land of Israel during part of the Second Temple period.

Hashkavah—'burial'

Hasid, Hasidim—members of the vibrant religious and social movement established by Israel Ba'al Shem Tov (1699–1761) in Volhynia and Podolia. The movement emphasizes the emotional and devotional aspects of Judaism.

Hatan Torah—refers to a man who is called up to read the last verses of the Torah on the festival of *Simhat Torah.*

Hatikvah—('the hope'); the national anthem of Israel.

Havdalah—ceremony marking the end of the Sabbath. It consists of blessings over wine, spices, and a candle, and the main blessing, which refers to the distinction between holy and profane.

Hazan, hazanim—the person or people leading the congregation in prayer in the synagogue.

Hiyyah—Aramaic derivative of the Hebrew name *Haim*, meaning 'life'.

Hok le-Yisrael—a book which is a compilation of short passages from the Bible, *Mishnah, Talmud* and *Halachah* and ethical texts; some people read it daily after prayer.

Hol Hamo'ed—the intermediate days of the festivals of *Pesah* or *Succot.*

Hoshen Mishpat—written by Rabbi Yoseph Caro; a section of the *Shulhan Aruch* that deals with civil and criminal law.

Humash—the first section of the Bible, the Five Books of Moses.

Ibn Ezra—(1089–1164) born in Spain; peripatetic poet, grammarian and biblical commentator. Also well known for his knowledge on secular subjects such as mathematics and astronomy.

Ima—Hebrew for 'mother'

Ish Hasid—a pious man

Jallabia, jallabias—the white smocks that were the habitual clothing of the Syrian populace, a combination of cloak and dressing gown.

Kabbalah—Jewish mysticism

Kaddish—the prayer for the dead

Kal Nidrei—the Sepharadi pronunciation for what Ashkenazim refer to as *Kol Nidrei* (see below).

Kashrut—laws pertaining to what is *kosher*; food prepared according to Jewish religious requirements.

Ketubbot—(pl. of *ketubbah*); marriage contract

Ketzot Hahoshen—the famous eighteenth-century commentary by Rabbi Aryeh HaCohen on *Hoshen Mishpat*, the section of the *Shulhan Aruch* dealing with civil law.

Kol Nidrei—('all vows'); the prayer that begins the *Yom Kippur* service, which asks for forgiveness for the vows between men and God that were not kept during the year.

Kuttab—Arabic term for the school where youngsters study Torah.

Kuzari—classic twelfth-century work of Jewish thought.

Maharam Schiff—acronym for Our Teacher Rabbi Meir Schiff, 1605–1641; German Talmudic interpreter.

Maharsha—Rabbi Shmuel Eliezer Edels; the sixteenth- and seventeenth-century Talmudist who lived in Poland; known for his extensive commentary on the Talmud and Rashi.

Makam Zaba—(also *makamim*); musical scales for Eastern music.

Maran Yoseph—see previous reference to Rabbi Yoseph Caro, the sixteenth-century scholar born in Toledo who later became Chief Rabbi of Safed, Israel.

Massora—see Ben-Asher

Me'ayen Pashtan—a method of Talmudic study that emphasizes the surface meaning of the text.

Menorah—the candelabrum used on the festival of *Hanukkah*.

Mezuzah—('doorpost', pl. *mezuzot*); the parchment and often the case attached to the doorpost of rooms in homes, containing various scriptural passages.

Midrash—ancient rabbinic elaborations of biblical texts which often emphasize moral lessons.

Midrash Nasi—fictive name of Aleppo synagogue

Minhah—the afternoon prayer

Minyan—'number'; a Jewish prayer quorum requiring a minimum of ten males, of bar-mitzvah age, thirteen, and up.

Mishnah—the early authoritative code of law divided into six sections, edited and issued by Rabbi Judah the Prince in Israel toward the end of the second century C.E. It is divided into six sections and covers all areas of Jewish law.

Mishneh Torah—the great twelfth-century comprehensive code of Jewish law written by Maimonides. This was the product of years of work and the first systematic codification of the entire corpus of Jewish law ever written. Unlike all of the Rambam's other works, the *Mishneh Torah* was written in Hebrew and was intended to provide the average Jew with access to the body of Jewish law. It is still used daily by students.

Mitnaggedim—'opponents'; opponents of the Hasidic movement.

Mitzvah—(pl., *mitzvot*); 'commandment' or loosely, a 'good deed', but referring specifically to the 613 commandments found in the Torah.

Mohel—the skilled person who performs the circumcision.

Moreh Nevukhim—The Guide for the Perplexed; the classic work of medieval Jewish philosophy written by Maimonides (the Rambam, 1135–1204).

Mussaf—the additional prayer recited on the Sabbath and other Jewish festivals.

Nehar Shalom—fictive name of a book.

Ninth of Av—the ninth day of the Hebrew month of Av marks the day on which the holy Temple was destroyed by the Romans in 70 C.E.

Parashah—one of the fifty-four weekly divisions of the Torah, read each Sabbath and studied during the preceding week.

Parochet—the curtain on the holy ark in the synagogue.

Pele Yoetz—a very popular book of moral guidance and advice, written by Rabbi Eliezer Papo in the eighteenth century.

Pesah—the Jewish festival of Passover

Philasuf—pet name meaning 'little philosopher'

Pne'ai Yehoshua—('Face of Joshua'), Talmudic novellae which are still studied in yeshivot today, written by the Ashkenazi rabbi, Ya'akov Yehoshua Falk, 1680–1756, also called the 'Gaon Yehoshua'.

Poskim—a term for generally accepted rabbinical authorities.

Prayer of Hannah—Hannah's prayer in the book of Samuel, in which she thanks the Almighty for granting her a son. In Sepharadi communities, this prayer starts the morning prayers.

Purim—the festival commemorating the story in the Book of Esther.

Rabba—a prominent figure in the Babylonian Talmud

Rabban Gamaliel—the name of several of the descendents of Hillel the Elder. They served as the religious and political heads of the Jewish community in *Eretz-Israel* during the Roman period.

Rabbenu—'our rabbi'; term of respect

Rabbenu Asher—(1250–1327) a younger contemporary of the Rashba. Author of an important legal compendium and Tosafot. The leading rabbinic authority of his time.

Rabbenu Hananel—lived in North Africa in the eleventh century; noted for his commentary on the Talmud.

Rabbenu Tam—(c. 1100–1171) Jacob Ben Meir, a grandson of Rashi. He was the outstanding rabbinical authority of his day, and the leading figure of the school of Talmudic analysis known as Tosafot.

Rabbi Isaac Halevi Herzog—Rabbinic scholar and the first Ashkenazi chief rabbi of the State of Israel. His grandson, Chaim Herzog, became Israel's sixth president in 1983.

Rabbi Israel Najara—(c. 1555–1625) Syria and Israel. A mystic, he is known for his poetry about the suffering and redemption of the Jewish people.

Rabbi Judah Halevi—one of the greatest Spanish medieval Hebrew poets, and a philosopher who lived in the eleventh and twelfth centuries. He is the author of *The Kuzari*.

Rabbi Shimon Bar Yochai—lived during the Roman period and was a student of Rabbi Akiva. An important halachic authority, he was also known for his studies in the field of Jewish mysticism and was reputedly the author of the *Zohar*.

Rabbi Solomon Ibn Gavirol—acronym, the *Rashbag*; Hebrew poet who lived in Spain during the sixteenth century.

Rabbi Yoseph Ibn Migash—(1077–1141) noted Talmudist who lived in Spain.

Ralbag—(1288–1344) acronym for Rabbi Levi Ben Gershon, also known as Gersonidies, who lived in Provence, France. He was renowned for his commentary on the Bible, and also famed for his work in the fields of philosophy and astronomy.

Rambam—(1135–1204) Rabbi Moshe Ben Maimon, also known as Maimonides, perhaps the most influential of the medieval Jewish philosophers. Born in Spain, he fled persecution there, and eventually settled in Egypt, where he was court physician. His principal works include his commentary to the *Mishnah*, codification of Jewish law, and his principal philosophic work, *The Guide to the Perplexed*. Among his other writings are the *Sefer HaMitzvot* (Book of Obligations), where he defined the 613 commandments, or mitzvot, and their principles.

Ramban—(1194–1270) acronym for Rabbi Moshe Ben Nachman, a profound rabbinic scholar. Author of highly influential commentaries on the Torah and the Talmud. Among his other writings were his criticisms of Maimonides' *Sefer HaMitzvot.*

Ramban Nahmani—the term used by the Aleppo community for Rabbi Moshe Ben Nachman.

Rashba—(1235–1310) acronym for Rabbi Shlomo Ben Avraham, the prolific author of responsa, a great Talmudic commentary and the leading legal authority of his time.

Rashi—(1040–1105) acronym for Rabbi Shlomo Yitzhaki, a great French rabbinical scholar. His greatest contributions to Jewish learning are his remarkably lucid commentaries on the Bible and the Babylonian Talmud. They remain the most popular commentaries on these works to this day.

Reshit Hokhma—a sixteenth-century encyclopedic work on morals by the distinguished kabbalist, Eliyahu Eliahu De Vidas.

Ribi—reverential form of address used by Syrian Jewry for their rabbis. 'Rabbi' is not used, since in Arabic it denotes 'God'.

Ritba—(1250–1330) acronym for Rabbi Yom-Tov of Seville, a distinguished Talmudist.

Rosh Hashanah—the Jewish New Year, starting with the month of Tishrei (around September).

Sabbath or *Shabbat*—the seventh day of the week on which God rested from the creation of the world. It is a day of rest and spiritual enrichment.

Sandak—the person who holds the baby during the circumcision.

Sanyat—'tray' in Arabic.

Second Temple—built on the site of the First Temple, on Mount Moriah. Built in 516 B.C.E. by the Jews who returned from exile in Babylon, and destroyed in 70 C.E. by the Romans.

Seder Taharot—the sixth and final order of the *Mishnah*. It deals with the abstruse areas of ritual purity and impurity.

Sefer HaBakashot—the 'Book of Supplications'

Sefer HaPizmonim—the 'Book of Hymns'

Sepharadi—('Spanish'); the name given to the descendants of Jews from the Iberian peninsula; also, recently and more loosely, the oriental Jewish community.

Shach—acronym for *Sifte Cohen,* the name of an influential commentary on the *Shulhan Aruch*, written by the European authority Rabbi Shabtai Cohen (1621–1662).

Shaharit—morning prayers

Shamash—a beadle, the man responsible for running the synagogue.

Shavuot—(The 'Feast of Weeks' or Pentecost); a Jewish festival commemorating the receiving of the Torah on Mount Sinai and the harvest of the first fruits.

Shehehianu—blessing recited at momentous times in one's life ("Blessed art Thou, O Lord our God, who has kept us and sustained us and enabled us to reach this time.")

Shekhinah—the divine Presence, (from 'to dwell').

Shevat—the fifth month of the Hebrew calendar, which falls in the winter.

Shevet Musar—('ethical rod'); a book of Jewish ethics which empha-sizes ascetic behavior, by Eliyahu HaCohen of Smyrna, Turkey.

Shmoneh Esreh—'The Eighteen Benedictions', which constitute the central part of the three daily prayers.

Shofar—trumpet made of a ram's horn, commemorating the Bind-ing of Isaac; blown on *Rosh Hashanah* and *Yom Kippur*, and other occasions of great solemnity.

Shulhan Aruch—('The Prepared Table'); the authoritative code of Jewish law written by Rabbi Yoseph Caro (1488–1575).

Shushan—the biblical city, in which the story from the biblical 'Book of Esther' takes place; is Hamadan in modern Iran.

Siddur—the prayer book

Sifra—a halachic midrash or exegetial commentary to the legal mate-rial in the book of Leviticus (Vayikra).

Sifre—halachic midrash or commentary to the fourth and fifth books of the Bible: Numbers and Deuteronomy.

Simhat Torah—a holiday immediately following Succot, celebrating the end and beginning of the cycle of the weekly Torah readings.

Six Orders—another term for the *Mishnah* (see Talmud). It is divided into six sections or orders that encompass all of rabbinic law. The *Mishnah* is the earliest compilation of the Oral Torah, which is the basis of the *Gemara*.

Succot—festival of Succot; the biblical festival in the fall, which com-memorates both the wandering of the Children of Israel in the desert and celebrates the harvest festival.

Sura and Neharde'a—the two leading Torah academies in Babylon at the time of the compiling of the Talmud.

S'vara—Talmudic logic or opinion

Tahanun—a prayer that is said after the Eighteen Benedictions, that originally was a personal supplication, but today has a fixed form.

Takanah—a ruling, a rabbinical edict

Tallit—a prayer shawl

Talmud—('teaching'); the name applied to both the Babylonian Talmud and the Jerusalem Talmud. It is the collected records of academic discussion and case law by generations of scholars during several centuries after 200 C.E. and is also referred to as the *Gemara*. The term 'Talmud' may also refer to the *Mishnah*, together with the *Gemara*. Study of the Talmud constitutes the largest part of *yeshiva* studies.

Talmud of Onkelos—an Aramiac translation of the Pentateuch written by Onkelos, a second-century Roman convert to Judaism.

Talmud Torah—a traditional Jewish school for young boys. It is a preparatory school for studies in a *yeshiva*.

Talmud Yerushalmi—the Talmud that was compiled in Israel at the end of the fourth century.

Targum—translation, usually referring to the *Targum of Onkelos*: a translation of the Pentateuch written in Aramaic, by Onkelos. (See above, Talmud of Onkelos)

Taz—acronym for *Turei Zahav*, an extremely influential commentary to the *Shulhan Aruch*, written by the European authority Rabbi David Ben Samuel HaLevi, who lived in the Ukraine and Poland (1586–1667).

Teban—the central podium on which the Torah scroll is read from, in Ashkenazi, the '*bimah.*'

Tefillin—phylacteries, or two small prayer boxes containing verses from the Torah in micrography written on vellum. The boxes are bound during prayer to the forehead and the arm, and worn during the weekday morning prayer. They are the sign of the covenant between God and His people.

Tevet—month of the Hebrew calendar, occurring in winter.

The Four Columns—(translation of the Hebrew, *Turim*); a classic compendium of medieval rabbinic laws. (See *Tur*)

Tikkun—a set of prayers that have mystical significance.

Tisch—(Yiddish for 'table'); the ceremonial meal led by the rebbe (leader of a Hasidic group). During a *tisch*, the rebbe eats and imparts wisdom to those attending, who are also given the honor of sharing the scraps from his table.

Torah—the Pentateuch, the Five Books of Moses, constituting the first section of the Bible.

Tosefot—a method of Talmudic analysis, developed by medieval sages, mainly from France.

Tosefta—an ancient collection of Jewish law that is parallel to the *Mishnah*, and more expansive.

Tractate—a section or grouping of material within the Talmud.

Tur, Turim—the name for Rabbi Jacob Ben Asher's (c. 1270–1340) classic code of Jewish law.

Tzizit—('fringes'); the Bible commands the wearing of ritual *tzizit* (Numbers 15:37–41) on the four corners of garments for all males.

Vatikin—the 'conscientiously pious', referring often to those who are meticulous in ritual observance, especially with regard to reciting the morning prayers at daybreak.

Yeshiva—traditional Jewish school for teenage and young adult males, devoted primarily to the study of the Babylonian Talmud and its commentaries.

Yerushalmi—(refers to the *Talmud Yerushalmi*, see above)

Yom Kippur—the Day of Atonement, the holiest day in the Jewish calendar, the tenth day of the month of *Tishrei*. It is the day on which Jews beg forgiveness for their transgressions against God.

Zevah Todah—fictive name of a book

Zion—another name for Israel, referring both to the physical land and the aspect of spiritual yearning for what the land of Israel represents to the Jewish people.

Zohar—the seminal work of Jewish mysticism, attributed to Shimon Bar Yochai during the Roman period.

Acknowledgments

The Publisher would like to express appreciation to Rabbi Raphael Groner for his invaluable assistance in preparing *Aleppo Tales* for publication, and thanks to Shoshana Sabato, Micha Witzel, Talia Gillis and Kaden and Joseph Harari.

About the Author

Haim Sabato

Haim Sabato descends from a long line of rabbis from Aleppo, Syria. His family lived in Egypt for two generations before moving to Israel when he was six. Rabbi Sabato, who served in the tank corps in the 1973 Yom Kippur War, today teaches Talmud at the *Birkat Moshe* yeshiva, in Ma'aleh Adumim, near Jerusalem, which he cofounded. His previous book, *Adjusting Sights,* (Toby Press, 2003) a bestseller in Israel, won the prestigious Sapir Prize for Literature and the Sadeh Prize for Writing. *Adjusting Sights* was recently made into a film of the same name. *Aleppo Tales,* in the original Hebrew *Emet MiEretz Titzmach,* appeared in 1997.

The fonts used in this book are from the Garamond family

Other works by Haim Sabato
are published by *The* Toby Press

Adjusting Sights

The Toby Press publishes fine fiction,
available at fine bookstores everywhere. For more information,
please contact *The* Toby Press at www.tobypress.com